MY HUSBAND'S PAST

BOOKS BY SHARI J. RYAN

The Bookseller of Dachau

The Doctor's Daughter

The Lieutenant's Girl

The Maid's Secret

The Stolen Twins

The Homemaker

The Glovemaker's Daughter

The Perfect Nanny

The Nurse Behind the Gates

LAST WORDS

The Girl with the Diary

The Prison Child

The Soldier's Letters

SHARI J. RYAN

MY HUSBAND'S PAST

bookouture

Published by Bookouture in 2024

An imprint of Storyfire Ltd.
Carmelite House
50 Victoria Embankment
London EC4Y 0DZ

www.bookouture.com

Storyfire Ltd's authorised representative in the EEA is Hachette Ireland
8 Castlecourt Centre
Castleknock Road
Castleknock
Dublin 15, D15 YF6A
Ireland

ISBN: 978-1-83525-892-7
eBook ISBN: 978-1-83525-891-0

To the most understanding husband in the world...
Josh, I promise this story has absolutely nothing to do with you.
Love you.

ONE

My ex-husband's head was as smooth as a bowling ball, a metaphor for the void in our marriage. Something was always missing—nothing to grab onto. But the problems in our marriage sadly ran much deeper than just Jack's baldness, which is why I now wake up every morning to the sight of Griffin's silky tousled golden-brown hair instead.

I gaze at the thin, sheer shades, watching shadows of tree branches flutter through the windows. The whistling wind snakes in through the cracked-open window.

"Time to get up." I run my fingers through my husband's thick, silky strands. "It's six."

Griffin rolls onto his back and stretches an arm around me. Old Spice wafts through the air with his warm embrace, a sharp contrast to the brisk mountain air whispering through the open window. Despite the chill, the comfort of his hold tempts me to ignore the world outside our bedroom.

He kisses the tip of my nose; his plump lips cool against my skin. "The most beautiful alarm clock a guy could ask for and yet, there's no snooze-button," he croaks, along with a tired chuckle.

"The older models don't come with that feature," I retort, my tone playful yet laced with fatigue.

"Older models?" He grins. "You're only forty."

"Some days it feels like a hundred," I reply with a snicker. "Hey, what happened to your phone alarm?" It didn't go off again.

Griffin peers toward his phone. "That's a good question." He wiggles the cord. "The charger's fried. I'll order a new one."

My gaze skates across his chest to where autumn-orange hues from the morning sun bleed onto the walnut nightstand. His lifeless phone and an unfamiliar wristwatch stand alone in the spotlight.

"Is that new?" I point to the brown leather strap and bronze-framed timepiece. It's out of character for him, not matching his typically casual style or fitting with his hatred for watches.

Griffin follows my outstretched finger toward the watch. "Oh, this thing?" He grabs and inspects it as if he's never seen it before. "Yeah, I—ah—found it last week when I was collecting boxes from my parents' house. It needs a new battery, but there's something about it. It has...kind of timeless look."

He's been living here with my kids and me since our wedding day, but had only moved belongings from his condo over. He still has a bunch of old stuff sitting in his parents' basement, but after being untouched for so long, he wasn't in a rush to drag it all over here. About a month ago, his parents told us they're planning to downsize and asked him to collect the rest of his boxes. He's been grabbing a few each week.

"It does. I love it. It'll look great on you—like everything does," I say with a sigh.

"Oh stop." He flaps his hand at me, smiling at the compliment.

Griffin rolls to the side of the bed, the warm high-thread-count linen bunching against my side. An achy groan follows his movements as he scoops up the phone and watch. In a pair of black-boxer-briefs, he pads across the white shag rug barefoot. When his heels scuff against the grainy bathroom tiles, the bathroom door follows, clicking shut behind him, shortly followed by the sound of the rumbling vent fan. Some days I find the need to pinch myself, a reminder that this is truly my life now. I didn't know a relationship could feel like it just *fit,* or if that would even make sense to anyone else.

I bend forward, reaching to grab my maroon "engagement" sweatshirt, donning the memory of our day at Mount Washington. I pull it on, and prop myself up against my plush pillows, lilac fabric softener whooshing past my nose. A day trip to the peak in the middle of summer heatwave sounded like a beautiful escape until we reached the summit. I knew there would be a temperature drop, but it felt more like winter, and I was freezing. Of course, I didn't know Griffin was going to propose, so I was in a rush to head back down the mountain toward warmth.

That's when he pulled me into the little summit gift shop and got me a sweatshirt, buying himself a few more minutes in the cold.

I love this sweatshirt almost as much as the beautiful ring he put on my finger.

The bright display on my phone lights up, summoning me with notifications. I grab it from its charging cradle on my nightstand next to my small glass jewelry box.

6:05: Ten minutes before kids need to be awake.

The pad of my thumb swipes down the screen, scraping a jagged crack I've ignored. The phone's haptics vibrate against my palm as my inbox fills. It's the same list of daily alerts and store sales.

Delete, delete, delete, delete.

I keep forgetting to unsubscribe to these. I need to just take the time to do it and get it over with.

Delete, delete, de—

My thumb freezes. Along with my pulse. The header for the last email in the list jolts through me like lightning.

IzzyBee83isMe@aol.com: Hey you…It's me…

Izzy's name unearths a hurricane of memories—agony and distress. The subject line, bold and white against the dark mode bear a crippling burden as memories flood my mind. My childhood best friend. I never thought anything could come between us. Until she disappeared, of course.

The thought of her gnaws at my stomach, the familiar pain of loss returning like a gust of heavy wind.

The air grows colder as I think about our final night together, a crackling fire in the distance—the laughter of friends celebrating the end of our high school days.

This email cannot really be from Izzy. I know this. She's gone. It's been over twenty years. I know she died that night—she must have. It's what the police decided.

Spam emails can look very real.

I should just leave it alone.

But—I can't stop staring at her name.

The *what ifs* are stronger than any other thought, they control me.

I tap on the email…

To: JessPetersonXoXo@aol.com
From: Izzy Lester
Subject: Hey you…It's me.

Hey Jess,

I assume you think I'm dead. It's OK. Even I still question how I survived.

You remember my stalker, right?

My heart thunders in my chest as the bathroom door bangs open. I gasp, jolted into the present, clutching my phone as if it were a lifeline. Taking a ragged breath, I glance up at my husband—still in his underwear. His toothbrush dangles from his parted mouth, foam collecting in the corners.

"I didn't mean to scare you." He presses his free hand to his chest and removes the toothbrush from his bite.

I'm not sure I can hide the alarm bells ringing in my head. "I —no, I'm—I'm okay." My lie is obvious. I take an extra breath of the heavy air to mask my unease. "Um—I'm sorry...what were you saying?" I swallow hard, desperate to get back to the email but needing to be alone when I do.

"I've just seen a meeting invite for tomorrow after school. It's an all-faculty meeting." His gaze drops and he taps his fingers against his lips. "After all the rumors about budget cuts and next year's incoming kindergarten class being much smaller than usual, I can't help but think the worst..."

"Honey, they're not getting rid of you. You've gotten the teacher of the year award twice in the last four years. You have nothing to worry about."

He just shrugs. "It's from three to six tomorrow. Could you grab the kids?"

I'm having trouble focusing on what he's asking. That email is burning in my hand.

"Jess?"

"Yeah, sorry." He needs help with my children, Jack's children—the two children Griffin has selflessly taken on responsibility for. "Of course. I'll close the shop early and pick them up." I know he hates to pull me away from the coffee shop. But I'm a mom first. That's never been a question.

"Sorry for the short notice," he says.

"No." I close my eyes to recenter my attention. "Don't apologize. I'm so grateful you help as much as you do with them."

"I love those kiddos." In the thirty seconds we've been talking, he's gone from pale to paler, work nerves eating away at him. "Be out in a few." He clears his throat and closes himself back into the bathroom.

My focus clings to the door for a minute, heart pounding, before shifting my attention back to the phone. The tips of my fingers are white from my grip on it.

I bring the email back up. Beads of sweat tingle along my collarbone. The sun's glow fades, leaving behind a murky light. The air around me constricts. Forcing myself to breathe, I start reading...

Jess,

I should have listened to your warnings about the way he was acting. I was blinded by silly teenage love.

I thought I was running away from him that night, but I only ran into his trap. He took me and held me captive. For years, every day was a living nightmare.

His charm masked his true intentions. What seemed like love and promises of a future was all a lie. He wasn't my boyfriend. He was my stalker—you were right all along.

But I escaped. I survived.

It's been years and I'm still terrified he'll find me again. So sometimes I search his name online, just to make sure he's still far away.

I'm risking everything by reaching out, but I couldn't just say nothing.

Jess, when I searched his name, yours came up too.

Because my stalker—he's your new husband. You married him, Jess.

You're in danger. You need to run, before it's too late.

Yours always,

Izzy

TWO

Every muscle in my body turns to stone as panic swirls within my stomach. The sharp words dance before my eyes, an unfathomable possibility of truths. I know this isn't Izzy. It can't be. She's gone. We all know she's gone—every person in this town will say the same. I don't know what kind of sick jerk could think up this elaborate story.

My heart ticks like seconds of a clock running out of time. I've come so far since losing her. The undefined "gone" was my main source of pain—the lack of any concrete closure, a wound that would never heal. It just kept bleeding. But I had to make my own closure, come to my own decision about what happened that night.

"This is impossible," I tell myself. This is not Izzy. She's gone.

I study the sender's email address.

IzzyBee83isMe@aol.com

There isn't even a typo to relieve me. I was with her when she thought up the rhyming email address. We giggled about it for an hour, repeating it, elongating the "me" at the end into a squeal.

It's been over twenty years since I've received an email from her. Her AOL account surely wouldn't still be active after going unused for that long unless she truly did escape. Maybe email addresses are recycled and made available again after a certain length of time.

An icy trill of fear shoots down my spine as I scan the email again.

I assume you think I'm dead.

She was the only real light in my life. But then, she was just gone. I always blamed myself for not doing something more to protect her. That's what friends are supposed to do.

My heart hammers against my chest, grief bleeding out like water from a cracked dam, gnawing at my stomach like it used to when I was still so raw. For years, every time the house phone rang, I prayed it was someone calling to say they'd found her. I'd held on to hope long after others suggested we come to terms with an unfathomable reality.

I refused to believe she could be gone forever.

There were search parties, investigations, and then more search parties.

It was years before the case went cold. All we could do was assume the worst.

Now her name pops up out of the blue heeding a warning about my husband, of all people.

The warning is enough for me to know this isn't Izzy. Whoever thought I might believe this email came from Izzy should have thought up a more believable reason for her disappearance. A more plausible lie. Izzy never got to meet Griffin—our relationship began so many years after she went missing. Plus, nobody who knows Griffin could ever believe he'd hurt a fly, let alone a human being.

"I miss you so much, Izz. It still hurts like I lost you yesterday," I whisper.

What a cruel joke.

I lie in bed, rigid with unprocessed emotions. The longer I stir over the email, the more rage fuels me like caffeine. Those infamous keyboard warriors think they can hide behind a computer screen, do whatever they want, and never get caught. I just don't know who would target me. Who would want to hurt me like that. Although, come to think of it...there was a large group of older teens who piled into The Bean Nook yesterday. They were making such a racket and disturbing the regulars that I had to ask them to lower their voices a couple of times. They were whispering and chuckling when they left. They'd surely know the history of the town—know my history with my best friend. It's what this place is famous for, after all. Maybe it was one of them?

I drag myself out of bed, my body heavy from the weight of unsettling thoughts. My feet shuffle along the floor as I head out of the bedroom and down the hall to wake up Abby.

The door is open a crack, allowing the blinking LED lights from my fourteen-year-old's faux nightly party bleed into the hallway. With a step inside her room, the alarm clock blares, assaulting my former moments of silence. Then I trip over a pair of jeans hiding in the shadow of her nightstand. It's easier to blame the shadows instead of my ragged thoughts about Izzy. I catch myself on the corner of her bed. "Abby, how can you sleep through this racket? Come on. It's time to get up." As predicted, her groan begins—a daily reflex.

I wrench open both sets of blinds, drowning the room with harsh early morning light.

"I'm tired," she asserts, her words muffled against her pillow.

"Well, join the rest of us. Up. Let's go." I yank the covers down to her ankles and she snarls.

"Why are we in such a rush?" She lifts her head, opening one eye with skepticism. Aside from not wanting to poke my head into her bedroom three more times to make sure she's truly awake this morning, I do need to be at the school a few minutes early. My other best friend Natalie is the only person I feel like I can talk to about the email in my inbox—the only person who knew Izzy as close to how I did. I need to talk to Natalie, and I know she'll be at drop-off.

"I need to give Natalie some notes from a school meeting she missed the other night. She's pressed for time on Mondays."

Abby relents, setting her feet on the ground, whining and groaning along the way. "Okay, I'm up."

"Thank you. Be quick in the bathroom."

She closes her door as I step out into the hall, hearing the shower from the en suite still running.

On to the next child. When I open JJ's bedroom door, the water pipe squeals through the walls. The piercing shrill sends another shock down my spine.

"JJ, it's time to get up."

At least my energetic seven-year-old still wakes right up. Chipper and full of energy. Abby was the same until she turned thirteen. Maybe JJ will always be a morning person. I can only hope.

"I don't want to be late today."

A smile stretches across his freckled cheeks as he stretches his arms over his scraggly hazelnut curls. "Mommmm," he drawls. "Can I have eggs today?" He knows his big hazel eyes can convince me to do anything. *I can't give in today*. I need to catch Natalie, which means I need to be on time.

I pull open the blinds, and he pops upright like a jackknife, rubbing his fists against his eyes. "Not today, buddy. I have bagels, like you asked."

"Oh yeah," he toots.

I rifle through his drawers, grabbing pants, a shirt, underwear, and socks. "Come on, I'll help you dress."

"Why? I can get dressed myself," he says. JJ can get dressed himself but also gets distracted easily. He often finds something more exciting to do than get ready for school. My reminders would need reminders this morning.

"Why don't I just help you so I can make sure we get to school a few minutes early today, okay?"

JJ shrugs and stands up, shooting his arms into the air, allowing me to dress him quickly. "But why?"

"I'm meeting Natalie at the high school. I need to give her something and she can't wait long."

"Ohhh," he squeaks. "Oh, Mom?"

"What is it?" I ask, tapping on his bed so he sits down.

"Um, um," he says, tapping his finger against his chin. "I forget." He plops onto his bed so I can slip his socks onto his feet.

"Are you sure, sweetie?"

"Yeah, I—forget..."

"Hmm. I'm sure you'll remember whatever it is during breakfast. Come on."

"Yeah, maybe," he says.

I step back into the hallway, finding Abby in the bathroom, applying a coat of clear mascara and batting her eyelashes at her reflection. "Save the lip gloss for after breakfast," I say, waving her into the hallway.

"Ugh, Mom," she groans, grabbing the pink tube to take with her downstairs. Her groans and grunts have become decipherable lingo to highlight her discontent over just about everything I say.

"Abbs, could you do me a big favor and throw two bagels into the toaster for me? I need to check something on my laptop."

"Do I have to?" she whines.

She has no clue how much harder life could be...

I wish I were eight so I could see the pantry shelves above my head, but I have to wait a year for that. I pull a wooden chair from the kitchen table over to the closet, its legs scraping against the tile floor. I look out from the kitchen toward the stairwell, knowing Mom is going to be mad at me for moving the chair. But I'm hoping there's something on a higher shelf that I can't see.

"Jessica! What's all the racket?" Mom screams from upstairs. "I was sleeping."

"I'm trying to find something for breakfast before the bus gets here," I answer. Daddy always leaves Mommy with grocery money, but she never goes shopping. If I were old enough to go alone, I would.

There are black bananas on the counter with flies on them. And there's a loaf of bread in front of me in the pantry, but there's black spots on that too. Daddy told me not to eat bread if I see black spots.

"Oh, for God's sake, lunch is in what? Three hours. You'll be fine."

I'm hungry.

I climb up on top of the chair and see a box of cereal. My tummy grumbles, hoping there's something still inside.

I hoist myself up onto the shelf to reach in toward the back and grab the box. I climb back down and peek inside, finding nothing but crumbs. They must have been whole pieces at one time. I find a sandwich bag and pour the crumbs inside. It'll have to be enough.

"You better not miss that bus, Jessica. I am not driving you to school."

"I won't," I tell her, slipping my coat on and making sure it's buttoned up tight, so I don't catch a cold. I hear Izzy's mom from across the street telling her to stay bundled up, so she doesn't get sick. I didn't know the cold could make me sick. Her mom got her a nice hat and gloves to go with her coat. I asked Daddy to get me the same. He told Mommy to buy them, but she's been too busy watching her soaps.

I meet Izzy at the base of the driveway, and she shivers with a loud "burrr." I feel the cold, but I try to pretend it's not so bad. "You must be cold. Do you want to borrow a hat or gloves?"

I glance back at my front door, wondering if Mom is watching me. Probably not, but she's told me to stop borrowing things from the neighbors. "No, that's okay. I'm not cold."

Izzy twists her lips to one side. "Okay. Well, my mom told me to give you this," she says, handing me a plastic bag with a muffin inside. It's still warm in my hands as I take it from her.

"Thank you so much." I stare up Izzy's driveway, finding Mrs. Lester at the door watching the two of us. I give her a wave to say thank you. This will be better than my cereal crumbs.

Izzy loops her arm with mine. "Ready?"

"Yup, let's go." I'm lucky to live across the street from my best friend. And even better, we're in the same grade, so we get to walk to the bus together every day, and have done so since kindergarten.

I made the kids a hot breakfast every single morning until Abby started high school this year. We're in too much of a rush to get out the door now, but they have never had to look for food. They never will.

"I'll get the orange juice," JJ says, following Abby into the kitchen.

"Do you want cream cheese?" she asks him, unwrapping the bakery bag of different flavored bagels.

"Mmm, no," he says. "Actually..."

"Make up your mind," she sneers.

"Yes. Wait, no."

"Ugh. You're so—"

"Abby," I say, warning her not to finish her statement.

The entire first floor is open plan, with only separated decorative pillars. It was nice to keep an eye on them, especially when they were younger.

The moment they're occupied, the words from the email slice through my head again. I can't believe someone would say those things. That someone would want to mess with me like that. But who?

I glare at my laptop, still sitting open at the dining room table. I might see more on the computer than my phone. Something different, maybe—a clue to the real sender. I take a seat at the table and jab my fingers against the keyboard like a child sitting at a piano for the first time, but my screen stays black, unresponsive. Frustration grows within me, threatening to boil over. I twist the laptop to the side, confirming I haven't attached the cord. Of course. After searching quickly behind my chair, I find the power cord neatly looped up against the wall. I lunge for it as if it might disappear before I can reach it. I have mere seconds left before the kids are fighting next to me at the table and I don't want them hovering.

"Ding...da...da...ding," the laptop sings to life. I watch the progress bar move at a snail's pace while listening to Griffin moving around the bedroom in his dress shoes against the hardwoods. He'll be down in a minute.

The screen turns blue, flashes with a white error message, then blinks back to black. No, no, not today. Come on. Don't crap out on me now. I summon the botanical wallpaper to fill the screen while drumming my fingernails against the table.

Another dialogue box pops up.

[Update in progress...]

I unclench my hand from around my phone to check the time. It's already 6:35.

While Abby sets two plated bagels on the table, my floral background stretches across my screen, allowing me access to my inbox. The email sync icon blinks like a cursor and I bounce my knee at least a hundred times before the emails populate.

"Mom..." Abby says with a mouthful. "You look like you're worried about something."

I check my watch again. This time just for effect. "Nope, just keeping an eye on the time."

My heart dips into my hollow stomach when Izzy's email address appears again. Before this morning, it's been so long since I've seen it, yet it might as well have been yesterday with how fast these years have flown by.

I swallow hard, knowing I'm going to regret opening a browser and typing in Izzy's first and last name. I've done this too many times before. It's never helped me. The act is compulsive once I start. I could find an update on her disappearance—or someone found her, or she...thought I'd be the best person to email first. *I doubt it.* I know better than to get my hopes up.

I click the check box to search for the most recent articles.

As the page fills with links, I confirm they're all the same articles I've read over and over—thousands of times in the last twenty-two years.

SPRING HILL DAILY

May 20, 2001, Spring Hill Teenager, Missing – Isobel Lester, 17, short brown hair, blue eyes, 5'3, and petite. Last seen wearing black carpenter jeans and a light-blue sleeveless, hooded shirt. An active investigation and search party are in progress by local and state police to help locate Isobel. If you or anyone you know have any tips or knowledge of her whereabouts, please contact...

MUDFORD COMMUNITY JOURNAL

May 21, 2001, 17-Year-Old, Isobel Lester, Missing from Spring Hill, NH – The town of Spring Hill comes together in search for "one of their own." Seventeen-year-old Isobel Lester was last seen leaving a school sponsored event from the Spring Hill Falls Campgrounds at approximately 9:15PM on Friday, May 18th. Isobel's family reported to the local police that their daughter never arrived home from the school event, and no one has any leading knowledge of where she might have gone...The community has organized a vigil at the town square for seven o'clock this evening. *"The heart of Spring Hill is broken. This town has always come together in times of need. We won't let the Lester family down, and we won't give up the search until we find our girl,"* —local business owner.

WESTERN NEW HAMPSHIRE NEWS

May 22, 2001, High School Senior, Isobel Lester, 17 and Missing – Isobel Lester has been missing for four days. Friends, family, neighbors, and community members say she is a smart, happy, loving girl who has never shown signs of discontent. Loved ones are pleading for help to help bring home their daughter. There are currently no tips or hints of where she could be or why she never came home from a school sponsored event last Friday night...

One minute we were having the best night ever, dancing

around a bonfire with our classmates, the next, she was gone. She never made it home.

I click the sort option on the top of the screen and search for the most recent articles, but there aren't any new articles. The latest one is from 2003, following the final press conference held by the local police. That was the end of the search. They said there was no evidence to aid the ongoing investigation and they had no choice but to put the case to rest. It felt more like they were putting Izzy to rest—without ever suggesting she had died, nor providing any hope that she may still be alive. The message felt strong. It was over. Time to move on. So strong that her family felt the need to move to Nettle, a town away.

I return to the email, staring at the words as if an explanation will pop out at me. Who and where could this have come from? I click on the options button in the top right corner of the email and select *View Source Code*. A white box of HTML unravels as I scan each line for an IP address to track. It's doubtful I'll find much information from it, but there could be something.

I'm less than a few lines in when the doorbell rings, breaking my train of thought. I shoot a sharp glance at the door as if it's offended me.

"Who would be ringing our doorbell this early?" Abby grumbles.

"Maybe it's a delivery!" JJ says. He always gets so excited for packages even when he has no clue what they are.

I doubt it's a package since I didn't order anything, but I don't know who would be at the door this early. My aggravation toward whoever sent me this email is enough this morning. I hardly have the patience to deal with another unexpected disruption.

A knock follows as I'm making my way across the living room. As I reach for the doorknob, a memory of Izzy waiting for me at my front door with her bike when we were JJ's age, complete with two long auburn braids, matching hair elastics, and stick-on purple heart earrings, tugs at my heart. We were around JJ's age then—not a care in the world. I'd do anything to find her waiting for me on the other side now.

"Jess, was that the doorbell?" Griffin calls out from upstairs.

"Yeah, I'm sure it's just—"

Another three impetuous knocks jolt me as I yank it open with matching urgency.

THREE

Mrs. Turble, the neighborhood's 6:00AM speed-walker, stands before me on my welcome mat. She unapologetically stares into my house as if there's something interesting going on behind me. She has no idea.

"Good morning, dear. It's a lovely autumn day, isn't it?" she says after scoping out the view of the woods in front of and to the side of my house. Then takes another gander inside the house.

"If only the rest of those pesky rain clouds would clear up," I say, bouncing my fist up. The clouds are an early morning accessory to our town nestled between two mountain peaks.

"It's Mrs. Turble," Abby shouts upstairs to Griffin.

She grins, one of those smiles I can't decipher–judgmental or maybe just a simple response to Abby shouting as if Griffin is a street away.

"The sun is out. It will be a beautiful day, I'm sure," she says. "Anyway, I'm sorry to be bothering you this early in the morning. It's just that I found this key chain on the curb next to your driveway. I always see your Abby with so many dangling from her backpack. It must be hers." As I nudge open the storm door, she moves back so I can join her on the front step. Between her pinched fingers, she holds the object up for me to see: a glossy black rock attached to a key chain.

I choke on the air flowing through my lungs. *What in the world is she doing with that?*

Confused, I reach forward to take the key chain from her outstretched hand. "Oh—wh—how thoughtful of you," I say. "Thanks—thank you so much."

"What is it?" Abby calls out from the table. "Did I lose something?"

"It's nothing," I shout inside, sounding more hostile than necessary. "Sorry. Mornings before school with her are—"

"I remember the days well, dear. But they do go by so fast. You'll miss these mornings too, I'm afraid," she says, humored with laughter.

"I'm sure you're right," I say, gazing down at the key chain. I find a reflection from the sunlight in the gloss of the rock and hues of colors swirling in the center. "Thanks again," I say.

"Oh—of course, dear. Have a good day," Mrs. Turble says, a floppy wave over her head as she turns to continue on her walk.

"You too." I wave to the back of her head and step back inside the house, then close the front door.

Odd. I drop the key chain into my pocket before returning to my laptop.

"Mom, what was it?" Abby asks again.

"I don't know. Mrs. Turble found a piece of old junk out front."

"Can I see it?"

"Not right now." This thing wouldn't belong to Abby. It's older than she is.

I need to know where this email came from.

With a refocus on the HTML sprawled out on my screen, I

grab the IP address, click edit and copy, then open the internet browser. The wi-fi connection must be struggling this morning. The page is loading slower than I can handle.

"What did Mrs. Turble want?" Griffin asks, jogging down the steps, clasping the buttons on the cuffs of his green button-down-shirt. He's less pale now, but red splotches from the hot water coat his fair skin. They aren't getting rid of him, even with budget cuts. I'm sure of it. He's the best teacher that school has. He makes his way across the living room and into the open kitchen.

"Nothing. Just her usual lost and found street-junk check-in."

Griffin snickers. "Anything good?"

"Nope," I chuckle.

While continuing toward the kitchen, Griffin holds his focus on me, his brows furrowing. "Are you already working at this hour? It's only the twentieth of the month, it's not time for bookkeeping yet, right?"

Aside from online shopping or scrolling aimlessly through social media, the only other time I use my laptop is to manage inventory and bookkeeping for the coffee shop. "No, no. It's not work," I say with a sigh. I consider telling him about the email, but when I look over at him, all I see is stress lining his eyes. He has enough on his plate right now. He doesn't need a petty email prank adding to it all. "There's just a form I forgot to fill out for Abby. It wouldn't pop-up on my phone."

I click back on Izzy's email to obscure the IP search page, facing those haunting words again.

You're in danger.

I click the X icon on the email, close my laptop, and pull the plug.

Glancing at Griffin in the kitchen, I watch him steal a

second of his time to smile at the kids as they eat. At least they *relieve* his stress.

"No cream cheese for those bagels?" he asks them, powering up the coffee maker.

"No," JJ mumbles.

"Ew, no. Cream cheese is gross," Abby says, making her sudden distaste for something she's always loved known. "And, Mom, what form are you talking about?"

I wasn't expecting her to ask. My face singes, heat flaring from my ears to my nose. "That thing...the—uh..." I pinch my nose and close my eyes, thinking up a quick lie. "The request for volunteers for the field trip to—um—the..."

"Art museum?" Abby asks, her eyes wide, perplexed that I could forget an important detail.

"Yes, that."

"You filled out that form a week ago," she says.

"Abbs, give Mom a break. She's juggling a lot," Griffin says, dropping his head to the side. He's the one juggling a lot.

Abby shoves the bagel into her mouth and fights an eye roll I can sense coming.

Griffin glances in my direction, a question lingering in his eyes. "You okay?"

"Yeah, why?" I sound like I ran around the block twice.

"Your cheeks are red," he says, making his way between the pillars toward the living room.

"I'm fine. It's the lighting."

We've only been together for two years, but it's like we've known each other forever sometimes. He knows me better than most ever have. He's taken the time to ask the hard questions most wouldn't ask, and some I won't answer.

I grew up in a dysfunctional household, then married young, falling into the same pattern, but with a different ending. I would have never considered a divorce had Jack not found someone to love more, and, in turn, replaced me as if I were an old, broken and useless appliance. It's kind of been the story of my life, I guess.

After a long court process of dividing our assets and handling the custody of our kids, I was on my own again—the thought of finding someone new and starting over seemed so far out of reach, but one conversation, and that one first date changed my forever.

* * *

I can't believe I agreed to a date. I'm thirty-eight and this just seems...odd. My divorce has only been official for four months. I told myself I'd wait a year before jumping back into the dating ring. I'm still raw. Although, I guess I've been raw for eighteen months at this point. For the first six months after Jack confessed his love for another woman, we slept in different bedrooms. Then I filed for an official separation. He moved into his apartment then. Until a judge signed our divorce papers, I didn't feel quite single.

It's not exactly like I was expecting to find a spark with a man during a fundraising event at the elementary school, but lo and behold, there we found ourselves in a casual conversation that led to an exchange of phone numbers. Now, I'm meeting Mr. Adler, or, Griffin, I suppose I should call him, for dinner at the steakhouse.

He offered to pick me up, but I prefer having my car nearby. Or it might just be that it's been a while since I've been on a date. A long while. Jack and I were married fifteen years. My God. I have no clue what I'm doing or should do. At least he already knows I have kids. I don't have to rip that Band-Aid off.

Griffin is waiting out front of the restaurant. A sports coat, jeans, his beautiful golden-brown hair framing his face. He smiles when he sees me walk toward him. The thought of someone admiring me in such a small way sends flutters through my stomach. I've always seen myself as a wallflower.

"You look gorgeous," he says, offering me his hand.

My face burns and I'm sure it doesn't go unnoticed. "I'd say you clean up well, but I get the feeling you always look this good."

Now we're even. Both of us and our blushing cheeks. He opens the door for me.

When we sit down, he pulls my chair out.

Jack wasn't that type of guy.

I'd say Griffin is already winning this first date.

"You know. There's something about you that strikes me as familiar," he says.

I glance down at my silverware, catching my reflection in the soup spoon. "I just have a familiar kind of—"

"No, you don't," he says, interrupting my automatic response when someone tells me I look familiar.

"Are you famous and lying low in the mountains of New Hampshire? Is it possible I've seen your face in a magazine or something?" He's a charmer. And his paper-white smile is alluring.

"I suppose, but only if there's a magazine for tired moms," I jest.

"Hey, be nice to yourself," he says, reaching his hand out to place over mine. "I was serious. It's like I know you, even though we've only crossed paths once. It's a good feeling. Comforting."

"Do you live in town? Or just work here?" I ask.

"I live in Anchoren. The commute isn't too bad."

Thirty minutes of driving through dense fog each morning would be rough.

"Did you grow up here in Spring Hill?" he asks.

"Yup. I'm one of those people who never left," I say with a chuckle. A chuckle that used to be a cry. If I got into college, I would have left.

"It's a great place here. After I got my teaching degree, I worked in Anchoren for a while, but it was time for a change. I love how small and cozy this town is, so when a teaching position opened at the elementary school last year, I jumped on it. I'm glad I did."

Me too.

FOUR

"Because my stalker—he's your new husband. You married him, Jess." I can hear Izzy's voice as if I last heard it yesterday. Except her voice would sound different now, twenty-two years later. I wouldn't be able to hear her voice through an email, especially one not written by her. I need to push this out of my head.

I'm smart enough not to fall for a spam-mail trap. People get emails like this all the time.

"Hey, where'd JJ just go?" Griffin asks as he steps away from the closing refrigerator door.

I whip my head to the left, knowing he was three seats down at the table a minute ago. His plate and bagel are there, but he isn't. "Abby, where's your brother?"

Her mom-blocking earbuds are in place, muting my every word as she scrolls through her phone.

"JJ?" I call out, trying my best to remain calm when I've already endured more than enough stress to last the week.

There's nothing but silence in response, except for a dog howling in the distance. I get up from behind my laptop, searching in every direction. "JJ?" I shout so my voice will carry up the stairs.

As my palms start to prickle, a flash of royal blue catches my eye. JJ's T-shirt. He's under the table; knees against his chest, face buried between them. I drop to his level and reach for him. "Buddy, what's going on? Tell me what's wrong."

He lifts his face and shrugs. "I don't think I should go to school today."

"What? Why?" I ask JJ, pulling him out from beneath the table. "Did something happen? You love school. Your teachers will miss you if you aren't there."

He stares at me, a blank look on his face. It's like he isn't hearing anything I'm saying.

"Sweetie, what's going on?"

He must sense the distress coating every cell in my body.

Why now, after so long? She would have resurfaced before today if she was alive, surely.

JJ continues to stare off into the distance, ignoring my question. I cup my hand beneath his chin.

He shifts his lost stare directly to my eyes, dropping his faint brows beneath his top lashes. "I don't know. I just have a bad feeling."

Me too, but I hope to God it's not about a prank email.

"About what?" I ask, trying to keep my voice calm. *We really need to get out of here.*

JJ glances up, above my head, his eyes glistening from the growing sunlight. "I think you know..."

I know? I don't even know when I cupped my hand around my throat, but the pinch from my nails tells me to take a breath.

He can't have read my emails.

Unless he snuck downstairs to use my laptop while I was asleep...but he's never done that before. Or, he could have been on my laptop and opened the icon with an envelope.

No, no. The email was unread.

It was definitely unread.

It was bold. I'd remember otherwise.

"I'm not sure what you're talking about, sweetheart. Can you tell me?" I release my hand from around my neck and stroke the side of his cheek, trying to hold my hand steady.

"JJ, buddy, what's going on? You'll feel better if you tell us," Griffin says, trying his hand at unraveling the mind of a seven-year-old.

"I don't want to—I'm just hungry," he says, standing up. He plops down on his seat at the table and continues eating as if nothing just happened.

I don't know what time the email came in, but they both went to bed before I did last night. At least, I'd told them to go to bed. They were in their rooms with the lights out.

Griffin drops the coffee pot into the sink and grabs his travel cup off the counter. "I have to run," he says, slipping his arm into the sleeve of his gray sports coat. I'm now holding my gaze on Abby, wondering if she knows what JJ is talking about.

With my phone placed securely in my pocket, I spin around, finding Griffin less than a footstep away. "Are you sure *you're* okay?" he asks, keeping his question inaudible to the listening ears.

I close my eyes and shake my head. "Yeah—I—I'm..." Griffin rubs his hand up and down my arm, gazing at me with a crease between his brows—concern. "I don't think I slept well last night. It's nothing. I'm fine." I press a smile on my lips, rising onto my toes to give him a kiss on the cheek. Any other form of affection will result in a teenage groan.

"I'm putting your laptop into your bag so you don't forget it," he says, taking the computer from the table.

"Oh—thanks, honey." It's a sign to let the email go. Just let it go.

"If you need anything today just text. I'll call you back during my break," he says, placing my laptop inside my bag. "Geez, this bag gets bigger and heavier every day, Jess. Do you really need all this stuff inside?"

"Yes. It's my work/Mom bag. I need everything inside. Or I will at some point. And if I don't have it, I will need it," I blab, forgetting to take a breath before speaking. It's the nerves. It's Izzy's name branded in my head.

"Okay, okay. Sorry for insulting the 'mom-bag'," he jests, holding his hands up in defense.

"Everyone knows to never insult the 'mom-bag'," Abby mutters, folding her fingers into air quotes.

Griffin chuckles. "You're right. I don't know what I was thinking," he says with a sigh. "Later, Abbs. Have a good day at school." He gives her a quick wave. One she doesn't reciprocate. One she may never reciprocate because he's the "jerk" who makes her mom happy. I tell myself she can't hear him, like she didn't hear me asking where JJ was. "JJ, buddy, you are going to nail your spelling test today. I just know it." Griffin holds his fist out across the table, waiting for JJ to bump his fist back. I love how hard he tries to be this person in their lives, one without a dad title, but still an authoritative figure. I'm sure it's harder than I can imagine.

"Thanks," JJ utters, mindlessly poking a hole into his bagel.

"Anytime, buddy."

Griffin moves my bag next to the coat closet, then coasts out the front door. It's as if everything around here is completely fine. It was until 5:59AM this morning.

"JJ, do you want to talk now? Tell me what's going on?"

"Mom. No. I said nooo," he grumbles, nibbling at his bagel.

"Okay, well I can't help you if you don't talk to me." I wish someone was offering to talk to *me* right now.

"Tell her," Abby urges JJ.

"Nooo," he argues.

"He thinks there's a ghost in the house," she says with laughter. *Good to know she can hear us now.* "I told him there's no such thing, right?"

"No, I don't," JJ snaps. "I'm seven. I heard 'sspstp sspst sspost' noises downstairs last night. Like whispering."

"Who? Who was talking?" I ask, interrupting what seems like a conversation only taking place between the two of them.

He shrugs. "I looked down the stairs, but the hallway was dark and—"

"He got scared," Abby says. "I told him to go back to bed because it was his imagination playing tricks on him. I didn't hear anything, and your door was closed so I assume you were asleep."

JJ flicks his head back and forth. "I'm not making it up. I heard it."

FIVE

On the drive to school, I ran out of questions and ways to ask JJ why he was so sure he hadn't imagined the sounds last night. I told him the house can make funny sounds at night because everyone is so quiet.

His steadfast belief of hearing someone whispering unnerves me more than I'll admit out loud. I wish he believed my excuse for random sounds in the night.

"How about we leave the lights on downstairs tonight?" I ask, pacifying him.

"Yeah, that would be good," he agrees, his voice quiet and unsure.

Abby still has her earbuds secured, blocking out any form of conversation I'd want to have with her before school. Peering through the corner of my eye, I watch as her thumbs tap wildly on her phone while blue bubbles flash across the screen every couple of seconds. Her oblivion to the world around her worries me to no end.

We pull up to the drop-off zone at the high school, and Abby jets out of the car before I have the gear in park.

"I love you. Have a good day—"

"Buh—" The car door slams without a chance for her to finish a one syllable word. Abby walks away as if the world around her doesn't exist, still staring at her phone. Yet, impressively, she manages to walk in a straight line toward her best friend Bella, Natalie's daughter. We always promised we'd have daughters around the same age who'd be best friends just like we were. But as we grew older, I knew the likelihood of that happening was slim. Except, it all seemed to work out just so. The kids have grown up together just like Natalie, Izzy, and I did.

The girls are getting so tall, I almost don't notice Natalie standing beside Bella, chatting with another mom. She's waving at me, walking toward me now, her keys dangling from one hand, a travel coffee mug in the other. I pull out of the looping line and up to the curb where cars aren't supposed to stop to let their kids out.

She leans down as I open the window. "Hey! You're never here this early."

"I just needed to chat with you this morning." I pinch my fingers against my thin edge of my eyebrow. I need a morning re-do already.

"Oh no. Is everything okay?" Natalie asks, staring at me for a long minute before leaning further into the car. "Jess?"

I take in a deep breath and let it out slowly. "Yeah—no, I don't know. It's a long story," I say, running my fingers through my blonde shoulder-length hair.

The lines on her forehead deepen as she continues to stare at me. "Can you give me a hint? You're worrying me."

I peer up at my rearview mirror, spotting JJ immersed in a kids' book club magazine.

When my eyes meet Natalie's again, she has her dark hair pushed back away from her forehead, her free hand pressed against her scalp with unease. "I'm just having a moment. That's all," I whisper, covering my hand around the side of my mouth. A car pulls up behind me and whoever's driving lies on the horn. I jump and my heart skips a beat.

"Ignore her. She can go around you. Did something happen? Is Abby okay?" she asks, her big brown eyes widening with curiosity.

I glance into my rearview mirror again, watching the mom behind me narrow her eyes and purse her lips. With a long blink, I push the angry mom out of my head, allowing my thoughts to return to the reason I wanted to talk to Natalie. "I—I, ah—got a stupid—prank, spam, whatever you want to call it, email from someone," I whisper, leaning closer toward the passenger window.

She releases her hand from her head and holds it out to the side. "What do you mean? What did it say?" Natalie is so thin and fit; I see her pulse thudding against the artery in her neck.

I stare at her for a long second, debating if I should pull her back into this pain too. But I need someone to tell me to delete the email and move on with my day.

"Izzy," I whisper, even quieter this time.

Natalie's olive complexion pales. She lifts her hand to her chest and her gaze darts around my head. "Our Izzy?" she confirms.

I nod. "There's more." Another car honks at me because I'm not supposed to be parked here. I look in the rearview mirror to see a van that isn't planning to go around me.

"My God. Do you think it's her?" Natalie stands upright, the car window framing just her chest and torso now. She's breathing so heavily. She must believe it's possible. Should I? The pain we both went through...Losing our best friend just before high school graduation. It's nothing we could have seen coming. The three of us had been as close as sisters since we were five.

The van honks again.

"I—I don't—"

She holds up her index finger to the van driver, asking them to wait a minute. I'm sure that won't go over well. "Listen, go drop JJ off, then call me."

"I will." She backs away from my car, her hand resting on her chest as she walks away in slow, contemplative steps.

Somehow, I don't think she's going to tell me I'm overreacting like I wanted her to. Like I needed her to.

SIX

My brakes squeal as I lower my speed to a crawl while looping around the elementary school parking lot. All eyes seem to be on me and my squeaking brakes until I come to a stop behind the line of cars waiting for the clock to strike 8:00.

I glance out my window at the staff parking lot, searching for Griffin's rust-orange hybrid SUV. The color is hard to miss, making it easy for me to see he's not here yet. He left over an hour ago, he should have been here by now. My mind races with concern.

Then the jarring words from the email slash through all other thoughts: "You need to run—before it's too late."

I blink for a long second. The email isn't real. I need to forget about it. The kids all run toward Griffin in the morning. They aren't afraid of him, nor should anyone be. He's the sweetest man I've ever met.

A car horn squawks at me, making it known I haven't pulled up close enough to the other cars butting up against each other in line. I hold my hand up to apologize for not paying attention.

A group of teachers step out from the front entrance,

inviting the kids into the school. A dozen car doors open at once as kids pile onto the sidewalk. "Hey, buddy, do you—"

"Love you," he shouts, unclasping the belt of his booster seat. He kicks open the door and jumps out of the car.

"I love you too," I tell the slamming door.

I pull my phone out of the cup holder in search of any missed messages from Griffin. Nothing. He'd call me if something was wrong. I glance up once more before pulling out of the looping line, spotting JJ waving toward the parking lot. I cut my stare to the left as Griffin pulls into a parking space. He rushes across the school grounds, his phone pinned against the side of his face as he struggles to put his coat on. He's smiling as he talks to whoever's on the other line. Before he reaches the school doors, he ends the call and stares down at his phone, a smile still lingering. He doesn't notice me in the parent line or JJ waving at him furiously. I pick up my phone once more just to see if I got a call that went right to voicemail, but there's nothing there.

I follow the train of vehicles out of the lot, stopping several more times before being given the chance to turn onto the main road.

"Siri, call Natalie," I prompt my phone.

There's hardly one complete ring before she answers the call. Her voice booms through my speakers. "That was the longest ten minutes of my life."

"I've been stirring over this email for just over two hours, and I feel like it's been a year. I am completely freaked out."

"What did the email say?" Natalie asks. "Do you think it could really be Izzy?" She seems as pessimistic as I'd be if she were telling me this story.

I don't pause intentionally, but her question is so casual, and the email is anything but. Whoever wrote the email would like me to end my blissfully happy marriage. That's why I should stop reading so far into this. I'm happy. He's happy.

I think.

I just need Natalie to say what I really need to hear. That this is some kind of sick prank. This entire town spent years searching for Izzy, only to leave the missing person case cold and closed.

"Jess?" Natalie says, interrupting my thoughts.

"I'm here. Sorry. She said she was sorry for losing touch and that she was afraid of the man who was stalking her. Even to this day."

"Oh...my God," Natalie says. "This is—wow. I just don't... Could she be alive after all this time?" Her inflection of hope adds a layer of guilt to my conscience. If the following words in her email didn't threaten to ruin my life, I'd want to believe it's her. I'd convince myself it's her. Just to believe she's okay. I could go on with my life, knowing she's okay. I'd feel awful for whatever she's been living through. But I'd also be terrified for me and the kids.

"She also told me the stalker's real name."

"Seriously? Do we know him?"

"She said that the stalker..." I take a breath. There isn't enough air to fill my lungs. "Nat, she—whoever—said Griffin was the stalker." The words are foreign on my tongue, or my tongue is numb, lodging in my throat. Never mind spilling out the rest of what the email said.

Her silence is understandable but also deafening.

"Jess," she says, with unexpected laughter piping through the speakers. "Come on. That is the most ridiculous thing I've ever heard. Griffin? Of all people..."

Tears fill my eyes because she's saying everything I needed to hear.

"I'm jealous that you met Griffin before me," she says, still laughing. "He's this gorgeous, perfect male specimen. It could be some jealous woman from his past trying to get under your skin. Ignore it."

"You're jealous?" I ask, rehashing the first comment she made.

"I'm kidding."

"Good because you're married, and so am I. To Griffin..." I remind her with a forced laugh.

"I meant if I wasn't already married. He's like the sweetest, most caring person I've ever met. And he loves kids. He's a teacher, and from what I've heard, one of the best."

"He is," I agree. "Which is why some woman from his past would want him back, right?"

"Okay, bad example. My point is...whoever wrote that email clearly doesn't know Griffin at all."

"Yeah," I say, wishing her words lifted more of the weight off my shoulders.

"Seriously, Jess. Don't lose sleep over this. These kinds of emails go around. People find your information on the dark web and exploit it, get under your skin, then try to get something from you. This person could be a totally random weirdo in a basement somewhere. Don't pay attention to it."

"What if—"

"Okay, I know you. If you really think there's a chance that this could be Izzy, somehow, someway, then just write a quick response, asking her a question you know only Izzy would have the answer to. If there's no response—that's your answer. If there is a response, well...wow, and we'll go from there. As much as I wish the email were true—apart from the Griffin bit, of course, I think it's unlikely to hold any merit."

"Yeah. I'll think about it," I say.

"Oh God, I gotta run. The school is already calling me about something. Call me later when you have an update. And breathe."

The call disconnects and I feel only the slightest bit of relief.

Natalie is right. Griffin hasn't given me one reason to question his character. I wouldn't have married again unless I was certain he was someone I could trust and happily spend my life with.

From the day we met at JJ's school, it all came so naturally. Our lives blended together as if we were always meant to be. I was sure we'd have some hurdles to clear along the way. With me bringing two kids into his life and this being his first marriage, I expected turbulence. But so far, the only person who's had trouble adjusting is Abby, not shocking at fourteen. Griffin has been amazing with them both. JJ loves him and I'm sure Abby will grow fonder of him over time.

I have no reason to question him or the validity of an email from someone who disappeared from my life over twenty years ago.

My compulsive questions travel with me to the parking spaces behind the coffee shop. I pull in between my two employees' cars, thankful Sam and Rachel are already here taking care of the café while I try to shake the million thoughts out of my head.

I pull down my visor to check my complexion in the mirror, realizing I forgot to put on mascara before leaving the house. At forty, I don't recognize the person I once was, especially not twenty-two years ago. I'm still as fair-skinned and covered in freckles, but the sharpness of my freckles looks more like blurry dots now. My hair turns grayer by the day, requiring upkeep with blonde highlights to fill my roots. Even my eyelashes have become ashy blonde. I look bug-eyed beneath my pale, thinning eyebrows.

God, I shouldn't have even looked.

A woman from Griffin's past would look like a better option for him these days. Who knew forty would come with so many fine lines?

I grab my bag and pull the keys from the ignition, the collection of key chains dangling together. Five deep breaths are all I get before stepping into the shop's storage space. The air is thickly flavored with a mix of hazelnut, vanilla, and dark coffee beans—a recipe to decompress on any other day.

Dropping my bag down on my desk in the corner of the back room, I push my hair back out of my face. The rush of energy from the customers and the sight of a long line at the counter always perks me up. Then I watch Sam and Rachel seamlessly dance in circles around each other, helping every familiar face. There's happiness everywhere I look.

This is my true reality, not that email.

"Morning, Jess! We're running low on sesame seed bagels, and caramel sweetener," Rachel says, multitasking in a way I've never been able to. The younger millennials have a way of doing ten things at once where I struggle to do a few. "I added it to the list on your desk, but we've had an influx of requests for those two items this morning."

"I'll get those restocked right away."

I find Sam topping a specialty coffee. "How are you? Do you need anything?" I ask him, placing my hand on his shoulder.

"Good morning! I think I'm good. I'll let you know if anything comes up," he says, whisking away to bring a customer their order.

Thank God I have these two running the show up front. "I'll be in the back if either of you need anything."

This little dream of mine to run a coffee shop came to life much quicker than I could have expected.

I thought the process would take years, especially in a small town. I took it as a sign of fate when a reasonably priced space became available on Main Street. I applied for a loan, the necessary licenses, and within a few months, I was up and running.

The pride of success fades to black as my gaze falters over my bag, knowing my laptop is a minefield waiting for me.

I open the laptop, finding the IP address search page still

open, and my heart thunders in my chest. I thought I'd closed this page down.

I hover my mouse over the red X icon to close out the screen. An IP address won't give me any information, and I'm not about to go looking for some bored teenager in a basement hacking email addresses. Natalie's right. I've heard of the dark web, but I'm content staying away from it—whatever it is. I imagine a black screen and green lines of text unraveling. *Nope. No thanks.*

I click the X on the top left of the screen, waiting for the window to close. But the cursor switches to a spinning circle.

The never-ending spinning circle.

My machine freezes again.

My gaze wanders along the lines of HTML. It's a rabbit hole I don't need to dive down. There's more logic behind this being some kind of phishing scam than anything else.

I'll just do a hard restart. I reach around to the side of my laptop, feeling around for the power button, when a line of the code catches my eye.

Domain: aol.com | Sender Id: xxxx0014.exc

Location coordinates Latitude: 43.9654°

N Longitude: 71.4824° W

Sender host: Spring Hill, NH

I stare at the name of the small town I've lived in my entire life, confirming my suspicion it's someone in the area trying to poke at me.

SEVEN

APRIL 2001 - TWENTY-TWO YEARS AGO

Izzy

The ear-splitting screech of Natalie's brakes as she backs out of her driveway six houses down, and then again when she stops between my house and Jess's, must rattle the windows of every house in our neighborhood. Dad said she's in desperate need of new brake pads. I was the one driving the three of us until my car battery died. And Jess is still saving up for a car. Of all the things her dad buys her to make her love him more, a car is not one of them. Our options are squeaky brakes, or the unthinkable school bus no high school senior wants to take.

I grab my backpack from my bed and catch a glimpse of Jess jetting out her front door and checking the doorknob to make sure it's locked. Her dad goes to work so early every morning that she wakes up to an empty house. It's sad she never has anyone to say goodbye to. She'll always say it's no big deal and that it's nothing new to her, but I see through her words. I see the sad way she gazes in my direction when my parents are giving me a hug in public. It breaks my heart. I feel guilty knowing how lonely it must be having no one around, especially when I do my fair share of complaining about Hannah being the most annoying sister in the world. I'm sure she'd do anything for a sibling, annoying or not. I try to be that to her as much as I can.

Jess and I couldn't be living more opposite lives even though we live just opposite each other on the street. As seniors in high school, she's been fully responsible for herself for longer than I can remember, and here I am with a mom who still waits by the front door in the mornings with two plastic baggies, a muffin in each, and two brown paper lunch bags in the other.

Despite my lack of hunger this early in the morning, she still insists on making sure I have something to eat now and later. "Make sure you eat," she says with forced cheerfulness, her voice tense and strained. "Jess too. You can tell her I said she looks too skinny lately." The comment will flatter Jess, but Mom doesn't mean it as a compliment.

"I know, I know. We will. I promise."

She presses her lips into a smile and curls a strand of my short hair behind my ear. "I love you, sweetie."

"What's wrong?" I ask.

She only fiddles with my white strands of hair, a unique anomaly among my auburn locks, when she's worried about something.

"Wrong? Nothing's wrong," she says with a scoff. "You're just growing up so quickly. It's hard to wrap my head around sometimes."

"I guess it happens to all of us," I say, kissing her on the cheek.

"Okay, well, just be careful," she whispers.

Her recent state of distress is palpable, giving me a chill to battle against April's morning wind. She'll continue to tell me everything is fine, but I know it's not. Dad told me she's silently grieving over a countdown of months until I leave for college in the fall. That's still months away, though. Plus, she still has

Hannah here. It'll be another six years before she leaves for college.

I step out the front door of my long and narrow one-story house. My gaze drifts directly to my dormant Nissan, a silent reminder that I need two more paychecks to get a new car battery. I hate depending on others to give me rides. I could take the bus, but it's a mile away and Natalie has offered to drive me until my car is working again.

As I adjust my backpack over my shoulder, a rattling tap, tap, tap, tap, tap catches my attention—an unfamiliar sound. A white envelope flaps under my wiper blade.

Our mailbox is at the end of our driveway. Why would someone stick something to my car? Plus, the hike up the mountainous driveway is a steep commitment. This is why Natalie and Jess are waiting at the bottom for me. I rush to my car and snag the envelope. My heart flutters as I inspect it while jogging down the driveway. It's unmarked on the front and back.

I slip into the back seat of Natalie's red Volkswagen Jetta, assaulted by a douse of Gap perfume. Jess curls her hands around the curve of the front seat, her long blonde waves flying everywhere. "Your hair looks super cute today, and I love those little butterfly clips with the pixie fringe," she says. Jess has been trying to cheer me up after chopping my hair short a few weeks ago, but I'm still in a state of regret.

Natalie peeks over her shoulder next. "Oh wow! I love it! You're so freaking cute." *Like a little girl.* The two of them seem to have blossomed into women this year and yet, I still look like a twelve-year-old.

"Thanks," I utter, staring back down at the mysterious envelope.

"What's in the envelope?" Jess asks.

"I don't know. I found it on my windshield."

I secure my seat belt, then hand the muffin and lunch bag

over Jess's shoulder. "My mom said you look skinny and to eat. Here."

"Well, thank you," she says, clearly flattered.

I catch Natalie's eye in the rearview mirror, her lips subtly quirking to the side. We've shared the same silent look for years, knowing Jess has no one making sure she eats three healthy meals a day. The older she's gotten, the less effort she puts into preparing food or meals for herself. She tells us she isn't a breakfast or a lunch person, but we both worry she isn't a dinner person either, many days.

Jess opens the plastic bag, the scent of blueberry mixing with the perfume. Natalie pulls away from the curb and the moment of quiet allows me to refocus on the weird envelope.

I pull out a piece of paper, covered in lines of neat penmanship. My name has been written over multiple times, to darken the ink, making it bleed through to the other side.

"Izzy, what is it?" Natalie asks, her brakes punctuating the question as we come to the end of the road.

"It's a letter to me..."

"From whom?"

"I have no idea. There's no name at the bottom."

"What does it say?" Jess asks, her mouth full.

"Holy cow...It's some kind of cryptic poem about stars, magnetic forces, and a serendipitous tango..."

Izzy,
We're two stars drifting through the night sky
I gaze and glimpse but cannot pause to say hello
It is your beauty, lingering like a shimmery sigh
Such magnetic force, your allure, impossible to forego
One day, valor will ignite me, and I'll soar up high
To cease this charming, serendipitous tango

No longer content to merely pass you by...
X

"A poem? Like, from a secret admirer?" Natalie gushes.

"I guess so," I reply. My cheeks burn as I reread the words.

"If it's a 'holy cow' kind of poem, I bet it's from Peter!" Jess shouts. "I saw him staring at you at lunch the other day."

Peter hasn't said a word to me in two years. I'm not sure he's the type to write me a poem.

"He is the quiet, smoldering type," Natalie adds. "Secret poet...I'd believe it."

The excitement of having a secret admirer battles with a sense of anticipation and apprehension as we walk in through the school's front doors.

My heart pounds in my chest, considering every person we walk by. Friends tug at my arm to say hi and each touch makes me jump. There's nothing wrong with a bit of mystery in life, but I know I won't rest until I figure out who wrote the poem.

I pass Peter, the lid of his baseball cap curled tightly over his forehead, hiding his eyes. We were sandbox friends when we were little. I think he'd talk to me if he wanted to. I can't imagine any of the guys in our school coming up with the idea to do this. It could be a prank. A good, believable one.

"See you after school," Jess says, looping her arm around my shoulders for a quick squeeze. "We'll figure out who this mystery man is. Don't worry." She veers off down another hallway toward her homeroom, leaving me to continue walking in a trance to the last hallway on the right.

A locker slams behind me, and I spin around to see who's there, but whoever it was is already out of sight. The hallways are quickly emptying as everyone spills into their appropriate classrooms, and the halls seem to widen as I take the last corner.

Footsteps speed up behind me and I whip around again, finding Sarah Adams, our class secretary who is never late for class, hustling down the hall. "Good morning," she says.

"Good morning."

I slink into my homeroom class, also science class, and discreetly take a seat. I slip my backpack beneath my chair and slouch to blend in between the rows.

The bell rings and Mr. Brown shuffles in, taking attendance without wasting a second. He stands beside the chalkboard, rolling back and forth from heel to toe, calling out names. The writing on the chalkboard includes a lesson plan for today.

The topics that make my skin crawl.

Lesson Plan Topics:
Behavior of Celestial Objects
Stellar Activity
Magnetic Force

My mind races as I recite some of the poem tucked into my pocket. The words "*Such magnetic force, your allure...*" haunt me.

Mr. Brown calls out my name, wrangling me back to reality. "Isobel Lester." I find him staring at me with an uncanny smirk as if he knew where my thoughts were.

"Present."

I suddenly can't breathe.

As the day crawled forward, the words in the poem replayed in my head over and over, puzzling me more and more. I needed to know who'd left that note for me.

I'm waiting at my locker for Natalie and Jess, watching everyone walk by, questioning if one of the guys I've known since kindergarten could be this person.

Jess scuffles down the corridor, her low-rise flared jeans, dragging beneath her Birkenstock clogs. She was wearing a sweatshirt this morning, but she's down to a camouflage patterned crop top now. Jess and Natalie like to flaunt their goods.

Me, on the other hand, I opt for chunky black heels with cargo pants and shirts that cover my belly button. Maybe if my goods ever grow in someday, I'll want to flaunt them too. Until then, I can continue to look "adorable".

"Natalie forgot she has a Student Council meeting today. Do you want to wait for her or just walk home?" Jess asks, adjusting her backpack over her shoulder.

"Her meetings run long sometimes, and I have a lot of homework tonight. Do you mind walking?" I ask her.

Jess purses her lips and sighs. "Well, I'm not going to make you walk alone," she says.

"It's okay. If you want to stay here, I'll be fine." Jess is never in a rush to get home, and I understand why. There's no one to go home to. Her dad won't walk in through the front door until at least eight tonight.

"You can come over and do your homework with me if you want?" I offer.

She shrugs. "Thanks for the offer, but I have to do the laundry and I left a sink full of dishes this morning."

I never know how to respond to her when she makes comments like that. I know my life is a cakewalk compared to hers and it makes me feel guilty. "How about I help you first, then you can come over and do homework with me?"

"No, no. You know how my dad gets if someone comes over," she says.

"Yeah." She can go wherever she wants but can't have anyone over. It's the exact opposite with my parents. They insist on me having friends over rather than me moseying around town with nothing to do.

"Enough about my chores. Did you figure out who the mystery man is yet?" she asks, nudging her elbow into my side.

"I have absolutely no clue."

"Can I see the note? I might recognize the handwriting." Jess mulls over the paper half of the walk home, squinting her eyes, pointing at words, shaking her head. "I don't know if we know anyone this smart." She laughs. "Dude, this is deep. Who is this guy?"

It's hard to keep the smallest secrets here in this town, never mind trying to pull off a mysterious anonymous note.

All I know is, the closer we get to our street, the more of an urge I have to look over my shoulder. I keep thinking this guy is just going to pop out from behind a tree and shout: "Surprise!"

EIGHT

I wish the confirmation of that email coming from someone in town had put my mind at ease, but now I want to know who would go to those lengths to send something so awful. The loss of Izzy is a sore subject to anyone who lived through what many of us did when she went missing. It's hard to imagine anyone using Izzy as click-bait, and for what reason?

The swinging door between the front and back of the shop squeals and moans before Rachel presses the ball of her foot against the brass kick plate. She latches her fingers around the edge of the wooden slab. "Sorry to bother you, but did you already order more bagels?" she asks.

"No, I was about to do that," I tell her, closing my laptop and the frozen screen with the map coordinates of Spring Hill I'd been staring at.

"We need more cranberry scones too," she says.

"Got it," I tell her, unable to form any more words than the few essentials, pressing an unconvincing smile onto my lips.

Her head falls to the side. "You're super pale. You feeling okay?"

I swallow before responding because there's a glob of

phlegm lodged in my throat. "Yeah, yes, I'm totally fine," I say, mirroring her casual tone. "JJ was up with nightmares last night. I just need—"

"A hazelnut Frappuccino with soy milk, two sugars, and one pump of mocha coming right up. Whip or no whip?" she asks, poking her finger into the air.

"No whip is fine," I say, holding on to the smile that's becoming heavier by the second. "Thanks, Rach."

"You got it, boss," she says, spinning back into the front of the shop. The door slaps shut behind her.

Some days, I regret not leaving town after Izzy disappeared. I thought about it. Leaving the pain behind would have been the easiest route to take. But like everyone else in this one stoplight town, life carried us forward to today. We had no choice. It was clear Izzy wasn't coming back.

Order form. I need to focus. I reach up to the wall of hooks beside me, finding the clipboard of order forms missing. I shuffle around the papers on my desk, wondering if I piled something on top of it, but it's not here either. I scoot my chair back and peek under my desk, finding it out of reach, but upright against the wall. It must have fallen off the hook.

I crouch beneath the desk, reaching for the clipboard.

"Jessica..." The familiar sound of my name on his lips strikes a nerve down the center of my spine. The unexpected visit stuns me into hitting my head beneath the desk as I try to stand up.

I cup my hand atop my head, and this time dodge the desk to get up onto my feet. There's only one reason he'd be here... The chill in the room seeps through my shirt as I face more unwanted trouble. "Jack, what's wrong?" I try to mask the emotional distress in my question, remaining strong in front of a wrecking ball. Yet a tremor in my voice reveals my true apprehension.

"Did you receive a call from the high school?" he asks, raising an eyebrow.

"No," I say, unable to hide the defensive tone. I grab my phone from the edge of my desk and flip it over, finding a missed call. I'm first on the guardian contact list and Jack is second. "What's wrong? Is Abby okay?" How did I miss this call?

"She's fine," he assures me. "But the principal would like to speak to us." All I can focus on is the word "us" as he rubs his hand over his glistening bald head. Are we still considered an "us" now that we're divorced?

"Is she in trouble?" I ask, dreading the answer.

"Yeah, why else would the principal want to talk to us? She was caught sneaking out of school between class periods."

Jack is so matter of fact and speculative. I refuse to jump to an assumption that our daughter is in trouble just because the principal calls. Abby isn't innocent by any means, but she's only been in trouble for breaking superficial rules up to now. A dress code violation when she decided to hike her skirt up after arriving at school. Then argued her case. There was also the time she "exercised her rights, *freedom of speech*," after a teacher scolded her for offering an opinion at the wrong time. She's a teenage girl, testing boundaries, and stands up for what she believes, too often maybe. But she wouldn't sneak out of school for no reason.

"Did they say what the reason was for this so-called attempt?"

"No, he said he wanted to talk to us in person."

It's not even ten in the morning and I can't catch a moment to breathe without my heart racing. "I'll meet you there," I tell him.

"I don't mind driving. The shop is on my way back to work anyway."

I spent fifteen years being the passenger in his car, but right now I need to be in the driver's seat. I also need to clear my head. "Thanks, but I'll take my car. I'll meet you there in a few minutes." I pack my things back into my tote haphazardly. Jack leaves the way he came in, the swinging shop door. I give him a minute to leave the building before sticking my head out to the front. "Rach, I have to run to the school real quick for Abby. I'll be back soon. Call if you need anything."

"No problem, boss," she squeaks. Her voice becomes a whisper as she says: *"I don't think she placed that inventory order yet. Her head is totally in the clouds—"*

Rachel must not think I notice the whispers as I walk out the door. But I've become very astute at hearing what I shouldn't hear.

NINE

The sky darkens, each heavy cloud mirroring my thoughts while navigating the back roads. So much for that "nice" day. Each turn a sharp hairpin bend between jagged cliffs. The closer I get to the school, the tighter my grip on the steering wheel, still trying to figure out how I could have missed a call from the school. I've never done that.

With my car in park, I head for the front doors, wondering why I don't see Jack's sporty BMW anywhere. He must have had to stop somewhere on the way. I can't help wondering what people think when they look at the two of us co-parenting. No one knows why we got divorced since I kept the news of his affair to myself. It's not something I want the kids to find out. Still, to the outside world, we seemed like the perfect couple, but no one wants to be a part of small-town gossip.

I hit the buzzer next to the front door, staring at the little speaker box, awaiting the questions about my reason for visiting during school hours.

"Come on in," the school secretary says instead of asking me why I'm here. There's a camera above me. They can see who I am, but now I've crossed the threshold of confirming my identity to the face of a problematic child. The door buzzes and I hurry inside, up to the front window. "Good morning, Mrs. Adler. You can go on back into the principal's office. He's waiting for you there. Will Abby's father be joining, as well?"

"Yes, Jack should be here shortly. He must have taken the long way," I say, rounding the corner and tucking my loose strands of hair behind my ears. He should be here by now. There really isn't a "long" way.

I knock on the door donning a "principal" embossed placard. Not that I didn't already know which office belongs to him since I've been invited to speak to him in the past.

"Come in," the muffled invitation carries through the closed door.

I open the door, finding Abby sitting in one of three chairs facing the principal's desk. She's pale and looks like she's been crying, and doesn't turn her head to look at me. "Sweetie, what happened?" I ask her, ignoring the brute square-jawed face staring me down from behind his desk.

"You might have better luck at getting an answer from her," Mr. Downing says with an aggravated sigh.

"I needed some fresh air," she utters, avoiding eye contact. "I wasn't trying to break school rules. I had five minutes before my next class."

"Our rules are clearly stated in every classroom and hallway, and repeated as reminders during every morning announcement," Mr. Downing adds.

"Why didn't you go to the nurse? Are you not feeling well? Is that why you needed fresh air?"

"Mom..." she says.

A knock on the door stops her from answering my question.

"Come in," Mr. Downing says.

I can smell Jack's woody aftershave before he even steps into the room. I turn to face him and greet him with a smile as if

I didn't just see him at the coffee shop, before moving to take the seat closest to Abby.

He leans over Mr. Downing's desk with his hand outstretched. "How's it going, sir?"

"Well. Very well. I can't complain. Nice to see you again. How are things at the firm?"

"Doing great. We're having an outstanding quarter."

"Fantastic," Mr. Downing says. *The coffee shop is flourishing too,* but I'll keep that to myself.

"What's going on, sweetheart?" Jack asks Abby.

"I needed air," she says through gritted teeth. "It's legal in most states I believe."

"Okay, okay," I say, trying to calm her down before she says something she might regret—we all might regret.

"I don't have any other answer other than the one I've given you," she continues. "I apologize for breaking school rules. I won't let it happen again."

She's covering up for something or someone. She doesn't ever apologize this quickly, not to anyone. It's a rite of passage of being a teenager.

"Abby, the issue here is, you stormed through the hallways filled with hostility, causing panic among the students. Several teachers and an administrator tried to help you, asking that you calm down and have a word with them so they could help you with whatever was upsetting you. By the time you reached the main entrance, you were warned of the consequence if you set off the security alarm and yet, you did it anyway. In setting off the alarm, you caused chaos that led to a lock down. While I'd like to believe your reason of needing fresh air, I'm afraid I can't let you walk out of here with just a lecture. We're going to need to involve the school adjustment counselor to work through whatever troubles you are experiencing. For now, I'd like you to leave the premises for the rest of today, and tomorrow, to think about your actions. I expect you to email your teachers, inform them why you aren't in school and catch up on any missed work by Wednesday."

"Is this truly necessary?" I ask Mr. Downing.

"Our rules are in place for a good reason, Mrs. Adler, and I can't make exceptions. With the number of school incidents on the rise, we take security very seriously."

"Of course," Jack says. "We'll make sure to have a talk with Abby about her behavior and sort through this at home. We appreciate you not taking any further disciplinary measures." He doesn't have to kiss the man's ass. He put a black mark on Abby's permanent files. My face heats up to a temperature that must be making me a nice shade of burgundy.

"We'll see to it that this doesn't happen again." I refuse to hide my bitterness. "Abby, let's go."

The three of us walk in silence until we reach the parking lot. Jack releases a heavy breath and folds his arms across his chest. "I expect better from you," he tells Abby.

"Well, stop expecting so much," she retorts, a matching raised eyebrow. "I stopped expecting to have two parents who live together. It's only fair, right?"

If we were still married, I'd tell her not to speak to her father that way, but that's not my responsibility anymore.

"Really?" He drops his arms and pulls his keys out of his pocket. "I'll speak to you after work."

I'll bring her with me to work. It's no problem at all. Your job is far too important to be affected by situations like these.

Abby's blank stare at Jack speaks volumes. It sometimes seems as though she's lost her faith in both of us since the divorce. She's asked each of us many times if the divorce was because of her. But no matter how many times we assure her that isn't the case, it seems like those thoughts still linger. I would never want to taint the kids' perspective of their father with the truth of why we're not together, but that notion makes this divide much harder to explain to them too.

I blame myself for her behavioral issues. I'm too easy on her, fearing the resentment she might have toward me for remarrying. A therapist has and will tell me that acting like her friend won't do her any good, but I fear what will happen if I don't.

Jack leans in and gives Abby a hug and a quick peck on the top of her head, then presses his key fob. *Chirp chirp* says the beautiful elite-class BMW.

I'm still standing in the parking lot, watching Jack peel out of his spot when I unlock my car, hearing the less-than-fancy stiff *toot toot.*

The car door of my SUV opens and closes, and Abby settles into the passenger seat. I follow, debating which direction to start my questions with.

It isn't until we pull out of the parking lot that I find a word to start with. "Abbs—"

"Don't," she says. "Now, go dismiss JJ from class. He's in danger as you likely already know."

"Excuse me? Why in the world would I pull him out of school? What danger is he in?" I quickly pull over onto the side of the road because I can't predict what her game plan is. The rubble putters beneath my tires and the brakes squeal to a stop.

"If I could have picked him up an hour ago, I would have," she says, staring at me with a dead cold gaze. "Why else do you think I was trying to leave?"

TEN

"Abby, what are you talking about? You tried to leave school so you could go dismiss your brother? Why?" My volume is growing despite trying my best to remain calm with her.

"Who is Izzy? Tell me," she demands in return.

"Excuse me?" She shouldn't know anything about Izzy. I haven't ever spoken about her to my kids. "Did you go through my emails?"

Abby drops her chin, staring down at her intertwined fingers. "I was trying to find the tracking number for the new shoes you ordered for me, so I logged into your email account. Everyone knows your password...it's not like it's a secret. I just wanted to know if they'd be here before the weekend."

"So, you figured you had free range to go through my other emails too?"

She drops her hands by the sides of her legs and clenches her fists. "I didn't mean to open it."

I highly doubt that's the truth.

"But I did see it, and—why would anyone talk about Griffin that way? He teaches at JJ's school. He's won teacher of the year like three times in the past five years. Why would anyone think that of him? He doesn't have a mean bone in his body." Abby has been her typical teenage self since Griffin moved in, but it's still nice to see her defending him. That speaks volumes alone.

The intention of the email is to get a rise out of me, and I know Griffin isn't a concern. All I want to know is why someone would dredge up Izzy's past and revive it through her old email address.

"Izzy was a friend from high school. I haven't spoken to her in over twenty years. The email is spam. You don't need to worry. I'm going to check into it."

"Just a friend, telling you you're married to a stalker? Who would do that?" she presses.

"Someone bored with a computer?" I reply. "I don't know why."

"Yeah, but whether it's spam or potentially Izzy, that email was obviously meant to scare you. Whoever it is knows about your old friend and Griffin. They know who you are—who we all are. What if it's not just some prank, Mom? We live in a world full of sickos. How many times have you told me this?"

Abby's questions ignite my stress to a higher level. I don't have it in me to argue with her over the details right now.

"You're not wrong. There are a lot of bad people in this world," I solidify the statement I've made to her many times over the years.

"That's why I was trying to get out of school so I could get to JJ. If someone's trying to get your attention, for whatever reason, what will they do next? It's all I could think."

I think Abby has watched too many murder mystery movies. But her explanations are getting to me. Am I brushing this off too easily? The thought of anything happening to JJ...Griffin can't keep an eye on him during the school day. He has his own class. They have recess at separate times. The school building is locked up like Fort Knox, but the playground is surrounded by short barn fences. Anyone could get through.

I'm sure I'm overreacting. It's a prank email.

I glance over at Abby for a quick second, watching her nibble at her fingernails, her eyes glazed over as she stares out the windshield. My stomach tightens, wondering what else is going through her head.

"You know what. I'm going to go pick up your brother and then I'll figure this all out. You'll see there's nothing to be concerned about."

What if I run into Griffin while I'm dismissing him? I'll just say I'm taking him to the dentist. An appointment popped up. I'll be lying. I never lie to him. We don't do that. I need to get myself under control.

None of this is logical. Yet, I'm taking my kid out of school.

I turn into an open spot facing the front of the school and glance over at Abby, tapping away on her phone. "Abby, this conversation does not leave this car, and not a word about it to your brother."

"But..." she says.

"Wait here," I interrupt her.

"Or you could let me come in with you. I can go to Griffin's classroom and simply ask him if he's truly some kind of psycho stalker on the loose," she shouts before I can close my door.

I wrench it back open. "Abby! Seriously?"

"Fine. We'll just sit here and wonder," she says.

My pulse races the entire time I'm waiting in the office for JJ to walk in through the doors. He'll be worried that I'm picking him up without warning him first. Then he'll be mad when I lie about going to the dentist in front of the front desk staff.

"What are you doing here?" JJ asks, walking in through the oak wooden door covered in encouraging educational posters.

"There was an opening at the dentist, and I needed to take the appointment. I'm sorry, kiddo." JJ drops his head back and whines.

"No. Please, I'll be fine. My tooth doesn't even hurt anymore."

"Aw, JJ, you're lucky to have a mom who cares so much about your hygiene. It's better not to let a cavity sit in your mouth. You can be brave, I know it," one of the front desk assistants says to him.

I scribble my initials on the sign-out sheet centered on the counter, then wave and mouth a "thank you" to the woman urging JJ to move along.

"Oh, Mrs. Adler, should I let Mr. Adler know you've taken JJ home? I know he drives him home after school."

"That would be so helpful. Thank you very much. I was going to leave him a message, but he might not get it before he goes looking for him."

"I'll let him know right now," she says with a smile, lifting the phone from the receiver.

"Thank you," I say again, pulling JJ out the door, into the main entrance, and out the front door as fast as I can without looking like I'm running from something.

"Are we in a rush too?" he asks, still whining.

"A bit. It's okay. I want to get into the car."

I urge him into his booster seat and secure the seat belt over him, blindingly trying to click it into place. "What are you doing here?" he asks Abby.

"None of your business," she says. I'll ignore the rudeness in exchange for her telling him the truth.

I close JJ's door before saying another word and slip into my seat just as fast. I drop my phone into the cupholder and scratch the metal frame of the keyhole several times before getting the key in to start the car.

JJ is asking question after question and I'm stacking them up in my head as I back out of the spot and leave the parking lot.

"Now what?" Abby asks.

"We're going to the dentist," JJ answers.

The amount of pressure against my chest is seeping into my stomach, causing cramps. "Actually, first we're going to the coffee shop."

"But you said we're going to the dentist!"

"JJ, shut it," Abby says.

"Abby..." I scold her.

Back into the same parking spot behind the coffee shop, replaying my morning routine again, but with the kids in tow. I grab the coat I've shed, my bag and the keys as we all pour out of the car. "Please keep your voices down and stay in the back room," I tell them.

Abby stops walking after stepping up onto the curb next to the back door and stares down at— "Is that my phone?"

"You left it in the cupholder," she says. "But...you should see what popped up." Her bottom lip falls as if she's surprised by what she sees.

"What? What is it?" I ask.

"I—I don't—"

I grab the phone from her hand and read the message.

Unknown: *You can't just ignore my email. Your husband keeps secrets from you. You should know...*

ELEVEN

"What in the world is this? Who would send me something like this?"

Abby shrugs. "If you knew them, you'd have their number in your contacts," she says, her words embraced with a sense of caution.

As soon as I get the kids settled inside the coffee shop, I pull my laptop back out at my desk. I have to reply to the email—it might be the only way I'll get any answers.

"Who even uses AOL anymore?" Abby says, taking a seat in the corner with her backpack and phone.

I've changed email addresses three times in the last twenty-two years but had them all forwarding to the new one. It's rare to see someone with the same email address they had so long ago, especially before the boom in social media.

"I don't know." I brush her question away, waiting for the internet to connect.

What should I say?

With the cursor blinking in the body of the email, I hold my focus on the white space until my eyes cross, blurring my vision.

To: IzzyBee83isMe@aol.com
From: Jessica Peterson
Subject: Re: Hey you...It's me.

Hi,

Is this some cruel prank?

After twenty-two years of mourning, convincing myself my best friend was gone forever, someone wants to pretend she's just reappeared? No.

Izzy's disappearance left everyone in shambles. We had no choice but to believe she was dead. How can you expect me to believe this is her?

Before I give another thought to anything in your email, I need some proof of who you really are.

If this is actually Izzy, you'd be able to remember the thing you left with me before you disappeared. Tell me what it was.

Otherwise, this correspondence is over.

Jess

I click send without rereading the email a dozen times like I tend to. Emails used to feel like a fast method of communication. But in this moment, it's as slow as snail mail.

"If you and Izzy were friends in high school, wouldn't you have seen Griffin before if he was stalking her? Wouldn't you have known who he was?" Abby asks from behind me.

"Who are you talking about?" JJ asks.

"No one," I say quickly. "Okay, Abbs, I can't do the questions right now..."

"I'm just trying to help," she mutters. "God."

"Did something happen to Griffin?" JJ asks. He's been quiet because he knows we aren't at the dentist and likely doesn't want to remind me. He must think I forgot. "I saw him at school this morning. He seemed okay then."

I'd love to ask him if he knew why Griffin was so late today, but I won't involve him.

"No, Griffin is fine, sweetheart," I tell him.

I didn't and still don't know anything about the guy Izzy was seeing before she disappeared. Their relationship was all a big secret. She didn't want anyone to know who he was. I even wondered if she was making the guy up for a little attention. But then I saw them talking from a distance, just once. His back was to me. It was clear Izzy was enchanted by him. But it wasn't like her to be so secretive. We'd always told each other everything until he came into her life. In a way, his presence made it feel like I was losing her even before I really did...

To anyone who asked me about the boy she was dating, all I could say was that he went to a different school. It was all I knew. Later, I told her mom and the police that she sometimes described unusual displays of affection, with the odd notes that showed up out of nowhere, and the tapping on her windows. For a long time, I wanted to believe she'd run off with him. Young love, stupid idea. If she had, she would be happy—and she would show up again somewhere later when she realized she missed us. She never did.

Griffin, on the other hand, graduated a few years before us and was away at college when Izzy went missing.

"Mom," Abby says, startling me into jumping in my seat. I didn't know she was behind me, never mind leaning over my shoulder. "There's another message from that number." She points past my ear to where my phone is sitting on the desk, a bright message illuminated on the display.

I scoop up the phone, whisking it out of Abby's sight. With dread slicing through my veins, I read the message.

Unknown: *I was hoping you'd be at the coffee shop earlier. I was looking for you. So was your husband. He's not looking for you anymore, though.*

"I'm blocking this number right now," I say, wishing I could.

"It's an unknown number. You can't block it..." she says.

"Well, I just deleted it. It's gone. Nothing to think about now." Until another one comes through.

I want to believe these texts are a coincidence. Bad timing, with the email coming in too. But this is too over the top.

I glance over at JJ, finding him on his stomach, perched up on his elbows coloring on printer paper. His legs are swinging back and forth and I'm thankful he has no clue what's going through my head. I'm envious of his innocence.

A sudden ding from my laptop strikes like a metal bell clanging against the side of my head. I grab my mouse and click to my inbox. I barely breathe as I read.

To: JessPetersonXoXo@aol.com
From: Izzy Lester
Subject: Re: Re: Hey you...It's me.

Jess,

It's a risk sending you these messages, but I don't want you to go through what I did.

You have kids. So, please, delete these emails and get as far away from Griffin as you can. I don't know how I can be any clearer.

The day of the senior bonfire party, when I was scared because of how possessive he was suddenly acting, you told me to tell him we needed space—a break. I did. I tried to tell him. But it didn't work. He just got more upset. More obsessive.

I could have never imagined he would do what he did to me that night. I'd have never believed it, just like I'm sure you don't want to believe me either.

You have to be smarter than I was.

I'm sorry, I don't remember what I gave you before I left. I wasn't in the best frame of mind.

Izzy

The memory of how distressed Izzy was that day sends prickling chills down my spine. It was the last time I saw her. I told her she needed some space from him. I was so worried about her. I had been worried about her long before that day, though. The guy she was seeing wanted her all to himself, or so it seemed to Natalie and me. Izzy spent all her free time with him. At first, we chalked it up to him being her first love and all the emotional highs that come along with it. Then, she started telling us she couldn't hang out because he'd be upset that she went somewhere without him. We told her to bring him along. We wanted to meet him, but she had so many reasons why we couldn't. We never did. Every time Natalie and I voiced our concerns, she pushed back—telling us we were being the over-protective ones, not him.

It wasn't until that last day we saw her that she confessed to fearing his erratic behavior.

Despite all this confusion though, there's no way she'd forget what she gave me that night before running off.

TWELVE

It's noon and I haven't gotten a stitch of work done today. Now, the door between the front and back of the shop opens again, this time with a warning knock. It's Rachel, reminding me I never put those two orders through for her this morning. I click away from the email to open my ordering app. "It'll be here soon," I say, focusing on the form in front of me. I knew it was only a matter of minutes before Rachel would come back here to check on the order again. She shouldn't have to be chasing me. I need to pull myself together today.

"What will be here soon?"

At the unexpected male voice, I quickly close my laptop and look up at the door.

"What are you doing here?" I ask, my throat constricting as I gaze at the man I love. The man being called a monster in these ludicrous emails. The man someone is trying to make me doubt...

"I tried calling you after Miss. H at the front desk told me you'd dismissed JJ for a dentist appointment. I thought...Did you already go to the dentist?"

"Nope," JJ says. "The tooth really doesn't hurt anymore."

"Mom didn't realize she had to call back to confirm she'd take the last-minute opening even though the message said: please confirm," Abby chimes in, adding an eye roll to her lie.

"After I picked him up, I got another message that said the appointment was taken."

"And Abby?" he asks, pointing at her.

"Sent home to think about my behavior," she says, raising her hand proudly.

"Dude, seriously?" Griffin says to her.

"I told you Mr. Downing hates me," she continues.

"It's a long story. We'll talk about it later," I tell him. "Why did you come down here? You never leave school for lunch?"

He chuckles as if my question is ridiculous. "Well, your GPS location said you were here at the shop, not at the dentist. I also saw that Abby was here too, not at school. Naturally, I got worried, especially when you didn't pick up my call."

Call? He never called. I've had my phone with me all day. I grab it from my desk and click to see if I have any missed calls, but there aren't any.

"I didn't get a call from you," I say, showing him my phone display with no missed calls.

"Hmm." Griffin dips his hands into his pockets and rolls back onto his heels. "Well, now that I know you're okay, how about we grab a quick bite and I'll bring JJ back to school with me?"

"Uh—" My phone vibrates before I can muck up an answer. "One second." I flip the phone around, finding another message from an unknown number despite blocking the last one.

> Unknown: *There's nowhere to run away from your problems now. It's too late. Your worst fear is happening right under your nose and you don't have any clue what's going on. Again. First, with husband #1, now with husband #2. Such a shame.*

My body becomes cold, and a shiver runs down my spine before nausea creeps through my stomach. *Someone's screwing with me.* That's all this is. Griffin is not Jack. I wouldn't question something like that.

"Jess," Griffin says, his head leaning to the side, brows furrowed. He steps in toward me and takes me by the elbow and leads me away from the kids toward the metal inventory shelves. "Something is going on and you're really starting to worry me. Please, tell me why you seem so frazzled today?"

Lying isn't my forte. I'm not sure if people can see guilt on my face or if it just bubbles inside of me until I break, but honesty is easier. Plus, I haven't had a reason to stretch the truth with Griffin. In fact, neither of us have much of a filter, and it's been nice never having to wonder what he might truly be thinking outside of what he's shared with me. Plus, his chipper personality, endless energy, and motivation to volunteer and help whoever needs a hand is what makes up this incredible man standing before me.

I'm going to tell Griffin about the email, but not in the middle of the school day with the kids sitting here. He'll want to get to the bottom of it too. Someone is clearly trying to screw with me or us. The text messages mean someone has my number. This is way too personal.

Why...to all of this?

I've convinced myself that Izzy is dead. I needed closure and the only way to find that was to jump to the worst-case scenario. The only one with any finality about it. It was only an assumption though, with no evidence to say for sure that she'd died. With these questions resurfacing, wondering if Izzy could still be alive...the thoughts are pulling me right back into a life I left behind.

"I—I'm not going to have time to step out for lunch right now. There's an issue with my vendor and we're out of more than a few items. I need to find a backup," I say, staring at the wallpaper picture on my phone rather than my husband's eyes. Lying is easier this way, I guess.

"Want me to take the kids?" he presses.

I should have known that question would come next. I look at him now, the innocence in his blue eyes. His brows knit together at a crease over his nose.

"No," I say, louder and more forcefully than necessary or normal.

"Oh," he says, holding his hands up. "No problem. I'm sorry."

I glance at him, remorse shooting through me. I'm letting this email get to me and he's an innocent bystander without a clue as to what I'm trying to ignore. "I'm sorry, I'm so sorry. I'm just—I'm stressed out, and..." I study him for another moment longer, a question poking at my tired mind. "Griff, didn't you have a green polo T-shirt on when you left this morning?"

The question fires out of me. I'm not sure how I managed to notice what he was wearing this morning, but I did. Green is his least favorite color, and I was wondering why he was wearing it. I must have gotten distracted before asking him. Now, he's wearing a long-sleeve lavender dress shirt with a tie. I wouldn't mix up the two.

Griffin peers down at his shirt as if he's confused by my question. There is nothing to be confused about. He's dressed differently now.

"Yeah, I had to change. It's just one of those days..."

"Why would you change after you left the house?"

A smile stretches across Griffin's lips as if my questions are cute or funny. "Jess, you're so cute when you worry." He steps in toward me, reaching for my hand. "The lid on my coffee cup came loose and that one and only stoplight became a coffee crime scene. I raced home to change, but you and the kids were already gone."

I drop my head into my hand and laugh. "I got you that new

coffee cup..." He refuses to get rid of the old cup. The lid doesn't twist into place properly anymore and one wrong move results in a disastrous short commute.

"I know, I know. I've been using the new cup, but I forgot to turn on the dishwasher last night and just grabbed the old one this morning."

I shake my head at him and laugh, trying to dispel the unease I feel. "What am I going to do with you? Aside from buying you a backup coffee cup."

"Maybe five cups, each labeled with the day of the week would be a good idea," he adds.

"Like JJ's underwear?" I ask.

"Hey!" JJ shouts, confessing his endeavor of eavesdropping on us.

Griffin storms around the corner, tackling him with stomach tickles. A fit of laughter ensues. "I told you what would happen the next time I caught you eavesdropping," Griffin jokes. I step out from around the shelves, watching them laugh together. A reminder of how lucky I am.

"I'm sorry you came down here." I glance down at my watch. "You don't have much longer for lunch, so why don't you just grab a sandwich wrap from the front counter to go? Don't worry about the kids. I promised JJ the afternoon off if he didn't fight me about the dentist, so I just need to—"

"I understand," he says.

"You didn't say—" JJ interrupts.

"That you didn't have to go to the dentist?" Abby argues. "They could call back at any moment and tell you to come right in. All because you don't want to brush your teeth twice a day. I told you you'd get a cavity."

"You're being mean," JJ argues with her.

"I'm just telling you how it is, kid."

The fact that Abby's trying so hard to help me makes me question things more than if she was arguing my concerns. I toss my head back with the appearance of frustration at my children fighting again.

"You'll have a much easier time digesting your food in the car than you would while sitting with them at a table."

Griffin scratches the back side of his head. "Yeah, they've been at each other's throats lately. They might each need some one-on-one time. We'll figure something out when I get home later."

"Sorry again for all the confusion and concern."

"I'm just glad you're all okay." Griffin steps in toward me and gives me a kiss on the cheek, knowing the kids are watching, and typically disgusted by any forms of affection. "I'll see you in a few hours."

The moment he walks back out to the front of the shop, my strength drains from my muscles. The stress from the emails, Izzy's name, the text messages—it's all too much. I fall against the nearest wall and slide down until I'm on the floor. I pull my knees into my chest and lower my head.

Feet scuffle across the ground, Abby's sole-heavy boots are hard to mistake. She kneels in front of me and grabs my shoulders. "We'll figure this out," she says. She hasn't been this pleasant to me in longer than I can remember. As much as I'd like to selfishly steal this unique moment with her, this situation cannot involve a "we."

I lift my head and toss it back until I thump the wall. "Thanks, sweetie. I'm okay. We'll all be okay." Now I'm lying to them too. This is awful.

Abby scoots next to me to lean her back against the wall and I take a moment to send Jack a quick text.

12:15PM

Me: *I need a favor. Can you take the kids tonight?*

Offhand he'll have a meeting, or a date planned, but I have

to ask him first, per our divorce decree, before I can call Natalie or any other backup. I need to get to figure this out, and I'll feel safer if the kids aren't home while I do so. Despite how ridiculous the accusations about Griffin are, there's no such thing as being too cautious with Abby and JJ.

12:17PM
Jack: *Sure. What time do you want me to get them?*

"Mom? Why?" Abby asks after peering over my shoulder at my phone. "He's probably working tonight anyway. Can we just go to Natalie's house so I can hang out with Bella? Natalie said I can come over whenever I want."

"No. You're going to your father's and that's it. He's not working tonight. You'll be fine. I need to spend some time with Griffin."

"Fine," she argues. "I'll get a lecture for hours on end about you two being called into the principal's office and being sent home. Why would you do that to me?" Abby has a habit of blaming all her mistakes on me. This action had credible intentions, I want to tell Griffin about the email and figure out where it's coming from, and why. "Should I just tell Dad why I was really trying to leave school?"

My jaw aches as my teeth clamp together.

"You were trying to leave school? I thought you were going to the dentist too?" JJ adds.

"Nope, I was sent home for today and tomorrow," she says, as if proud of the consequence.

"But why?" he asks.

"Nothing for you to worry about," I interrupt.

"I was trying to keep him safe," she utters to me.

"I understand what you were trying to do, but the email is obviously some kind of prank and I'll find the reason. If you tell Dad why you were sneaking out of school, he'll ensure you stay with him until he gets to the root of this email too. We might not be married anymore, but he still loves the two of you very much. He will go to the ends of the earth to protect you. Just like I will. Does that make sense?"

Her *"huh"* and grunts are the only forms of a *yes* I manage to get out of her lately, so I'll take it for now. She gets up and storms back across the room, finding her earbuds in her bag before pulling her sweatshirt hoodie over her head.

12:18PM

Me: *Can you pick them up at the shop at four?*

12:18PM

Jack: *Sure. See you then.*

At least he doesn't pry. He doesn't pry, so I won't pry. It works for the sake of co-parenting.

My stomach curdles as I pull into my driveway. My car is empty, no kids, no knowledge of the truth, and no direction on where to go from here. Griffin is already home. It's a matter of seconds before I need to explain why I'm here without the kids on a night when they should be with us. But I just need to tell him what I've read. I just need him to reassure me that this is all a big mistake—a stupid prank—so we can go back to our normal lives. So that niggle of doubt, that seed of something uncomfortable, can go away for good.

The house is quiet, and I don't see Griffin anywhere when I go in. I glance up the stairwell, finding our bedroom door open. If he was changing his clothes, it would be closed, fearful of one of the kids barging in on him.

He might be in the bathroom. I drop my bag by the door and walk up the steps toward our room, spotting the bathroom door open from the hallway. The door to the bathroom next to Abby's room is also open.

"Griff?" I call for him.

No answer.

I head back downstairs and walk toward the back porch. "Griffin?" I walk out onto the empty seasonal porch and search around the small back yard, seeing nothing but grass and trees. "Are you out here?"

I pull my phone out of my pocket, checking for a message or a missed call. There's nothing.

I didn't get his missed call this morning either.

I turn back for the porch's French doors and step back inside. A waft of window cleaner assaults my nose just as I run right into Griffin's chest, face first. He grabs hold of my shoulders and pushes me back.

"What the hell are you doing?" Griffin shouts.

THIRTEEN

APRIL 2001 – TWENTY-TWO YEARS AGO

Izzy

The second half of our walk home from school has been unnaturally quiet between Jess and me, making the distance seem longer than usual. We haven't walked this many consecutive days since the beginning of last year before Natalie got her license. She was the first of us. But now she's tied up with student council meetings all the time because they're in charge of putting together all the end-of-year senior events.

I keep reminding myself that I will appreciate my broken little car more than ever once I have enough money saved up to replace the battery.

"Is everything okay? You seem quiet today," I say to Jess.

"Yeah," she sighs. "Well, I guess not. I don't know. Nick is going to break up with me. Again."

"Holy cow! What? Did something happen?" I ask her. They've been on and off for months. She wants romance, dinners, and long walks, and he wants to play video games and watch sports. Like most high school boys.

"Aside from telling me we need to talk about something

important—something he doesn't want to talk about at school... no." Jess laughs, sounding more annoyed than upset.

"Maybe it's something silly or embarrassing. I'm not sure I'd just assume..."

Jess grabs the straps of her backpack and scuffs her shoes along the rubble. "Eh. If he's over me, I'm over him. No big loss. Plus, haven't you noticed how many breakups there's been lately? At least Nick and I have only been dating this school year. Some of the other couples have been together for two years now."

She's not wrong. Summer is just around the corner, and it's the last summer before everyone takes off for the real world. Apparently, no one wants to be "tied down" to this town. Most of us are going to out-of-state colleges or just moving away. I can see why relationships would be falling apart. But for Jess, people leaving this town is just a reminder of her mother abandoning her at seven. She protects herself from getting too close to any guy, assuming how it'll end up.

"Well, if Nick stupidly decides to end things with you, which I still wouldn't just assume, your consolation prize will be taking me to the prom as your date."

We both laugh at the thought, knowing full well this was our plan if none of us had dates.

"You'll have a date," Jess says, nudging me with her elbow.

"I doubt that. I'm pretty sure I'm never going to meet the guy writing me these notes," I say, pulling the latest out of my pocket.

She peers over and chuckles. "How many does that make? Five or six?"

"This is number seven," I correct her. "It's so annoying! He's a beautiful writer, one with his words, and he makes me blush. But how can I blush when I have no clue who's holding the pen? I keep thinking he'll confess his identity, but he's sticking strong to this mysterious presence."

"Can I see?" she asks, locking her gaze on the folded note.

"Sure."

She reads through the words, her eyes narrowing as if she's trying to understand what she's reading. "Is he an artist?"

"I'm not sure, why?"

Jess shrugs and crinkles her nose. "The way he writes...it's like all his words are meant to have double meanings but are also abstract. Hmm."

"What part makes you think that?" I ask, curious about what stands out to her that didn't to me.

She points to the paper. "This part here where it says: '*Your being, an addiction I cannot relinquish, bestows a remedy albeit with caution of an undoing.*' Do you think that's kind of creepy?"

I shrug. "I read it as: he can't stop thinking about me and though there's a solution, it might ruin him. He's shy and trying to get the nerve up to approach me. I don't think it's creepy."

"You don't think it sounds like he's addicted to you or obsessed with you and if he can't have you, it will be the end for him?" Jess asks.

Now that she points it out in that way, I can see how it could be taken out of context, but...his notes have highlighted his anxiety about getting the guts to approach me. I'm not sure I'd take his words for much more than that. "I don't think he's crazy or obsessed with me," I say. "We don't know each other all that well obviously."

"Do all of his notes have poetic lines like that?" Jess asks.

I snatch the note out of Jess's hand and shove it into my pocket. "Most but not all. It usually just seems like he wants to show me the poem he'd been working on."

"Oh, okay," Jess says. "I'm sure you're right." She forces a small smile as we reach her driveway. "And I'm sure he'll show himself to you soon and you'll live happily ever after."

She doesn't sound very convincing. Probably because we have no clue who this person is, and this could go on and on.

"As long as I don't have to stay in Spring Hill forever," I say with a whiny groan. After realizing what I said, I wish I could take the words back. I try to avoid the topic of leaving.

"Like me?" Jess says with a shrug. "I guess my mom must have felt the same way. This place isn't cut out for all of us."

I set myself up for that one.

I grab her hands and squeeze them tightly in mine, something I've been doing since we were little girls. Whenever she's down or upset, I remind her of other possibilities, hope, reaching for more. She forgets these statements so easily. "I sound like a broken record, Jess. But you don't have to stay here. And leaving wouldn't make you like your mother. You can leave and start your life somewhere else. She left her family, not just this town. It's not the same."

"Yeah, but, Izz, I didn't even get into college, remember? Leaving this place just isn't in the cards for me," she says, pulling her hands out of mine.

I wish she said this stuff for the sake of being dramatic, but it's not the case. I'm not sure if she's scared to leave the area because she doesn't know anything different, or if Spring Hill is home and the only staple that she clings to in life. She loves her dad, but he's never around. It's hard to blame him when he does everything he can to support her as a single parent. She has a roof over her head and means to live comfortably, but the feeling of neglect seems to run deep with her. It's understandable since she's been essentially living alone since her mom left ten years ago. No kid should have to grow up that way. It's not fair. She's spent years watching me live a common life just across the street and I can only imagine what that makes her feel like.

I worry about how lonely she'll be when Natalie and I leave for school in the fall.

"If you want to come over for dinner tonight, call me," I tell her.

"Thanks, I'll call you in a bit."

Jess pulls her long blonde hair off her neck and twists it over her shoulder before reaching into her backpack for the house key attached to her collection of loud, jingling key chains.

I approach my front door and wiggle the knob, finding it locked. Mom must have picked up an extra shift at the hospital, Dad's at work, and Hannah doesn't get out of school for another half hour. I twist around to reach into the small pocket of my backpack for my key and catch a glimpse of my car. Not just my car. A new note waiting for me on the windshield.

I scan the area, thinking this guy will pop up and reveal his identity. But no one's in sight. There's nothing but silence and dried leaves scraping across the driveway. A rush of excitement flickers through me as I race to my car and grab the note before heading back to the front door.

I jab my key into the lock and push my way inside, eager to read whatever this note says. I hurry down the hall toward my bedroom, flipping the letter from side to side, as usual, checking for hints. Of course, just like the other seven letters, there's nothing written on the outside but my name.

Hannah's closed bedroom door catches my eye as I pass by. She never closes her door before leaving in the morning. I stop and take a step back and hold my ear up to her door. "Hannah?" I call out, knocking.

There's no answer, so I open the door and poke my head inside. I recoil just as quickly, finding her room an even bigger disaster than usual. Mom must have closed the door so she wouldn't have to look at the mess when walking by. With laundry everywhere, the stench of mildew reeking from a pile of damp towels, and dirty cups stacked up, she's an anomaly to me. A twelve-year-old little bookworm with a bookshelf twice her height, dozens of books organized by genre and author name, and yet the rest of her room looks like the aftermath of teenage house party. I'm not a big reader, but I couldn't read in the middle of a pigsty. I close the door, keeping the mess hidden.

The comfort of my tidy room is far more inviting than my sister's. I drop my bag and curl up on my bed to open the envelope. My heart titters with excitement as I pull the paper out.

A car door slams from outside my window, jolting me off my bed. The house is too quiet when I'm home alone and my imagination often gets the best of me. I peek out from behind my curtains in search of a car, but I don't see one within my viewing distance. My driveway is empty, aside from my Nissan, and Jess's driveway is also free of cars.

I drop to the carpet and lean against the wall, pulling open the letter:

Izzy,

I'm starting to think I'm a bad writer. You've never written back! And you're probably laughing because you think there's no way to write back when you don't have my address. Either that or the poems I write make no sense.

How about this...If I'm annoying you, don't write me a note. If I'm not annoying you, leave me a reply note on your windshield. Deal?

I promise I'm trying to find the courage to approach you, but my nerves get the best of me at the worst times.

We aren't strangers and our paths have crossed when you've waited on me at the diner. I haven't been able to stop thinking about you. I even see you in my dreams. That must mean something, right?

And I don't mean this in a creepy way. I'm not some old guy preying on young girls, I swear. That's gross {{the thought made me shudder}}.

I hope you had a good day today and an even better night ahead.

Maybe soon, will be the right time to make our encounter official.

Yours truly,

X

I hold the note against my heart as warmth runs through my blood again. Every one of my shifts at the diner is non-stop, table after table. I've waited on too many people to even consider assuming who I might have met over the last month.

Clouds roll outside, casting a gloomy shadow along my walls. My thoughts are just as murky as I debate whether to write back. I do look forward to the notes and I'd be disappointed if they stopped. But at the same time, what if this person isn't who I want him to be?

I pull myself up along the wall and grab my backpack to pull out my notebook, a piece of paper, and a pen.

X,

First things first: Please tell me your real name. It's only fair since you know mine.

Second, I'm not big on mysteries or secrets. I would much rather know who you are. Also, I'm afraid my parents are beginning to wonder about the notes. My dad has spotted a couple before leaving for work in the morning. I've made up a story or two, but they might not be too thrilled with the idea of a "secret admirer," especially in a small town where everyone knows each other.

If you decide to write again, please leave me your name and phone number. Maybe soon, isn't soon enough.

I do appreciate your flattery, and your poetry is beautiful. Don't ever doubt your ability to write.

Izzy

With a blue envelope from my stationery box beneath my desk, I seal up the note and bring it outside to place on my windshield. I peer across the street, debating whether to bring the second mystery note over to show Jess, but a low moan from a motor tells me she might be vacuuming and wouldn't hear me at the door.

On my way back inside, I hear a stick crack behind me. No one was around just a few seconds ago. The quiet on the road and the breeze snaking up my back gives me chills, hurrying me along.

With just one foot set inside the house, a man calls out my name.

"Izzy—"

My grip is tight around the doorknob, and I freeze, heart pounding, unable to turn around. I don't recognize the voice.

"Wait...don't close the door."

FOURTEEN

I recoil from Griffin's grip on my shoulders as he jerks them away upon realizing it was me coming out of the porch. The startling moment steals my strength and I cower against the hallways wall. "Why are you shouting?"

Griffin huffs and presses his hands to his hips. His chest heaves in and out, in and out, before responding. "You scared the crap out of me. What do you mean, why am I shouting?" He's speaking so fast, and his gaze is darting in every direction.

"Where were you? I was looking for you, calling your name, and no answer."

"I—I didn't hear—I was...in the basement fixing a fuse. Why are you home early, and where are the kids?"

"A fuse? We haven't had issues with fuses. What's wrong?"

"It was just the—what's it called—" he closes his eyes and runs his forearm along the beads of sweat on the side of his face. "The light bulb blew in the hallway upstairs, but it was new, so I shut the fuse off before changing it out in case there was something wrong with the wiring. I was turning it back on just now. It was just a bad bulb—so wait, why are you home early again?"

I didn't know we had spare light bulbs anywhere. It would

make sense that we did, but I don't remember getting more after we changed out a bunch of old ones last month.

He's staring, waiting for my answer while I'm still questioning our inventory of light bulbs.

"Because..." I take in a lungful of air, wishing my pulse would slow so I don't get to the brink of passing out. "Uh—" I swallow hard and close my eyes, trying to straighten out my thoughts. "The kids are with Jack tonight."

He holds his hands out in front of him, puzzled by everything I'm saying. "It's not his night," Griffin says.

"I'm aware. I just—" My breath shudders, an obvious sign of concern I wasn't ready to share. "I needed a break. The whole thing with Abby and school today, then—" JJ was with me too. "The mix-up with the dentist. I got behind with inventory at work and—"

"Hey, hey, it's okay," he says, taking my hands in his. "I'm sorry for scaring you on top of everything else you have going on. Let me help you. There's no need to stress this much." His hands are warm, encompassing, loving, and offer a sense of calm I can't find on my own. "I'm going to start a pot of tea, I'll make us some dinner, then I'll help you catch up with whatever you need to do for the shop. How about that?" He presses a small smile onto his lips, peering down at me with an empathetic glimmer in his eyes.

I nod. "Yeah, that—thank you," I say, returning the hint of a smile.

Griffin presses a kiss against my forehead. "Go sit down. Give yourself a minute." He steps into the kitchen, grabs the teapot off the stove top and holds it beneath the running faucet.

"It wasn't just the kids and work that wreaked havoc on me today. I got this—" The words are stuck in my throat. How do I just tell him I'm supposed to get as far away from him as possible? I make my way over to the kitchen island and take a seat on the stool behind him.

"What did you get?" he says, turning around to face me, staring, perplexed.

"I got this email. It was supposedly from an old friend, but, well, that's impossible because—"

With a deep breath, a bit of relief fills my body as I prepare to spit out the information. However, the relief is short-lived as a muffled buzz whirs around us, making me question where I put my phone when I came inside. Even though I don't feel the vibration on me, I pat down my pockets, confirming they're empty.

Griffin leans to the side and pulls his phone out, inspecting the display before connecting the call. "Griffin speaking," he says.

His gaze shifts toward the ceiling, then down past my shoulder, and finally catches my stare. "Yeah, no, not tonight." He chuckles with whoever he's speaking to. "No worries. Of course." It's rare for Griffin to get calls after the school day, and he's not big on phone calls unless it's an emergency or work.

The lack of care Griffin has for his phone is a blessing after what I went through with Jack for years. Toward the end of our marriage, there were days I wondered if he was more in love with his phone than me. That was only until I figured out who was on the other side of the phone notifications.

* * *

Jack's car tires crawl up the driveway like fine sandpaper against concrete. It's almost midnight, but his headlights don't flash against the front window. He shut them off before turning down the street. I've been waiting up for him, worried. He hasn't answered my calls or returned my text messages. It's the latest he's come home without a reason.

The lights are off in the living room too. I don't want the kids to wake up. Abby will think something's wrong, and it's hard enough to get JJ to sleep through the night as it is at three years old. I also don't want Jack to think I've been waiting up for him before he's had a chance to step inside.

The door swooshes open, then closes with a hush. The scuffle of Jack stepping out of his loafers as a faint scent of unfamiliar perfume wafts over me, makes my stomach ache. "Did you have a nice night?" I whisper from the couch, in the pitch darkness where he can't see me.

"Jesus Christ!" he yelps. "What are you doing down here? You scared the crap out of me."

"Who is she?" I remain calm, somehow despite shattering inside. I've guessed that something was going on for the last couple of months but haven't had any valid proof to make an accusation. I was hoping it was all just in my head.

"Who?" he asks.

"The woman whose cheap perfume you have all over you."

"Jess, don't start this again. I'm not cheating on you. We were all stuck in a meeting room. I'm sure I smell like the shitty cologne from the men sitting around me too." I don't smell cologne.

"Who was the meeting with?"

"George, Paul, Stacey, and Charlie—the team."

"Hmm," I say, pressing my hand to my neck. He can't see the way I'm feeling. He doesn't understand that I want to collapse to the ground and sob because he's just another person to tell me I'm not good enough for him. I wait for my breaths to slow before speaking again. "Well, I called Paul's wife, Alicia, tonight to ask her if we should bring the 'team' some dinner since you've all been working so late. Paul was already home from work. In fact, they were already sitting at their dinner table having the dinner she prepared."

"Why are you putting me in this position, Jess? You didn't have to drag Alicia into this."

It's always my fault, of course. I'm an easy target—previously broken, fragile pieces.

* * *

The unease of not knowing what was happening right under my nose was a feeling I learned to live with for too long. But I let it go when Jack and I went our own ways.

"Sorry I can't help tonight. Good luck, though. See you tomorrow," Griffin says, ending the call.

I hate having to remind myself that Griffin isn't Jack, and he hasn't gotten tired of me and found someone more interesting to spend his time with. Yet, I still have a burning desire to ask who was on the other end of the line. The fear of betrayal is the one thing that can weaken me at the knees and tear me down. The burning question is like a lit stick of dynamite clenched between my teeth.

"Everything okay?" It's as passive as I can be.

"Oh yeah, the—uh—the school has a fundraiser tonight and they need a couple more hands on deck because someone backed out last minute."

I'm familiar with the difference between his professional speaking voice and his friendly, casual tone. They're wildly different. I should have known the call was about work, but I didn't notice that distinct difference this time.

"Oh, that's too bad," I say. "I—I know you were offering to help me tonight, which I appreciate, but if you need to go, it's okay. I understand. Work is work and I know you were stressed out this morning over the pop-up faculty meeting tomorrow anyway. If someone asked you to help, you should go." I just wish I knew who that someone was. *But it shouldn't matter.*

Griffin's shoulders drop and his head falls to the side. "Jess, you've had a rough day. I'm not just going to take off on you. Finish telling me about this email..." The teapot whistles, reminding me he put water on the burner. He places his phone on the island, face down, then rummages through the cabinets for teacups. "Wait, first—do you want lemon?"

"No thanks," I tell him, staring at his phone as if I can see through the back side, doubt niggling at me. Is he telling the truth? I don't remember hearing or seeing anything about a fundraiser tonight. JJ would have brought a paper home with him, one with large bold print asking for everyone to attend. That school has killed a forest worth of trees from sending home so many reminders about fundraisers, raffles, and school-wide events. And I'm the one to empty his backpack every night. I would have put the event in my calendar. I try to be an involved mom. "Actually, I will take a slice of lemon."

I wait until Griffin's digging through the produce drawer in the refrigerator before snatching up his phone, finding a new text message, but with a generic alert saying he has one new message. His messages have always popped up in full text on his display screen, even when locked.

I tap in his password—the same four digits he's had since we met. The four little circles for code blink and clear. The numbers don't work.

I type them in again, faster this time, knowing I'm running out of milliseconds before he finds the one last lemon hidden beneath the apples. The empty circles blink again, keeping the phone in lock mode.

He changed his password.

FIFTEEN

I stare dumbfoundingly at Griffin's blue-green gradient background with only the date and time on display, until a new message pops up:

You have one new message.

On my phone, the content of my messages pop right up on the screen. His messages used to do the same. But not now. I turn his phone over and place it back in the spot he left it, crossing my hands and resting them on my lap. My heart races and a chill wraps around the back of my neck. I'm staring through the decorative pillars between the living room and dining room, unable to blink.

"Got it. It was hiding," he says.

"What was hiding?" I ask.

"The lemon," he says. "You said you wanted lemon, right?"

I shake my head, trying to brush away my thoughts to think straight. "Oh yeah, sorry. I—I can slice it up."

"I've got it." He makes his way back toward the sink and pulls out a cutting board to slice the lemon. "Okay, so, the email...Also, what did happen with Abby? Why in the world was she sent home?"

"She needed fresh air," I say, using the same reason she gave the principal. "Walked out of the building. The alarms went off."

"Ouch," he says. "That's a big no no." *So is keeping secrets.* He spins around, the wet knife gripped in his right hand. Lemon seeds trickle down the blade. "Now that you mention it..."

"What?" I ask, watching the one seed that slips off the knife and falls onto his fist.

"Actually, never mind." He turns back for the lemon. "I was thinking it could have been some kind of freshman skip day."

She was leaving school on her own accord for reasons that still feel very unexplainable.

Buzz. Buzz.

Griffin peeks over his shoulder toward his phone but continues slicing the lemon. "Want me to see who it is?" I ask, staring at his shoulder blades as they move up and down with each slice.

"It's all right."

The metal clinks against the sink and he rifles through the cabinet for tea bags and teacups. The sound of steaming water whooshing into the cups normally puts me at ease, but there might be more steam spouting from my ears than from the teapot right now.

Griffin places the cups down, one in front of me and one across from me. He takes the opposite stool, sighs, and grabs his phone. His momentary glance equates to no change in expression. He just places the phone right back, face down in the spot it was in.

"Was it the school again?" I say, wishing I had more strength to keep my nagging thoughts to myself, but he's changed his password, and hidden his messages. And all of a sudden, nonetheless.

"Uh—yeah..." he says, taking a careful sip from his cup.

The ding from the doorbell interrupts us this time. What now? We stare at each other for a long, unwavering second. "Stay here, I'll see who it is."

"Are you expecting someone?" I ask.

"No, are you?"

"No." Although after Mrs. Turble's unexpected visit this morning, I might not be surprised to see her here at this hour too.

Griffin's posture stiffens as he opens the door. I can't see past his tall, broad-chested physique, taking up most of the open doorway. My pulse thrums through my ears and my cheeks turn to ice the longer he stands at the door. Between the emails from Izzy's account and anonymous text messages earlier, I can't take any more surprises.

Griffin reaches for something and nods his head. "Thanks. Have a good one."

The door closes and he turns back for the kitchen, walking toward me. "There's a package for you. I had to sign for it. What'd you order?" he asks, eager with curiosity. Everyone in this house loves getting packages, or it could be just the act of opening them, I guess. It's like Christmas morning every time we get a delivery regardless of what's inside.

Although, I'm positive I didn't order anything aside from Abby's shoes, especially not something that requires a signature. "I—I didn't order anything..."

"Want me to open it?" he offers. "I'm sure it's just something you forgot ordering. It's like last week's Jess sending this week's Jess a surprise." He laughs because we have each played the game of what's-in-this-mystery-box too often. The days of physical shopping seem long gone with how easy it is to have everything appear at the front door now.

"Right, a surprise to myself. Those are the best," I say, my words unbelievable even to my ears. I need to decompress and get a grip. This does happen often enough. But truly, I haven't ordered anything in the last couple of weeks and Abby's shoes aren't due to arrive for another few days. I even made a mental note, congratulating myself on fighting off my bad shopping habit for so long.

Whatever. It's just a box.

He just changed his shirt after leaving for work this morning because of a spilled coffee.

It's just a surprise teachers only fundraiser. Only a changed password, hidden text messages, and the lovely emails from my supposed dead best friend.

There's nothing to worry about.

"It's okay," I say. "I got it."

I try to shake the thoughts away as I find a small corner to peel. I wedge my fingernail beneath the tape and yank it back, the sound screaming through the room as I try again to remember what I could have ordered. The flaps give way, and I peer inside.

My heart jumps straight into my mouth.

I guess I'm not losing my mind. I know I didn't order these.

SIXTEEN

From the box, I remove a gardening shovel, then a handful of crusty bronze pyrite rocks.

"What the—" I set the random objects on the island table, scrutinizing them as I do.

"A shovel and rocks?" Griffin says, scoffing through a confused laugh. "That explains why it was heavy. Imagine the price for shipping rocks?" He continues to laugh.

I'm not sure I'm finding the same humor.

I turn the box from side to side, searching for a clue to its origin, but only find my name and address among a sea of obscure numbers. "I don't get it. Why would anyone send something like this?" I'm not directing my question at Griffin, but I'm stunned and speaking out loud.

"It's gotta be a mix-up..." he says, inspecting the rocks. "Speaking of which, I've been waiting on a check in the mail. It should have been here by now. Did you see anything today?"

His lack of concern for this ridiculous package is irritating me. "No, I haven't seen a check." I sigh and shove my fingers through my hair, pressing the heels of my hands against the sides of my head. "God, my name and address are on the shipping label. I don't—I'm not sure how it could be a mix-up."

His gaze softens and his shoulders fall. "I wonder who'd send you a box of rocks?" He's trying to hide his smile and stifle a laugh. I wish I could find humor in this, but I can't.

People don't send boxes of rocks for no reason.

The air around me is stale. I can't take in a full breath. "You know what, I think—I need to go for a walk. It's stuffy in here."

Griffin steps toward me, shaking his head. "Wait, what? Why?" he asks, a tentative chuckle lacing his words. "It's getting dark out there."

"I know—I just...need to clear my head." My words feel stuck in my throat.

"Sweetie, what are you trying to clear your head from? Is it this email? I'm sorry we keep getting sidetracked. Just tell me what happened?"

I look up at him, his relaxed stance, leaning against the back countertop, ankles crossed, arms folded over his chest.

In contrast, the muscles in my neck tighten and I clench my fists, trying to slow my breaths. "I know you didn't grow up in Spring Hill, but do you remember someone named Isobel Lester?" My entire body becomes cold and numb, unsure of how he'll react or what he'll say. If he'll say yes or no. The fork in the road leads to two dark, blinding paths right now.

"Isobel Lester?" he repeats, narrowing his eyes as if trying to recollect a person by that name. "Is she a friend of Abby's or something?"

I'm staring at my husband, holding his gaze. Izzy's name burns my tongue. The pit in my stomach I thought would never heal is back, burning against my organs. "No. She was my best friend in high school." I let my words linger for a moment, wondering if that will change his expression.

There's no change. No movement. Not even a blink. "A best

friend you've never mentioned before. Was she close with Natalie too?"

"Yeah. I—" I gasp for air before continuing. "I don't talk about her because—" I clear my throat. "It hurts to say her name out loud. We were a few weeks away from graduating high school. There was a class party for the seniors at the bonfire near the falls. Everything was going great. We were having the best night ever. Then Izzy walked away for a few minutes, came back in tears, told me she had to go. I begged her to stay, but she wouldn't listen. She just ran off." I pause, recalling the seconds I questioned what to do. "I question whether I tried hard enough to make her to stay. If I had...She never made it home. No one ever found her. She was just gone without a trace."

Griffin drops his head back, peering up at the ceiling as if in thought. "I vaguely remember my parents mentioning something about a missing teenager in Spring Hill, but I was in college then."

"Yeah. The whole town knew who she was. Everyone was looking for her. Despite all that, she never turned up."

"That's awful," he says. "I must have been buried in my studies, and I never followed up with my parents after they first mentioned someone was missing." Griffin's shoulders fall, his eyes heavy and mournful. "I'm sorry I wasn't aware you were living with this pain. I can't imagine. Every time I've asked you about friends from high school or other things from back then, you change the topic unless it's about Natalie. Is this why?" Griffin walks around the kitchen island to sit beside me and wraps his arm around my shoulders. "What reminded you of her today?"

"Well, yes." Aside from having a horrific childhood, Izzy's disappearance isn't a topic I enjoy talking about. "I grieved and mourned her loss for years. I had no choice but to assume she was dead. Until this morning...when I received an email from her."

Griffin's head recoils, shock weighing over his forehead and against his dark brows. "So, she's not dead?" A look of relief settles across his face, but it'll only be a temporary reaction.

I lower my head, swallowing back the grief swelling in my throat. "I don't know. To just show up out of nowhere more than twenty years after going missing...I can't believe the email could really be from her."

"But if it is her...that means she's alive. Did she give you a way to contact her? What did the email say?" Griffin's rubbing his hand in circles along my back, trying to help me work through this resurfacing trauma.

My eyes fill with tears, knowing what I must tell him next. "The email was a warning to stay away from the man who was stalking her—the man who caused her to run away from us that night. For me to run and get away before it's too late."

Griffin's posture changes now. His shoulders straighten and he lowers his hands by his lap. "Why would she, or whoever, send you an email like that after being missing for so long?"

"That's just it. I've spent the day trying to convince myself that someone is pranking me—could be an unhappy customer from The Bean Nook. There were some rowdy teens yesterday. I told them to quiet down. It's dredging up a lot of old feelings and I'm not sure what to think," I say, taking in a stifled breath.

"No wonder you've looked so spooked all day. You should have said something this morning. You didn't have to sit with this alone all day."

"You were stressed out over the faculty meeting this morning. I didn't want to add to it with something I should be able to convince myself is a scam. My friend isn't alive and cannot send emails."

He leans his head to the side to catch my unsettled gaze. "I get it. Do you feel threatened by the email? Was there anyone else you grew up with who knows—"

"No. No one I know would send an email like this."

"Okay. Well then...Did the email mention who this stalker person was? A name? Anything?"

Griffin's hard stare shows his investment in this situation, but I feel like this might be a short-lived moment. "There was a reference to a specific person..."

"Why don't we bring it to the police? You're obviously spooked over this. It can't hurt to involve them." He picks up his phone from the island, holding it firmly in his hand.

"Possibly, but—"

"Also, how about I order a new security system for the house since the old one stopped working?"

"That would be good too."

He swipes down the screen on his phone, the bright light illuminating the concern edged along his face. "Okay, I'll see if I can get a new system delivered overnight so I can hook it up tomorrow."

"Yeah, that's—that's a good idea—"

His fingers move wildly across his screen, his focused stare following each movement. "There, purchased. All set. The alarm system will be here between noon and three tomorrow."

"Thanks. That'll be good," I say, tangling my fingers together on my lap.

With his phone still clutched between his hands, he peers up at me. "Did you already do a search for the person? What's the name?"

I gaze at him, knowing I have no choice but to clear the air at this point. "Griff...the stalker...she said it was you."

His fingertips lift away from the phone, hovering in a long pause. "Me?" he asks, pointing at himself before erupting with a high-pitched laugh. "Jess, that's crazy." He sighs with relief and wraps his arm around me. "Sweetie." He peers down at me, his big eyes glistening as he sweeps a strand of hair away from my forehead. "Block the email address. It's not real. People get these spoof emails all the time."

A spoof email with a detailed story and reason for why someone has been missing over twenty years...Does that really happen all the time?

People change their passwords all the time too, switch shirts in the middle of the workday, and hide messages from their wife, and make up fake fundraisers. Of course someone can spoof an email. Whoever this someone is...doesn't want Griffin and I to be together.

He could be unaware. Or I could just be naïve, as I've always seemingly been.

But it's Griffin. I love him. He loves me. We've been more than happy together. He's been my miraculous second chance at a good life. How can I just question us?

"I know. You're right. The whole thing is ridiculous. Anyway, that's why I want to go for a walk and clear my mind."

"I understand, but it's getting dark out. A bath might be better than taking a walk outside with the bears?"

The thought of walking alongside a bear puts a small smile on my face. "You have a good point."

"That's what I'm here for," he says with his charming, quirky smile. "We have a bottle of white wine in the fridge. How about a glass to bring upstairs with you?"

"No, that's okay," I say with a sigh. "You should go to the school fundraiser for a bit, though. They clearly want you there, which is a good thing following your concern about the faculty meeting tomorrow, right?"

"You have a good point," he says, peering up at time displayed on the oven display.

"That's what I'm here for," I mock his charm from a moment earlier.

He leans down and gives me a kiss, muttering "I love you," against my lips.

"I love you too," I utter. "And after my bath, I'll put dinner together so we can eat when you get back."

He taps his fingers against his lips and stares at me for a long moment. "This doesn't feel right." He presses his fingers against his temple and rumbles a quiet groan. "I can't leave you when you're feeling so uneasy."

I stand up from the island, making the difference between his tall height and me sitting on a stool narrower. "I—I'll be fine. Baths and cooking always relax me." I rest my hands on his shoulders and press up on my toes to give him a kiss on the cheek. "I promise. I'm okay."

He continues to stare down at me, his eyelids heavy with reluctance. "It'll be ninety minutes, tops. I'll make sure I'm not gone longer. If you want me to stay here—"

"No, you should be there." *At this never-before-mentioned fundraiser*. "I'll be okay."

"Will you call me if you change your mind?" he asks, pleading with his eyes.

"Yeah, of course."

"Okay, go relax," he commands while heading toward the front of the house. He closes the couple of blinds that are still open between the kitchen and living room. "You know what I always say about times like these...*Stressful days make the rest feel easy*."

"Yup." I wish his favorite saying would give me the same amount of relief as it usually does.

As the door closes gently behind him, the quiet of the house becomes suddenly oppressive, heavy with haunting fears.

A warm bath might help. *Proof of a fundraiser tonight might also help*. Dinner won't take more than a half hour to put together. *If I find out there's no fundraiser tonight, I won't be making dinner*.

Just as I turn for the stairs, a shadow along the front blinds pulls in my attention. But there's nothing there when I face it straight on.

I wait and watch, thinking I'll see something else.

If I had a sense of logic moving through my head right now, I'd assume Griffin was just picking something up in the yard. I haven't heard his car engine yet, so I make my way to the front door and glance out the peephole.

He's already left. No one's out there.

I turn away from the door and hear gravel against quick moving feet. I grip the frame of the door again and look outside, still finding nothing.

It's clear my anxiety is getting the best of me. But what am I supposed to do with all these lingering unanswered questions?

SEVENTEEN

I haven't been alone at night in longer than I can remember. Jack only takes the kids on the weekends, so they're most often here, even if Griffin isn't. The house seems bigger without a scuffle or clacking of a video game controller. I make my way around the lower level, closing the other blinds that we don't walk past as often as the front ones.

I hope the hallway light bulb works. I'm not sure he tested it out since I scared him on his way up from the basement. I step back into the kitchen and pop open the wastebasket, looking for the padding that comes around a light bulb. Griffin doesn't leave unnecessary junk or trash lying around. Nothing in there.

I go to the closet next to the basement door where we keep all our extra household products. It's the only place either of us would put light bulbs. Upon opening the door, all I see is that I'm overdue to go shopping for toilet paper and paper towels. And light bulbs because there isn't a box of them, or a trace of any others.

Why lie about a light bulb? Why would the wires suddenly be malfunctioning?

An excuse to be down in the basement? He knows I hate

going down there and avoid it at all costs. It would be the perfect place to hide something if he were keeping it from me. And after today, I feel like there's something he's keeping from me.

I reach for the doorknob to the basement door, wishing I could talk this idea out of myself. With each step I take, I'm reminded of the cold musty air and the pipes that make awful noises.

Who knows, I could find the box of light bulbs down here. And there could be a fundraiser and I've been too busy to remember seeing the paper.

But the way he startled when we ran into each other after I got home—it was out of character for him. I know I'm being dramatic, sensitive, or just exhausted from every erratic thought that's crossed my mind today, but it would be nice to cross something off my growing list of concerns.

I yank on the dangling cord from the ceiling that controls the utility light, and a buzz from below vibrates the handrail of the unfinished wooden stairs. The rail is tight between my grip as I descend each step toward the cement floor. Large plastic containers of my stored belongings and Griffin's line the walls. All are neatly stacked and color coded like he wanted when he moved in with us. Each with a label. It's a pleasant change from my multi-colored assortments of different sized containers without labels before I met him. I could never find anything. Not that I wanted to come down here and look.

I don't see any rogue boxes of light bulbs, just the few new boxes Griffin moved down here last week from his parents' house. I'm sure he'll organize them into his color-coded bins soon too. There's nothing loose hanging around. It's much tidier than it ever was when Jack was living here.

I spot the gun-metal-gray fuse box in the corner. I unclasp the hinges on the left side and open the panel, finding the switches all facing the left with small, printed labels to the right.

Except one. One switch is facing the right with a label that reads: doorbell.

I flip the switch to turn it back on and the basement lights go dark with a dying buzz.

No, no, no...Please go back on. I run my fingers down the column of switches, trying to feel for the center where I hit the switch. I reach for my phone in my pocket, but I don't have it on me. I must have left it upstairs on the island. I flip a switch and hold my breath. It's not the right one. The lights are still off.

I hit the switch above. Still, nothing.

I move two down, trying that one, praying the light will turn back on.

I move through the entire column, flipping all the switches back and forth. None of them relight the basement.

My heart thunders against my rib cage and my stomach knots as I try to make my way toward the direction of the stairs. Though I have my arms out in front of me, feeling around the empty space, they don't prevent me from walking into a box. A clatter of clunks and clangs echo around me while I struggle to regain my balance. I manage to stay upright, but a startling crash tells me the box wasn't so lucky.

A light strikes from the back corner, outside the sliding door that leads into the wooded backyard. It's a motion detection light. What the hell is behind our house?

With the light offering a glow, I spin around and return to the fuse box. *Please be enough light to let me see these damn labels.* I thwack one of the switches I was sure I already toggled, and a metallic pop follows, then the lights flicker on. I was hitting the switches on the right column before. They're all facing the wrong direction now. I return them to their correct position, hoping I didn't just screw up every electrical device in the house.

My chest aches as my pulse tries to find a normal rhythm again and I press the heel of my palm into my sternum.

I shouldn't have come down here. All I ever say to the kids is to follow their gut when it comes to making decisions, and I can't take my own advice.

I glance back toward the sliding door, wondering why the back light went on. Griffin said skunks and raccoons will set it off. It must be an animal.

The box I kicked over is nowhere near the stairwell. I'd never make it out of here in the dark. I stand the oversized brown box upright. I didn't see it earlier. I thought we got rid of all the boxes when we switched over to our color-coded containers. This must be one of the new ones he hasn't sorted through yet.

I kneel to pick up the loose items that fell out. A flashlight (how ironic?) is the first thing I grab. Then a couple of primary education textbooks. Lastly, a shoebox. The shoebox isn't full of shoes, and it isn't empty. There are lightweight items shuffling around inside. I don't release my grip on the shoebox just yet but toss the books and flashlight back in on top of the mess.

I pop the lid off the shoebox, finding a pile of envelopes and triangular-folded lined-paper notes. I haven't seen a paper folded like this since junior high school. I flip one of the envelopes over, finding it blank. I shouldn't be doing this. These are his old memories.

Curiosity takes over and gets the best of me as I slip out a note from an unsealed envelope. I unfold the blue-lined notebook paper, finding bubbly writing with curls and swirls.

Hey handsome,

I'm sitting in class right now, sleeping with my eyes open so I figured I'd write you a note to pass the time.

Did you know that a man thinks about...you know what... like seventy times a day. That's almost once every twenty minutes. Is it true? Curious minds want confirmation.

By the way, I have the house to myself on Saturday night. Do you think we could convince one of your friends to get us a case of beer? We can rent a bunch of movies and binge them all night.

Oh, and I'm sitting next to your favorite girl (ha ha ha). She's totally daydreaming about you right now, drawing little hearts, x's, and o's all over her notebook. You should think about telling her things are over between you. I wouldn't want her to have a broken heart when she finds out we're an item. Plus, I kind of want you all to myself, remember?

You're such a player! But I luv ya.

Xoxo,

Me

A player. That's an interesting choice of words. I'm having a hard time picturing him as that type of person, even back in high school. He told me he was part of the math club, drama club, band, and in student council. That person can't be the same person addressed in this note. Could someone change that much?

We might be a few years apart in age, but I don't think the cliquey groups changed all that much. According to Abby, it's still the same as I remember it being.

I continue rummaging through the shoebox, wondering if the stack of notes are all from the same girl.

I don't care to read them if they are, but I peek into a few envelopes. They all hold notes with the same flowery handwriting.

Beneath the pile, there's a bleached-out photograph. A girl wearing a baseball cap too large for her head. She's holding her hand out in front of her eyes and sticking out her blue-stained tongue.

The photo is torn in half, impossible to make out details of where the photo was taken. I flip it over, searching for a date. *May 11, 2001*, stamped by the photo printer.

This was snapped just a week before Izzy went missing.

We all have a past. I know this. Although I don't have old notes from high school boyfriends in any of my storage bins. They weren't that important to hold on to. Griffin might be more sentimental or doesn't even know these are in here. Although he found that watch in one of these boxes. He must know what he still has in his possession. I grab the box and glance around the cement-clad surroundings once more. I was curious about where the light bulb came from, but now I'm wondering what else I'd find in these letters. What if Izzy's name is mentioned somewhere, confirming some part of that email? On the other hand, I could prove he didn't know her at all, like he said.

I drop the shoebox filled with letters back into the bigger box. The heavy displacement causes the other contained belongings to tumble around. A scratched-up leather jewelry box falls to the side of a pile, drawing in my full attention. I snag it and pry it open, holding my breath while I do. It's empty, but holds a little suede watch stand. So then, this must have been the box he was going through when he found the watch—the timeless accessory he's decided to start wearing again.

I turn the leather box from side to side, looking for a label, but it's unmarked except for a pen-engraved heart on the bottom.

EIGHTEEN

I escape the suffocating basement, and my pulse races as I close the door. I flip the light switch and spin around to the contrast of the well-lit, quiet and empty first floor. I could imagine eyes staring into every window between the small cracks of the blinds.

My phone, abandoned on the living room coffee table, lights up, a beacon and reminder that I never leave it behind. I scoop it up, finding three missed calls from Abby, and two from Griffin. I have unread texts too. I never forget my phone anywhere, and the one time I do, my child needs me.

I tap the messages, finding ones from Griffin and Abby. I click on Abby's first:

7:35PM

Abby: *Mom, where are you? I need you to come pick us up, please. Call me back right away.*

7:37PM

Abby: *Mom, why are you ignoring me? We need you!*

7:38PM

Abby: *MOM PLEASE!*

Abby's escalating fear through her messages is palpable, making my heart hammer against my rib cage. My God. What could have happened?

I click Griffin's messages before I call Abby back:

7:46PM

Griffin: *Hey babe, you must still be in the bathtub but give me a call when you get out. Nothing to worry about.*

8:15PM

Griffin: *Just checking in on you. Give me a call, maybe before you call Abby.*

Knowing the calm in Griffin's messages seems forced only causes me to panic more. My fingers fumble over the buttons as I try to call Griffin as quickly as I can. I hold the phone up to my ear, looking for the nearest chair to sit down in so I can pinch against the nerves in my stomach. The house that seemed entirely too big just a minute ago might as well be closing in around me now. I need cold air or water.

"Hey, honey," he answers after just one ring thankfully. "I'm sorry if I worried you. I've just gone and picked up the kids from Jack's house. We're on our way home. Everything is okay, but Jack had some chest pains, so Abby called 9-1-1. She's freaked out and JJ isn't much better. They know their dad is going to be just fine after he gets a quick check-up," he says, accentuating his words. I'm sure he's trying to keep the kids calm. I appreciate him starting the conversation with "everything is okay" but it's truly not.

"Oh my gosh. I—I'm a horrible mother. I can't believe—"

"Hey, hey, it's fine. We're in this together. Right?"

"Did Abby call you when she couldn't reach me?" After earlier today, I'm not sure what to expect from her.

"Actually, Jack did. When Abby told him you weren't answering, he didn't want them to be at his apartment alone when the ambulance came."

"Can I talk to Abby?" I press.

The phone rustles against fabric and a few seconds pass before another rustling sound. "Mom, why didn't you answer? I was so scared. You weren't there and I wasn't sure what to do." All I hear is my own negligence in not answering her call when she needed me. My biggest fear in life is letting them down.

"I'm so sorry. I was—" Oh God. I can't lie to her. "I left my phone on the coffee table and forgot I didn't have it with me. I would never do that intentionally."

"I'm so worried about Dad. He was in so much pain." Her voice breaks, the emotional pain clear.

"I'm sure he'll be just fine. This happens to people all the time. It's a smart idea to go to the hospital to get checked out to make sure he doesn't need any kind of medication."

"I'm so sorry for what I did today. I'm so sorry, Mom."

"It's okay. You didn't do anything wrong. I get why you did what you did."

"No, you don't. There's something else I didn't—" she coughs into the phone. "Mom, I'll talk to you when I get home. I love you."

I'm still staring at the "call ended" alert on my phone. I want to call Abby back and press her for information on whatever it is she hasn't told me, but I could hear the hesitation. She didn't want to tell me, not in front of Griffin. Or maybe JJ. I hope the latter.

I pace back and forth between the dining room table and the stairwell. I should have told him to stay where he was, and I'd get them. Abby must be panicking. It's my fault. I should have locked my email down so she couldn't snoop. I know she was as surprised as I was about the accusation against Griffin, but still. She's a kid—I'm sure what she read must have scared her.

I clutch the neckline of my T-shirt until it digs into the back of my neck. With my phone pinched in my other hand, I flip it over to check the time. It's only been five minutes since I called Griffin. Jack lives on the other side of town. It's only a ten-minute drive, but the roads are narrow and pitch black at night. Plus, there are wild animals that like to mosey across the streets at night and cause car accidents for anyone driving too fast.

I remember the locator app Griffin set up on my phone. I don't use it much. I haven't had a reason to worry about where they were. I still don't. Abby is known to be dramatic.

That email told me to get away from him. And he has the kids.

My thoughts are irrational. Griffin takes care of the kids all the time. He's a teacher. He's not a former stalker I should be running away from.

My pulse throbs in my head, a pain wrapping around my face from ear to ear. I can trust my husband.

My imagination can't.

I scroll through the list of apps on my phone trying to remember what it was called. After going through the list of apps twice, I spot an icon with a location marker.

Abby and Griffin are both near the center of town, five minutes from here. I continue watching the live motion of their GPS turning down streets I don't usually take. More of the dark, narrow, winding ones. They aren't shorter or more direct. What is he doing?

I try to breathe. He works at a school. He's gone through background checks. I should have run a background check on him before accepting his marriage proposal...

I shake the thoughts from my head. I'm being silly. *This isn't about him right now.* It's Jack. Jack called Griffin to help him with his kids because I couldn't be reached. There was no one else to call.

I'm not sure what Jack would think about Izzy's email. He'd likely tell me it's spam or junk mail, to ignore it. He's quick to brush things off—a trait I've never liked about him. Still, Jack knew Izzy. He was there when everyone was looking for her.

Abby and Griffin's location has stopped updating. I refresh the app, watching the progress circle spin over and over.

I restart the app, hoping it updates quicker, but the spinning circle returns.

Over and over, and over and over again until the map turns into a solid shade of green and the text next to their names says: *No Location Found.*

NINETEEN

My tires burn against the driveway, screeching as I back out into the street. I speed toward their last recorded location. I hate the way the road morphs into a cave of over towering trees. The branches are long enough to stretch from one side of the road to the other. The night was already dark with full cloud coverage. Now, it's a black hole without a hint of headlights in the distance.

Fog spills onto the road, the moisture in the air becoming trapped within the constraints of the trees. I'd never drive this way at night. The closer I drive to the foothill, the denser the fog. I can't see more than a car's length in front of me. A deer or moose could be standing in the middle of the road, and I wouldn't see it until I'm slamming on my brakes.

I want to go faster, find them quicker, but they could be driving around the corner behind a wall of fog too.

My phone rings, Abby's name pops up beneath my GPS screen and I hit the answer button, blindly, making sure not to take my eyes off the road. "Abby, where are you?" I ask before she says anything.

"—where—you?" Her words are broken up.

Beep. Beep. Beep. The call ends. There's no reception on this godforsaken road. I press the call-back button, listening to the ring again and again until her voicemail message begins.

The road climbs back upward after passing the valley and the fog becomes less dense the farther I go. Not one car has passed me this entire time. There's no other way to get home after turning in this direction.

I make it all the way to Main Street without passing another car. I take a right, my eyes unblinking as I pass by the grocery store, gas station, coffee shop, bank, and—police lights are up ahead. My body aches, praying the lights have nothing to do with Abby and JJ. I come to a slow crawl as I creep up closer, knowing I'd spot Griffin's orange SUV if it was on the side of the road.

I don't see a car, just flashlights shining into the local bank. Once I pass the scene of whatever is happening in our small, mostly crimeless town, I tap the phone icon on my GPS and press Griffin's name.

More rings, one after another, without an answer. Just a voicemail.

I pull off to the side of the road, grab my phone and open the locator app to see if it's updated.

It has.

They're home.

Tears I didn't realize had formed spill from my eyes, as the terror I've been holding on to like a lifeline fades in relief. I step on the gas, heading down the road faster than I usually go, but make it home within just a few minutes. My tires screeching once again as I pull back onto the driveway.

Before I can step out of my car, Griffin is coming toward me, from the front door. I can't make out his expression, but it's not calming like his voice was when he told me he had things taken care of.

"Where have you been?" he calls out as I make my way toward him.

"Looking for you!"

"What? Why? I told you we'd be home in a few minutes."

"Abby sounded so upset and I got worked up and tried to meet you."

Griffin's brows knit together, making me feel ridiculous. "She's inside, crying, hysterical because you're not here and her father is in the hospital."

I jerk my head back, surprised by his sharp words. "Do you think I was trying to make things worse for her?" I snap.

"Jess, you have a lot on your mind right now. I get it."

"What do you get?" I'm baffled by this conversation and the fact that he's standing between me and Abby crying inside. I didn't mean to say that. I've been internalizing everything that's been eating away at me today.

"Abby isn't okay. She wouldn't come near me and didn't want to come home with me. I've never seen her act like this before. We need to help her."

I race past Griffin into the house as Abby barrels toward me, her face red, wet with tears. Her body is overheated, and her arms are trembling as she squeezes them around me.

I spot Griffin taking a seat with JJ on the couch, pointing at something on the game he's playing. JJ seems unaffected by whatever he saw with Jack tonight. I hope that's truly the case.

"It's okay, it's okay," I say, as she rests her cheek on my shoulder. "Come on. Let's go upstairs and talk."

"Me too?" JJ asks, dropping his Nintendo Switch onto Griffin's lap.

"Yeah, you too, buddy. Come on up."

"Mom, I need to talk to you alone," Abby says, her eyes big and round.

"Bring your game and headphones up, JJ."

I give Griffin a quick glance, mouthing an apology. I know

he just raced to get them, and I just snapped at him outside. "Just give us a minute to chat, okay?"

"Of course," he says with one solid nod.

With the three of us closed inside of Abby's bedroom, the orange light from the lamp replaces the usual LED light show. The mood shift is firmly highlighted. "What did you want to tell me in the car?" I ask, holding my arm around her as we sit on the edge of her bed. "Does it have something to do with your dad? He's going to be okay, I'm sure. I'm going to call the hospital after we're done talking to check on him."

She stares down at her hands as she tugs at a jagged hangnail. "No, it's not about Dad. He'll be okay. He promised. It's about Griffin," she says, clenching her hands.

"What is it?" Why is this all so drawn out? I want to tell her to just tell me what she knows and not deliver it in piecemeal. Except I think she's coming to these realizations as she tells me.

"I saw him talking to some woman last week in the parking lot after school. I didn't recognize her. She's not from this town. I told myself she was just someone's mom, but I don't think that's the case. Not after the email. I think she might be Izzy."

I touch my fingers to my lips as my blood runs cold.

"Izzy?" The email she read and has apparently actually believed every word of, despite her protestations about Griffin. The email I refused to believe. The email that's getting harder to ignore.

"She could still have short brown hair, right?"

TWENTY

The longer I study my daughter, the more questions arise. I don't want to ask the wrong one. Like, how does she know what Izzy looked like?

"Abby..."

"You're going to say I wouldn't have any clue what she looks like. I'm not dumb."

"Then how?" I beg for an answer.

"I asked Dad if he had any old pictures of you. He did. He had some old photos from back when you were in high school. Most of the pictures were of you with this girl. I asked him who she was, and he told me her name was Izzy."

I drop my head into my hands. "Abby, please, please tell me you didn't mention that email to your father."

"No, I didn't. I told him I was curious if we looked alike at the same age. You said you don't have any old pictures here." I find it hard to believe he wasn't suspicious of her asking him for pictures and not me. I'm curious why he still has old pictures of me.

Our divorce was anything but simple. There was pain and

regret. I refused to sit by while he had an affair. Yet, he couldn't understand why a divorce was necessary.

Some people can't go back in time after their relationship hits rock bottom. I'm one of those people.

"What type of conversation were Griffin and this...person having?" I ask, my words muffled against my hand.

Abby swallows against a dry throat and shrugs. "I couldn't hear anything. It seemed serious, but not in an angry way."

Her description, as brief as it is, stiffens me, shakes me, and makes me want to cry. "Oh."

"I didn't think it was a big deal until I saw a picture of you and Izzy."

Izzy is dead, I remind myself. There's no other explanation for no one being able to find her over the course of more than twenty years.

"If you saw them from a distance, you wouldn't recognize a woman over twenty years older than someone in an old photo you were looking at. It wasn't Izzy."

"My gut says it is," she says, avoiding eye contact. "I know I've been a handful to deal with lately, but you're my mom, and I wouldn't want you to be hurt." Abby rests her cheek on my shoulder. Sincerity isn't something I've gotten from her recently.

"Abby, I appreciate you trying to help me, but whoever you saw, it wasn't Izzy." I have to put her out of my mind. I wish Abby had never seen that stupid email. "Let's focus on Dad getting better right now. Okay?" I unclench my hand from around my phone and close my eyes, trying to think of how to reach Jack. "Can you tell me what happened tonight?"

"It's my fault, Mom," she says, tears spilling from her eyes.

"No, it's not. That's not possible. Tell me what happened."

"I told him I thought I saw that girl, Izzy, from the photo recently," Abby says, wiping tears from her cheeks. "Then—uh

—his face became pale, and he grabbed the picture from me and said there was no way I'd seen her. But I argued."

"And then..." I prompt her to continue, my palms dampening from the sweat.

"He grabbed his chest and started groaning," she cries out. "I was so scared. I tried to help him onto the sofa, but I couldn't move him. He told me to call 9-1-1, then you. But you didn't answer."

I wrap my arm around her and press my lips to the top of her head. Jack knew Izzy, but not well. He was a quiet kid in school who kept to himself. Back before we were together, everyone talked about Jack like he was some kind of hermit, but that's because no one really knew much about him or his family. He was kind of a wallflower until we both found ourselves being one of the very few who weren't leaving the area for college with the rest of our class. Jack gained confidence and became more sociable as he found his talent in running a financial investment agency. He changed a lot between the time we got married and divorced. Loneliness brought us together and loneliness pushed us apart.

Griffin opens the cracked door, knocking while pushing his way inside. He points at JJ who must have fallen asleep with his headphones on at some point in the last fifteen minutes. His Nintendo Switch is still flashing away on his lap. "I'll put him to bed," he says. "Poor guy has had a long day."

Abby's staring at the side of my face, making it obvious she's still thinking about the email, Griffin, and his parking lot conversation last week. There must be a logical explanation for all of this. Griffin must have reasons for everything that I questioned today—the change of shirt after leaving for work this morning, the new password on his phone, the hidden messages... I'm just on edge because of the email dredging up old feelings about Izzy.

I press my hand down on her lap and squeeze until Griffin leaves the room with JJ curled in his arms.

"Mom," Abby hisses.

"Listen to me," I reply in a whisper. "I'm aware there's a lot going through your mind right now. Just as there is with mine. But until I have some answers, we can't feed into what is more than likely a prank email, same with those texts, and I'm sure there's a reasonable explanation for Griffin's encounter in the parking lot." Why is it so easy to say but impossible to convince myself of?

Griffin returns before we can finish our argument. "Mind if I join your conversation? I can leave if you're still talking," he says, pointing toward the stairwell.

"It's okay. You can stay," I tell him.

He steps into Abby's bedroom and closes the door slowly, making sure it doesn't make a clicking noise as it shuts.

"Are you going to hurt us?" Abby asks, whimpering.

Oh—wow. If I thought Abby was going to come out with this, I would have told him to wait downstairs.

"Abby!" I scold her.

"Wait, what?" Griffin replies, haste drenched around the word. He presses his hands against his head. "What in the world would make you think something like that? Why—how could I ever hurt you, any of you?" Griffin presses his hands into his stomach, leaning forward as if she's just punched him in the gut.

Abby narrows her eyes either with frustration or contemplation. The expressions are often the same. "If that's true..." she says. "Why did I see you with another woman in the school parking lot last week?"

Griffin's bottom lip falls, shocked—surely not as much as I still feel.

My heart throbs against my rib cage. The dead air between the three of us deafens like the aftershock of an explosion.

TWENTY-ONE

APRIL 2001 - TWENTY-TWO YEARS AGO

Izzy

"Don't close the door..."

It must be him...Eight notes later, he finally has the courage to meet me.

Holy cow. He's behind me, and this...suddenly freaks me out. I didn't think I'd be freaked out, but I am. With one swift move, I close myself inside the house and lock the doors. I lean against the front door and clutch my hand around my mouth.

I'm the one who said I wanted to meet, but there's no way he already read that in the one and only note I left for him just a minute ago. He's turned up without invitation.

The sound of the doorbell sends a spark through my nerve endings, making me gasp.

"I wasn't trying to scare you." His voice slips through the crevice of the doorjamb.

I press my hands against my mouth, dread threatening a shriek to escape. "I see you left me a note. I'm opening it right now."

I want to know who this person is and what he looks like. I

don't know if he's my age or an old creepy guy like he joked about in his letter. Jess's thoughts about his poetic words are playing through my head now: "*You don't think it sounds like he's addicted to you or obsessed...?*" I see horror stories that start that way on the news all the time.

"No more secrets, I promise. My name is Roe and I live in the next town over. My phone number is 203-212-7232. It's my house number, so my parents will likely pick up. But be warned...they'll tell you you've got the wrong number because girls don't call for me." It takes me a minute to pick up on the dry joke, but it's cute. "I go on long hikes and like to sit up on my roof at night staring up at the stars. I still live at home even though I'm twenty, but it's because I'm saving up to get my own place."

Being low to the ground, I take the opportunity to peek out the narrow window to the right of the door. A pair of worn brown mountain boots and baggy forest green cargo pants confirms the love for hiking.

We live in New Hampshire. Most of us who can, hike.

I crane my neck to get a glimpse of his upper body and head. A fitted black fleece, skin paler than mine, and a bad bleach-job on his overgrown shaggy hair. There doesn't look to be anything critically insane about him. He's tugging at a woven bracelet on his wrist and his chest is rising and falling even quicker than mine.

"Roe? That's your name," I respond, still from the safety of the other side of the door.

I watch as he blows a slow breath of air out from pursed lips, then smiles. "Yeah, Roe. A strange middle name to go along with my worst first name. I picked the least bad. My parents were trying to be unique."

"I was thinking more like Roe as in Romeo. One with his words."

"I'll take that as a compliment," he says, a nervous laugh follows.

Pulling myself up off the ground, I open the door a crack and he steps back as if I might be the one to jump out at him. "You really wanted to be my secret admirer?"

"It's lame. I can go with the Romeo thing and call it old-fashioned chivalry, right?"

He squints an eye and chuckles. I open the door the rest of the way, following desire rather than my common sense. Roe touches his hand to his chest and opens his mouth to talk, but nothing comes out for a second, before: "Wow, you're more beautiful than I even remember from the diner."

My cheeks burn in response to his compliment. Now that we're face to face, a faint recollection of him rings from the diner. I think I made a mental note about his bleached-hair that night too—I have a thing for bad blonde hair dye, I guess. It also suits him. "You're sweet," I tell him, sweeping my short strands behind my ear.

"So, now that we're not strangers, would it be okay if I asked you out?"

Holy cow. Again. Act cool, Izzy..."Yeah, I think that would be nice."

He tears a part of the envelope from my note and pulls a pen out from his pocket. "Am I pushing my luck by asking for your phone number?"

I take the scrap of paper and pen and jot down the digits. "It's only fair, since I asked for yours."

"I'll call you tonight if that's okay?"

"Yeah, definitely," I say, finding myself running out of air.

"Cool." With a cute wink, he turns around and walks away.

I wonder if Jess can see what's happening from her front window. If so, I'm not sure if she'd assume this is the mystery guy or just some stranger trying to sell me something. She'd definitely yell across the street and ask me if everything is okay. She's protective of Natalie and me. I'd do the same to her.

I go and sit on my bed with my phone cord pulled across the room, phone sitting on the bedsheets in front of me. I want to make sure I'm the one who picks up the call when it rings. It's too soon for questions from Mom and Dad. Worse, Hannah. She needs to know everything that's going on, and if she thinks someone is hiding something from her, she'll go on a hunt to find the information. It's been hours since I met my admirer for the first time, and I haven't even told Jess or Natalie yet. I've been too busy daydreaming and keeping the line free for his call.

I check the time on my alarm clock, wondering how it's already nine. The hard part is over. I can't imagine making a phone call would be a big deal. What's taking him so long?

I bounce off my bed to close my curtains. Before I pull the shade down, a tap against the glass sends me flying, a shrill scream escaping from my mouth. I rush back to the window to see what the noise was. Hurrying across my lawn is a figure in a dark hoodie, face turned away.

TWENTY-TWO

I stand up from Abby's bed and pull Griffin out into the hallway. "Who is the woman Abby's talking about?" I whisper, other questions threatening to vomit all over him.

The pause that follows is insufferable. Griffin meets my gaze squarely, his eyes an open window to his soul.

He holds his hands out to the side and steps back into Abby's bedroom to confront her accusation. "Abbs, I talk to parents in the parking lot daily. I never leave the school without being pulled into a conversation. Parents like to know how their kids are doing and think by catching me in the parking lot, I'll divulge. In truth, I'm so burnt out by the end of the day, I'd more than likely mix kids up and say the wrong thing to the wrong parent."

Griffin goes on and on, his explanation, rational, sensible. As a parent, I'm aware I've done the same thing to the kids' teachers if I caught them alone after school.

"So, do you hug all your students' parents?" Abby's question douses the burning conversation in gasoline.

My eyes bulge, staring at Abby, wondering why she would accuse him of something like that.

Am I just as bad, wondering why he changed his password on his phone?

Again, I need air.

"A hug?" he repeats, his disbelief doing little to soothe my growing rage.

"I would never touch a parent," he says. The narrowing of his eyes and his pressed lips tell me he's offended by the accusation. *Is Abby lying?*

"You touched Mom. She's a parent, isn't she?" Abby's sharp interruptions cut through Griffin's simple responses, leaving us white-knuckled, hanging from a ledge.

Dear God. This girl is destined to be an attorney. She shouldn't be involved in this conversation, and I need to remove her now.

"My relationship with Griffin did not take place on school property," I tell Abby, doing my best to mediate this new unnecessary tension between the two of them. I see how easy it can be to make assumptions since we met there. "Nothing ever happened between the two of us at school. We ran into each other at the grocery store *after* meeting at a school event. That's when he asked for my phone number."

The appalled look in Abby's eyes makes me feel like I switched sides to gang up on her. I don't want her to think that, but I want her to know the facts before making assumptions. If that's what she might have done in this situation.

"Whatever," she says. "I know I saw you hug someone." Abby crosses her arms over her chest, stating her firm stance.

"It might have looked that way from where you were standing, but I assure you, that did not, nor will it ever, happen."

Abby leans back into her bed, groaning with frustration. "Okay."

Griffin turns toward me, closes his eyes and takes in a deep breath. He gently pushes his palms out, his natural gesture of reclaiming peace. "Have you reached Jack?" Griffin asks me.

"No, I was going to try his phone before you came in."

I tap on his contact and hold the phone up to my ear, waiting to hear the rings. They never begin. Instead, his voicemail plays.

"His phone is off."

"What does that mean?" Abby asks, sitting upright, her shoulders tense and fists curled by her sides.

"Nothing. His phone could be dead. I'll call the hospital to get an update."

I search for the number and call the main desk to be transferred. I'm put on hold twice, the second time to the accompaniment of classical piano.

"Is that watch new?" Abby asks Griffin while I stare toward the dark window in her room.

From the corner of my eye, I watch him cup his hand down over the face. "No, I found it with some of my old things last week."

"It's nice. Was it a gift?" she continues. She's asking the questions I should have asked before finding the box with a heart etched along the bottom.

"It was," he says, leaving the rest of his answer dangling with a question mark.

"From whom?" Abby is relentless. Her curiosity knows no bounds. I should take note.

There's a taut silence between her question and his answer. The music on the phone stops abruptly and a woman answers.

"Yes, what is the patient's name you are trying to get an update on?" No hellos. No greetings. No warmth. It's the way the world operates now.

"Hi, I'm looking for an update on Jack Wyland. He was transported by ambulance earlier for chest pains—"

"Are you family?" the woman retorts before I can add a period to the end of my sentence.

"Yes." Though, I'm not sure I qualify as a member of his

family now, but we share children. That makes me eligible for an update.

"Okay, one second," she says, placing me back on a musical hold.

"My parents gave it to me for my twenty-first birthday," Griffin tells Abby. I catch his gaze, wondering about the truth. His Adam's apple bobs along his throat, and his weight shifts from one foot to the other. *His parents etched a heart onto the bottom of the box?* He could have had more than one watch.

"You didn't mention your parents—" Before I can finish my sentence the classical music scratches and stops. "Hold that thought." I hold my index finger up to tend to the nurse on the other end of the line.

"Hi there," the woman resumes our conversation. "You're waiting for an update on Jack Wyland, correct?"

"Yes, that's right," I reply.

"Okay, one more second please..."

"It's actually the only watch I've ever owned," Griffin continues talking to Abby, his words a whisper so as not to interrupt me.

"Really?" she says.

"Yeah, I'm not big on wearing things around my wrists." He inspects it like he did this morning. "Plus, who needs a watch with all those large metal clocks in every classroom. Right?"

"True," Abby agrees.

He's only ever had one watch. One watch box with a heart etched on the bottom...One watch I have a feeling he's lying about.

Still on the phone, the hospital's mundane melody blares in my ear—a sharp contrast from the silence among the three of us. The sound grumbles and stops again.

"Okay, ma'am." The assumable nurse clicks her tongue against the top of her mouth and mutters something unintelligible. The delay, the slow pace, the unnerving answer lingering somewhere is drumming up my heart rate. She must be reading his chart. "Mr. Wyland has said to tell you there's nothing to worry about. Everything is under control. He also said it was okay to share that he's under observation to rule out myocardial infarction."

I push my finger against my free ear as if I'm standing in a noisy space. I can't focus. "I'm sorry—what's that?"

"Presumably, Jack has your number, so I'll ask him to update you as soon as he can."

"Yes, thank you."

The call ends, still with nothing more to tell Abby. She'll want to march down there and demand answers. "He's being taken care of as we speak. She said he'll give us a call when the results come back."

"Mom, no. That's not good enough. I need to be with him," she says, standing up. "Please take me to the hospital. I'll sleep in the waiting room. I don't care."

"You're not allowed to do that as a minor. Plus, your dad wouldn't be too happy to find out you've been sleeping in the waiting room all night," Griffin says.

"I can't go to school tomorrow anyway. What's the difference?" she says. I forgot about the second day home to think about what she's done. Today has felt like an entire week shoved into fifteen hours.

"Why were you sent home today? Something about needing air?" Griffin asks.

Abby steadies her stare on my face. Suddenly she's short on words. "I needed air. That's all."

"Something more must have happened. Why did you need to go against the rules and set the alarm off?"

Abby shrugs, still staring at me.

Griffin runs his fingers through his hair and cocks his head back. "Okay. We'll talk about this more in the morning. I can't do much to help you with the principal if you aren't telling me the entire story."

"It won't matter. Mr. Downing is a monster," Abby says.

"Sleep on it, okay?" Griffin asks.

"Fine." Abby falls backward on her bed, her arms still crossed as she scowls and stares up at the stars glued to her ceiling.

"Get some rest," I tell her, giving her a kiss on the forehead. I close her bedroom door and follow Griffin down the hall to our bedroom.

It's just like any other ordinary night. Except, clearly, nothing is ordinary right now...

TWENTY-THREE

"I feel like I was just sucked up into a tornado and spit back out," Griffin says after I close our bedroom door. "Why in the world would Abby make up a story like that about me hugging a woman in the parking lot? I'd never—"

"I know," I say. It's what I want to believe.

"Do you?" he asks. "Because I can read the look on your face, Jess. Between that crazy email and now this, you're clearly not okay. Nor should you be. I'm at a loss for what to even say at this point."

His words trigger my other concerns from earlier—the changed password and hidden messages. It's all too much to think about at once. That and a hug in a parking lot—a speculation by my daughter with perfect vision. I just want to scream. "Speaking of being locked out," I say, twiddling with my wedding band. "I noticed you changed the password on your phone and your messages are popping up in private mode. Not that I'm ever really looking, but I noticed today." I sound like the guilty one now.

Griffin replies with a nervous chuckle, an unexpected reaction. Though his expression doesn't match the hint of humor.

"Yeah, I had a bit of an incident at school today. I left my phone unattended and, well, let's just say my students got creative with it. I had to change everything for security reasons."

That's logical. It would also be logical for him to share his new password since we're husband and wife. If I ask, it might sound like I don't believe him. I'm sure he'll give it to me. Not that I often go scrolling through his phone. We just know each other's passwords for everything.

I do know Jack wouldn't have thought up a story that fast if I asked him why he made a sudden change like that. "Oh. A teacher's worst nightmare, I assume?"

"Pretty much," he agrees with a sigh. I slip my shoes off and bring my feet up to the bench, pulling my knees into my chest. My tense muscles all ache as I hold on to these ramped up thoughts of spoof emails, and the unfathomable question: is Griffin hiding something from me? And on the same day that someone posing as Izzy wants to tell me he's hiding something from me. The coincidences are uncanny. And yet, there's an explanation for it all. I should believe that and let it go.

I can remind myself that Izzy is dead. She can't be the one sending me emails. Therefore, Abby couldn't have seen her in Spring Hill. It could have been a different woman...

I figured I'd be lying awake all night. After staring at the ceiling fan for hours, wishing it would hypnotize me into believing I'm asleep, the sun is starting to rise. Not even the blades on the fan could keep up with the thoughts whirring through my head.

Griffin was more than compassionate about the email, especially after the accusation of him embracing a woman in the school parking lot. He's done everything he can to reassure me. Even with my questions about the hidden texts and changed password, he's understood I'm feeling paranoid because of the emails. Those things are just coincidence, bad timing.

Except, I can't shake the idea that Jack always acted overly understanding and loving when he started sneaking around.

Lipstick stains on his shirt. Hushed phone calls out in the backyard. Late night unplanned meetings popping up. But that was the only time throughout our marriage that he attempted to help around the house, acknowledge how much I do, and say things to make me smile.

I remember asking myself why he was trying so hard all of a sudden. It had been years and years since he'd paid me that amount of attention.

It wasn't long before I learned it was just the guilt.

However, Griffin has always been doting and considerate, making this all harder to judge. He knows what I went through with Jack. He swore he wasn't that person. He didn't have it in him, he said. I believed his every word.

I still want to believe his every word. I don't have any concrete evidence that says I shouldn't. Anyway, the email accused him of stalking, not cheating. This is just my paranoia spiraling and trying to latch onto something new...

Lying on my side with my hands folded between my cheek and the pillow, I watch the time change, minute by minute on my phone. It's 5:59. Then it will all start again.

Griffin's alarm goes off promptly this morning with the help of a new charging cord. His hand swats at the nightstand, the sound of his wedding ring clunking against the wood as his phone stand falls on its side. I wish I could pretend I was still asleep. He knows me better. The thrumming melody on his phone stops just before he tosses his phone on the bed, a mute plop. The sheets rustle beneath him and the touch of his hand on my back causes me to flinch. "You can't possibly still be asleep," he says, his voice gentle while feathering his hand up and down my back.

"I'm awake," I reply, my voice tired, worn.

"Morning, sweetie," he says with a throaty sigh. "You didn't sleep, did you..."

"I'm fine," I lie.

"I can see you're not," he says, brushing a strand of my hair behind my ear. "What can I help you with this morning to make sure your day goes better than it did yesterday?"

Tell me about the woman Abby saw you embracing. Tell me more about that one watch you've owned with the heart engraved on the underside of the box. Tell me this is all in my head.

"Really, I'll be okay. You have a lot going on and I understand," I say, rolling onto my back.

"Jess..." His whisper of my name reels in my attention. "I'm not cheating on you, and no one is going to scare you into running away from me either. I won't let that happen." He sweeps his thumb against my cheek. "I love you. You don't have to question that."

His eyes tell the only story I want to believe. "I love you too."

"Mom!" Abby calls from down the hall. She doesn't sound angry or distressed. More like she needs something. It's enough to pull me out of bed and grab my fleece robe hanging on the back of the door.

"I'm jumping in the shower. Be out in a few," Griffin says as I dart out the door.

I hustle into her room, finding her hanging half out of bed with her phone grappled between her hands. "What is it?" I'm clutching the edges of my robe together, pressing my fist against my pounding heart.

"Dad sent me a text message. He's okay. The doctors let him go home last night. He said his blood pressure is too high and they put him on medication that will help."

"Thank God he's all right," I say, falling onto her bed. "How did he get home?"

"Taxi, I assume," she says.

I pull her into my arms, silently thankful she still loves him as much as a daughter ought to love her dad. I hope he doesn't screw that up with her like my parents did with me.

Jack is like my dad: Work before family. Money before love. I didn't see the similarities until it was too late. Until Jack became so obsessed with growing his agency that I realized I was rewatching my dad's life fifteen years earlier.

But unlike my dad, Jack had a devoted wife, willing to support his endeavors. I was everything my mom wasn't.

* * *

Sometimes, I hold my breath when I walk in the front door after the school bus drops me off. It's like when I get a shot at the doctor's office. I tell myself if I hold my breath, it won't hurt.

"Jessica," Mom shouts from the family room. "Is that you?"

"Yes. I'm home," I say, hanging my Big Bird backpack up on the short hook of the coat rack.

"Good. Go to your room."

My stomach growls, responding to her demand. I haven't eaten anything since lunch, and she only gave me enough lunch money for a grilled cheese. No milk, and no fruit slices.

"Could I just have a snack?" I ask, walking toward the family room.

The icky smell of smoke blows into my face as I turn the corner. Her head looks like it's in a cloud and she's laying down on the couch with the TV set at the loudest volume. "Are you talking back to me? I just told you to go to your damn room. Now go."

I do as I'm told because anything else would result in a spanking—the kind that makes it so I can't sit on my bum for days. I close myself into my small bedroom and fix the rose-patterned wallpaper that has rolled down again. The Scotch Tape isn't working anymore. If I can find some glue that might work,

Dad said he'd try to fix it up soon, but he works so much he never has time to fix anything in the house.

I pull the dark green curtains away from my window and stare outside, watching kids play hopscotch, or roller-skate. Isobel has a new hula hoop. I asked for one for my seventh birthday, but Dad just gave me something called a savings bond.

"Isobel, sweetie, come here. What happened to your pretty braid, silly girl?" her mom calls out from the front step across the street. Isobel drops her hula hoop and runs to her mom. She squeezes Isobel's face and kisses her nose before spinning her around. Her mom removes a hair elastic from the end of her braid, then pulls a hairbrush out from beneath her arm. Like magic. I didn't even see it before. She brushes Isobel's hair, over and over, and I wonder what that might feel like. I always have knots and they hurt when I try to get them out. Mom told me to figure it out.

Isobel's mom re-braids her hair and replaces the elastic. "Okay, you can go back to your hula hoop now. How would you like your favorite macaroni casserole for dinner tonight? I have cookies baking in the oven too."

"Yum!" Isobel shouts. "Thanks, Mom!"

She has no idea how lucky she is. I do tell her all the time. Sometimes, her mom invites me over to have dinner with them. I love their house. I wish Mom would make me cookies. Or something other than a sandwich for dinner. Maybe someday she'll change, but I don't think Mom loves me like the other moms love their kids.

* * *

"Will you take me to Dad's house before work? I want to help him today," Abby asks. I struggle to push my thoughts into gear before answering.

"Griffin said he was going to talk to your principal so you could return to school."

"Dad needs me. School doesn't want me," she argues.

I'm not sure I have the energy to argue back. "Okay, just for today."

"I'll go tell JJ Dad is okay." I give her a kiss on the forehead and push myself up from her bed.

I open his door and poke my head inside. "Good morn—JJ?" I race around to the side of his bed and tear the comforter down. "JJ?" I drop to my knees and yank the dust ruffle up, finding nothing but a few scattered Cheetos and a handful of Lego.

I nearly fly down the stairs, calling out his name louder and louder, not finding him anywhere.

I'm making my way to the basement door when Abby's heavy footsteps charge down the stairs. "Mom? Where's JJ? Why are you shouting for him?"

"I don't know where he is." I didn't go in and say good night to him after Griffin put him to bed last night. I didn't want to wake him up. How could I not at least check on him? What kind of mother am I?

I flip the light on in the basement and grab the railing, hurling myself down the steps. "Justin?" I shout.

Still no answer. The basement is orderly, aside from those few boxes Griffin moved down there. The boxes aren't big enough to form a barrier so there's nowhere to hide. He wouldn't hide down here. He hates the basement.

As Abby steps foot onto the stairwell, I race full speed up the stairs. She moves out of the way, making way for a freight train without brakes.

At the front door, I find the deadbolt still locked. *Where the hell could he be?*

The back porch and door are next, empty and locked.

"JJ, we can't play hide-and-seek if that's what you're doing. I need you to come out right now, buddy." I'm running out of ideas on how to corral a child out of wherever he might be because I've never had to do this with him.

"What's all the commotion?" Griffin hollers from upstairs.

"JJ is missing. I can't find him."

Griffin comes running down the hallway, a towel wrapped around his waist, a hand securing the towel. He bolts into JJ's room and yanks the closet door open. "JJ?"

The way he calls his name, unsure, unsettled, confused...my heart stutters to a stop.

TWENTY-FOUR

My feet slip on the carpet runner in the hallway in front of JJ's bedroom. I catch myself, my hands slamming into the ground before catapulting myself into his room to look for any clue as to where he could be. I check under the bed, before wrenching open his closet. On the floor of the closet lies a crumpled sleeping bag and his Baby Yoda pillow. JJ is clutching the glossy blue fabric beneath his chin with his right hand. His knuckles whiten as he stares up at us, his eyes blazing with shock.

A mere few seconds pass before I notice his other arm, free from the sleeping bag, resting to his side. The handle of a butcher knife secured within his grip.

Oh no. How. Why—why would he have this? Please don't be hurt. The thought...knowing what could have happened, chokes me.

No sudden movement. Scaring him would cause a reaction.

Both Griffin and I, shoulder to shoulder, stand in silence, staring at him staring back at us.

"Did you find him?" Abby shouts up the stairwell. Her shrill makes me jump just after telling myself to remain calm.

She can't come up here. "Yup. We're fine. Go eat your

breakfast," I call down to her, keeping my focus frozen on the knife in JJ's hand.

I bend my knees, slowly folding in toward the ground. "Sweetie," I say, gasping for air that won't pass through my lungs. "Why do you have that?" I charade a sense of calm, praying it's enough to keep him at ease.

"In case," he says. His answer is meticulous, containing no helpful information.

"May I have it?" I ask, speaking through a whisper.

His eyes lock on mine, staring with quiet thoughts I can't decipher. He peers back and forth between Griffin and me. "It makes me feel safe," he says.

My stomach cramps and acidic bile rises up the back of my throat. "Knives are dangerous, sweetie. You know this." I want to grab it. I want to act like this isn't happening. Have a normal morning. None of this seèms possible at the moment.

"That's why it makes me feel safe," he replies, his croaky voice laced with innocence.

Griffin hasn't said a word. I'm not sure he knows what to say.

I reach for the knife, making a show of my slow movement toward JJ. In response, he grips the black handle tighter. "Did you hurt my dad?" JJ asks, shifting his sharp gaze to Griffin.

Griffin recoils, his head jerking back with shock. "What? I—buddy, I'd never—I could never, ever, ever do something like that. I wouldn't hurt anyone. No one. Why would you—what made you think that?" Griffin asks, kneeling beside me.

JJ's eyes gloss over, pain or disappointment is all I can see. It's the same look he had when he was five, watching Jack move out of the house. He doesn't understand, but he feels let down. "You were there when the ambulance took him away. He was okay before you were there."

"Oh, no. No. JJ, your dad called me for help," Griffin replies before I can wrap my head around the accusation.

"But Dad was fine before you got there."

Griffin is shaking his head. "No, that's not true."

My mouth falls open as I glance between the two of them. A cold sweat slithers down the back of my neck. JJ didn't say any of this last night. He didn't seem concerned or worried about Jack or Griffin. He was occupied with his Nintendo until he fell asleep.

"Why don't you give me a minute to talk to him?" I mutter to Griffin. I need to be alone with JJ. Though, I don't want Griffin alone with Abby downstairs. "Wait in the hall for a second, okay?" I give him a wink, a sign that I want to smooth things over for JJ.

Griffin presses his hands against his knees to stand upright and walks out in a trance-like state.

"JJ, drop the knife right now," I tell him, making my demand firm.

He does as I say, and I slide it away from him, keeping it to my right.

"Do you have any clue what that knife could do? Not just to someone else but yourself?" I lecture him, the fury boiling through the flesh of my face. "Griffin did not hurt Dad." *Am I sure about this or just pacifying his fears?*

"You would believe him over me?" JJ asks, tears filling his eyes.

My lungs burn as I try to take in a sufficient amount of air. The light-headed sensation is getting to me. "This isn't about believing you or him." I'm terrified to admit that I believe JJ more over Griffin at the moment. For no other reason than he's been accused of disturbing behavior by two sources over the last day. I don't have a clue as to what's going on right now. "Dad is okay and coming home from the hospital in a bit. No one hurt him."

"If Griffin hurt Izzy, how can we be sure he didn't hurt Dad too?" JJ has been so quiet about all that's happened since yesterday. I stupidly assumed the context was drifting over his head, making him the lucky one in all of this. I didn't want to broach the subject if it wasn't affecting him or if he didn't understand. I'm sure he heard Izzy's name mentioned between Abby and me. But neither of us said anything alarming in his presence. I can't be sure of what she said to him while with Jack last night, though.

"We don't know that someone hurt Izzy. Did you think this from listening to Abby and me talk?"

JJ glances around uneasily. "No," JJ says, straightening his neck to stare up at the high closet shelves above his head. "The person I heard talking in the kitchen the other night..." he whispers, holding his hand to the side of his mouth. "It was Griffin. I heard him say the name Izzy. Then something about hurting someone."

I press my fingers to my temples and close my eyes. "Why didn't you tell me this yesterday? You said you didn't recognize the voice you heard downstairs."

"I didn't want to get in trouble with Griffin." He's never been in trouble with Griffin. A voice has never been raised in this house in the time Griffin and I have been married.

My next thought is if it's Griffin or Abby he's worried about getting into trouble. I can't help but wonder if Abby is filling his head with her thoughts.

All of these assumptions sparked from an email that can't be traced.

I still have no tangible proof about any single concern regarding Griffin's past or present. How can that be? How did I get to this point where I'm on edge inside of my own house?

I hold my arms out for JJ to get up and out of the sleeping bag. "Come on. Let's have some breakfast. Today will be a nice normal day for you."

JJ takes my hands and kicks his feet out of the sleeping bag, the zipper whirring from the force. He ducks out of his closet and stands in front of me. I take his hands in mine, staring up at him from still kneeling. "Buddy, where were you when Dad started to feel sick last night?" JJ stares through me as if I'm a pane of glass, taking a long moment to respond.

"I was sitting with Dad on the couch, watching *SpongeBob* until Griffin got there. As soon as Griffin came inside, he told me to go sit in the kitchen. Then suddenly I heard Dad groaning in pain."

My fleece robe is like an inferno draped over my body, sticking to the back of my legs as I stand up from kneeling so long. I take the knife and step out of JJ's room. "Get dressed and come downstairs please," I tell him, closing his door behind me.

Griffin hasn't made a peep since I asked him to give me a minute with JJ. Although I'm sure he heard every word JJ and I said, given he's standing to the side of his door.

The knife dangles from my hand as I peer up at Griffin, pain and fear slicing through my heart. "Do you know what he is talking about?"

I can ask and accept whatever answer Griffin gives me, but then I'll be forced to choose the truth. Abby didn't say anything about Griffin being at Jack's house before calling 9-1-1.

She was clear about calling for an ambulance because Jack was groaning in pain. Yet, Jack called me, then Griffin, so the kids wouldn't be left alone when the ambulance arrived. Why didn't Jack call for the ambulance if he was well enough to call Griffin?

Griffin holds his palm out. "Take it easy. I got there seconds before the ambulance and police car pulled up. I ran inside and made JJ go wait in the kitchen. I didn't want him to watch Jack being put on a stretcher," he whispers, moving toward the stairwell with me.

"I don't understand how he could think Jack was okay before you showed up." It's all I can say while holding the railing tightly, walking down the steps, fearful of tripping with this massive butcher knife in my hand. The thought of JJ walking up the stairs with this, in the dark...I could vomit.

"Whoa! Why do you have that?" Abby shouts as I walk into view. I didn't see her at the dining room table. Not that there's any way to conceal this thing.

"Don't worry about it," Griffin says. "I'll be down in a minute. I just need to get dressed."

"Okay. Abby, come with me to the kitchen," I tell her, keeping my focus on the knife.

"Um—" she says.

"Now," I assert.

TWENTY-FIVE

The legs of her chair scrape against the hardwood before she drags her feet into the kitchen. I rinse the knife, dry it on a dish rag and place it back into the knife block, then move the block on top of the refrigerator, out of JJ's reach. "Seriously...what's with the *Psycho* knife being upstairs?" she asks, leaning her elbows down on the kitchen counter.

I ignore her question, trying to maintain my composure. "Last night, when you and Dad were looking through old pictures, Dad said it was impossible that you saw Izzy recently, right?"

"Yeah," she says, shrugging.

"And that's when he grabbed his chest in pain and fell?"

"Right."

"Where was JJ when this happened?"

Abby straightens her posture, moving away from the counter. "Right next to me on the couch, why?"

"You told me you were trying to help him onto the couch, but you couldn't move him. That's when he told you to call 9-1-1, then me, right?"

Abby tilts her head to the side and peers up in thought. "Oh yeah. That's right. I did call 9-1-1 then you," she repeats. It's the only part she repeats.

"Was Dad unable to talk at that point?"

"He was in a lot of pain and wasn't saying much except to call 9-1-1 and you."

"Who called Griffin?" I press.

"Not me. He just showed up right before the ambulance did."

"Did your father call him or not?"

"I don't know!" Abby shouts, her face burning red. "I don't remember seeing him make a call, but I was panicking."

"Was JJ panicking?" I follow.

Abby's forehead scrunches, her gaze shifts to the side. "Not really." This is ridiculous. I cannot get a straight story from the two of them.

"Why didn't you call Griffin when I didn't answer my phone?"

Abby holds her hands out to the side, her eyes widening. "Why would I? We were at Dad's place because of him, weren't we?"

Griffin lets out a loud sigh as he jogs down the steps. "I'm going to be late for work," he says.

JJ is hobbling down the steps behind Griffin and Griffin steps to the side to let him by. Just after JJ passes him, Griffin shoots me a hard stare. "Hey, do you think..." He nods his head toward JJ, "he'll mention the—you know what at school?" He stares at me, hoping I know what he's trying to ask.

I hadn't gotten so far as to consider this fact yet, but he's right. Griffin knows he's right. It's obvious by his flushed cheeks and colorless lips.

"Even if I tell him not to..."

"He will," Abby finishes my statement, not knowing the exact question she's answering.

Griffin releases a heavy sigh and pinches his chin. "This is a tough one," he says. He clears the phlegm from his throat and wraps his hand behind his neck. "Um...Oh, man."

"Yeah, you're right. I'm keeping him with me today. A call to his doctor might be in order too."

"His doctor?" Griffin repeats. "You mean to get a reference to a therapist?"

"Well, yeah. If I have a question about the kids' health, physical or mental, I always call their doctor."

The look on Griffin's face says he doesn't agree with my decision, but he would never vocally disagree when it comes to the kids. Or, he hasn't yet.

"Keep me updated. And don't forget I have the faculty meeting after school today," he says. "But if you need anything at all, please call me." He wraps his hand around my arm and leaves me with a kiss on the cheek. "Love you."

Like a tornado, grabbing his coat and bag, both tossed into different spaces, he whips toward the door, leaving us behind with a gust of wind. I didn't even have the chance to debate a response to his parting words.

"Why is JJ staying home?" Abby asks after we hear Griffin's car pull out of the driveway.

Her question makes me stop and think before I answer her in a way that doesn't scare her to death. JJ said he was sleeping with the knife because he was afraid of Griffin. Despite what he might or might not say at school today, I can't leave him in that building with him.

"Just because. Last night was a little overwhelming for you both." *And the whole sleeping with a butcher knife thing...* "Why don't you go get ready so we can leave on time? I still need to drive you to your father's and get to the shop."

Abby and JJ pass each other on the stairs, and I hear the muttering of, "Nice going, kid." It's hard to tell if it was sarcasm or some type of compliment. JJ doesn't respond, which means he doesn't know what to make of it either.

"How would you like another day off school? You can come to work with me again."

"What?" he asks, his shoulders falling in defeat. "We're watching a movie in science class today about the solar system."

His pouts could put me into a state of depression. He's perfected them to be used as a secret weapon. "I'm sorry, sweetie. I'm sure I can find out what video they're watching, and we can watch it together tonight."

I drop the plates onto the dining table, one in front of JJ and the other across from him. "Abby, breakfast," I shout up the stairs.

"She's in the bathroom putting on makeup so she can take selfies all day," JJ says, mocking her with a squeaky voice.

He's probably right. I make my way to the banister. "Abby. Breakfast is ready!" I shout again.

A drawer closes, and another. Something small falls into the sink, followed by seconds of stillness. Frustration simmers inside of me. I have no fuse left to burn at this point.

The sound of a pebble hitting the window behind me makes me scream and jump. I spin around as JJ is shoving his chair away from the table. He runs toward me without looking back.

"What was that?"

"Someone was at the window," JJ says. He's breathless, shock filling his unblinking eyes.

"What? How do you know? Did you see someone?"

"I saw a blob of black out of the corner of my eye when I turned around for a second. Then it was gone. It was a person. I'm sure of it."

With JJ's shoulders gripped beneath my hands, I shuffle him around me, holding him behind my back as I peek through the narrow slit between the blinds.

"Stay here," I tell him.

My body shivers as I walk around the table toward the

window. Goosebumps cover my arms and neck as I pull open the blinds so I can get a better look around.

The trees are swaying along with the light wind. "Do you think it could have been a bird? Sometimes, birds see their reflection in the glass and think it's a friend."

"Yeah, if the bird was the size of a grown-up and wearing a sweatshirt," he says.

TWENTY-SIX

The longer I gawk at the mess of trees, the sharpness of my vision diminishes. "I don't see anything." Or anyone, thankfully. I bite the inside of my cheek and clutch my throat as I press the tip of my nose to the glass. Peering down below the window, I'm grateful to see only spring weeds.

I release the pull attached to the blinds, letting them fall closed, completely. I close the other set in the dining room and the three in the living room too.

"Why is it so dark down here?" Abby asks, making her way down the stairs.

"Mom closed the blinds," JJ says.

"Why?"

"Someone was tapping on the window," he tells her.

"Did you see someone outside?" Abby asks him.

I shake my head, subtly, hoping only Abby notices. I don't want to disqualify JJ's perception in case he did see someone, but no one is out there now.

"I'm sure it was a bird," I say again. "They fly into windows all the time."

I wish I could believe my own words.

"You know...there's an old tale that says a blackbird will fly into a window when it's trying to warn someone about a death in the family." Her words send another sharp chill across my limbs. "Dad wouldn't say he was okay if he wasn't, right?"

"Dad is fine. He wouldn't lie. It's called an old wives' tale for a reason. It has no current day merit. No one is dying."

"Then someone was definitely out there," JJ says with a gulp.

I want to call the police and ask them to do a perimeter check. I don't even have a garage—a way to get into the car without having to go outside.

The police in this town, though...Half of them are the same group of men who were appointed to find Izzy. The other half are their offspring who will eventually step into the higher roles. They'll scan the area without getting out of their cruiser because they'll assume it was a bird too. Plus, JJ loves police officers, and he would proudly tell them that he slept with a knife last night to protect himself like they do from bad guys. Another sure-fire way to ask the Department of Children and Family Services to come knocking on my door today.

I am drowning in this mess.

"I didn't see anyone out there. We're safe here. Don't worry."

"But I did see someone," he argues.

He's also sure Griffin hurt Jack last night. He's heard too much and understands too little.

"Both of you grab your breakfast plates and bring them upstairs. I need a few minutes to get ready before we leave."

The two of them march up the stairs with their plates in hand. I grab their napkins from the table and turn to follow them.

With the lights on and the blinds closed, a short, jagged sheen of light across the wooden floor catches my eye on the way to the stairs. Upon closer inspection, I find a thin, dry trail of blood drops and a streak of red smeared into a circle.

I take in a ragged breath and try to steady my thoughts. I want to ask myself where the blood could have come from, but the image of JJ sleeping with a knife stuns me all over again. Oh God. I hope JJ didn't slice himself on that goddamn knife.

Another ding clanks against the glass window in the dining room. I spin around and run to the window, pulling apart the blinds to look outside again. All I see are squirrels chasing each other, sprinting toward the grove of trees, the space vacant of any other movement.

There's nothing out here. The stress is just getting to me.

"Mom!" JJ screams. "I'm bleeding!"

TWENTY-SEVEN

There it is: a minor slash under JJ's forearm, dried blood streaked down to his elbow. He isn't actually bleeding anymore, but his sleeve is rolled up and he's holding his hand in the air like his arm is about to fall off.

"JJ. We need to get you cleaned up."

"No, no, no! None of that stingy stuff. I don't like it!" he says, backing away from me as if I might attack him.

This is going to be a nightmare. I hope to God this thing doesn't need stitches. "Okay, let's just take a breath. Did you not realize you had cut yourself earlier?"

"I don't know," he whines. "I thought it was just a scratch. I tried to turn over while going back to sleep and my arm rubbed against the sharp part. But I thought my pajamas were protecting me."

They must be torn. He must not have noticed when he changed into his clothes.

JJ shrugs, probably because his sleeve is rolled up above his elbow now. "I don't know, and I don't want to know. I don't want to see blood again!"

"Let me put a Band-Aid on it so you don't have to see it

anymore," I offer, hoping he'll bite the bait and scoot closer to me from the middle of the bed.

"No! I don't want you to touch it!" he continues, screaming.

It's minutes before I can calm him down enough to bring him into the bathroom to clean up the mess and inspect the wound. It's a surface scratch, a couple layers of skin but nothing gaping open. I cover the wound with antibacterial ointment and wrap his forearm with a strip of gauze.

"Are you okay now?" I ask JJ.

He pauses before answering. "I think I'll be okay."

"Promise me you'll never touch anything sharp again."

"I promise," he says, his words phlegmy after crying.

"We're lucky that's all that happened."

To avoid the blood and first-aid work-up, Abby took their breakfast plates downstairs and tossed the bagels into plastic baggies to take with us. "Is it safe to come back upstairs now?" she calls up from the first floor.

"Yes, but we're coming down. We need to go. Grab your things for Dad's."

It's another ten minutes before we make it out of the house. I take a back road behind Main Street to skip past the morning traffic and pull into the small parking lot in front of Jack's apartment building. It's the only apartment building in Spring Hill and fairly new by about ten years.

It wasn't my intention to stay in the house after our divorce, but Jack was insistent that the kids didn't lose their home.

Jack doesn't pay as much for postmarital support now that I'm remarried. So, I don't feel as bad that he lives in an apartment while Griffin and I split most of the bills and the mortgage. Jack covers a portion on behalf of the kids.

Divorces are messy, not something I intended to go through a second time.

As I shove the gear into park, Abby jumps out. Her backpack slings over her shoulder and she's heading right for the front door. JJ jumps out next, chasing after her, and I follow them both.

"I want to stay here today too," JJ says as we step into the lobby.

The smell of old lady perfume and window cleaner gnarls at my stomach every single time I walk in through these doors. It's not often since Jack will meet me outside to get them, but there have been a few times I've had to go up.

Abby is texting while walking up the two flights of steps, making me wonder who she's talking to at this hour when everyone else is being dropped off at school. "Are you telling Bella you're staying home today?" I ask.

"No. She already knows. I'm telling Dad we're here."

No sooner than she finishes her statement, the door at the top of the stairs opens. Jack steps out in his flannel pajamas, a sight only for Sundays when we were married. "I don't need to be taken care of," he says, as if continuing a conversation he must have been having with Abby.

"Well, I can't go to school anyway, so..."

He gives her a quick hug and a kiss on the top of the head before she walks inside.

"What about me?" JJ whines.

"You need to go to school, little guy," Jack says.

"Nope. Not today. I was going to go to work with Mom."

I knew this was coming. Jack raises an eyebrow at me, wondering why I'd decide to keep JJ home on a day he clearly doesn't seem sick. "Can we talk for a minute?" I ask.

"JJ, go inside with your sister," he says, nodding his head toward his living room. "And don't touch that broken lamp. You hear me?"

"Yup!"

"The wires popped out of it. He wanted to try and fix it while it was still plugged in yesterday. It's unplugged now. I just—"

"I get it," I say, cutting him off. "Are you okay? Your heart?"

"Yeah, yeah, I'll be fine. It's the blood pressure thing again. I stopped taking my meds last year. I thought I was better after losing some weight." It's no longer my place to lecture him on how to be healthy and stay that way for our children. But I wish he would think that way on his own. "Were the kids okay last night? I probably scared them both to death."

I drop my gaze to the thin, green and blue paisley carpeting between us. "Abby was pretty freaked out. JJ seemed a little confused."

"What do you mean?" he asks, crossing his arms over his burly chest.

"He thought Griffin hurt you. He said you were fine before he got here."

Jack lets out a belly laugh. "He thought Griffin hurt me?" Another wave of laughter follows. "Oh God. That's a good one. That guy couldn't hurt a fly if it landed on his nose. I'm the one who called Griffin, from the floor, because Abby was a mess after she said you didn't pick up her call."

"So why does JJ think—"

Jack tugs on his ear, then runs his hand over his glistening head. "I don't know, Jess. I don't think JJ even saw me fall, thankfully. Just before it all happened, we were watching *SpongeBob* together. The episode ended and I told him to go wash up and get ready for bed." He sighs, staring past me as if trying to recollect the rest. "If we're being honest here, that show is probably what did me in." He laughs, gripping his hand over his stomach. "Anyway, yeah, he had been in the bathroom getting ready for bed, taking his time in the tub. Whatever the case, it was enough time for me to call Griffin and for him to hightail it here from the school. In fact, Griffin arrived before the paramedics. By the time JJ came back into the living room, all he must have seen was me on the ground and Griffin standing by my side. Bad timing, I guess."

"I'd left my phone on the table," I say, feeling like I need an excuse for missing Abby's call.

"No big deal. It all worked out."

For him. Not so much for me.

"I'm glad you're okay."

"So, why isn't JJ going to school now?"

"At the moment, he's afraid of Griffin," I say.

Jack starts to laugh again, but I hold my hand up. "Just, hear me out. Abby said she told you about seeing Izzy."

Jack clears his throat and shifts his weight around to lean back against his doorframe. "Yeah, she said that. Took me by surprise. I mean, we've all thought—"

"Jack, I got an email from her email address. I'm still trying to make sense of this..."

"Wait, wait, you heard from her? Izzy?"

I nod. "Yeah."

Jack doesn't laugh this time. He places his hand over his mouth and drags his finger down the length of his chin.

"There's no way, Jess."

"I thought so too."

"No, I mean, really...someone must be screwing with you. Did you call the police or anything?"

"And say what? A girl who's been missing for over twenty years emailed me out of the blue to tell me my husband is some crazy stalker?"

"I suppose. They'll start hunting around Griffin. That won't be good for anyone. But still, I'm sure someone is messing around."

I pause the back-and-forth chatter, knowing this will go around in circles like it did with Natalie yesterday. I can say it's some sick joke or I can be vigilant until I'm sure. "Abby saw the email. She was trying to find a tracking number for a shipment. So, she knows. JJ woke up with a butcher knife in his hand this morning. Jack, they're freaked out over—all of it at this point and I couldn't send him to school, wondering if he would—"

"Wait, wait, a butcher knife? How the hell did he get that up to his room?"

"He walked to the kitchen and grabbed it at some point last night. He was sure Griffin hurt you."

"Holy shit," he says, leaning his head back against the doorframe. "Leave him with me. I'll have a talk with him. Go sort through whatever you need to sort through. I'll take care of them until you figure things out."

I hate being without them. It's the first time they both wanted to stay with Jack without me trying to convince them it would be fun. It's also the first day Jack hasn't gone into the office in God knows how long. It's a win-win for all of them.

The coffee shop is only a few minutes from Jack's apartment. I won't be staying long today, but I need to check in for a bit.

I park around the back and pull the key from the ignition. The momentary pause before stepping out is enough time to feel the intense exhaustion pulling me under like a riptide. I lean back against the headrest, promising myself just one minute and then I'm getting out and going to open the shop.

A car door closes nearby, startling me into a whiplash as I search for who else is parked back here in the shop-owner reserved spots. Off to the left, I find an unfamiliar white sedan with tinted windows.

I watch as a woman steps out of the car. With shoulder-length brown hair, red cropped pants and a gray T-shirt, she walks along the curb of the back door entrances to shops toward the corner. This isn't public parking back here. She's parked in one of the two reserved spots for the owners of Spring Hill Cleaner's, and I know that's not Mr. or Mrs. Glover, or their car.

What is this woman doing?

I lean forward, set on watching her until she's out of sight. While doing so, my chest presses against the car horn, shrieking a long, obnoxious BEEP. I flinch away, but as I do, the woman turns to face my car.

The seconds she's facing this direction are so brief, and yet, this sense of overwhelming familiarity strikes me like a hammer to my ribs.

TWENTY-EIGHT

After stumbling out of my car, I made a beeline for the coffee shop, closing myself into the back room. Without even a second to catch my breath, I race to the door separating me from the front. I nudge it open a crack and peek out at the swarm of people.

I gaze across every person, searching for a unique streak of white streak of hair, an inch in width framing the right side of someone's face. She's not in here.

Izzy is the only person I've ever met with that rare genetic trait. Except I can't accuse anyone of parking a white car in a private spot because it's impossible that Izzy would be here. *It is impossible, right?* I know better than to question something like this.

Just as I make a second scan around the space, I notice red pants moving past The Bean Nook's window-length sign. She continues past my shop door.

With curiosity raging through me, I make a beeline for the entrance, wondering where she's going.

"Oh, Jess, hey!" Rachel shouts after me. "I could use a hand for a minute. This lovely lady right here—"

I hold up my index finger, telling her to wait a minute.

"I'm so sorry, ma'am. I'm not sure what's going on right now. I'm sure she'll be back in just a moment," Rachel says to the customer.

I'd never ignore anyone in my shop. I just have to make an exception at the moment.

"Did you hear about—" A whisper, gossip—the most common form of conversation between these walls. "Jessica's daughter was suspended from school. I heard it's because—" *Nope.*

I rush out the door, follow the woman in the red pants, wanting to see if I truly saw a white streak of hair tucked behind her ear. It could have been a glare, the morning sun playing tricks on me.

The woman walks into the Spring Hill Cleaner's, a storefront down from mine. The bells on the door jingle as she disappears inside. I'm left to decide whether I want to corner this woman. She could be a random brunette who can't read a bold "Shop-Owner Parking Only" sign, or she could be related to Mr. and Mrs. Glover, which doesn't make much sense since I would have seen her around before. Or she could be someone I know. *Knew.*

This is ridiculous. I pace between the coffee shop and the cleaner's, watching my shadow ping and pong from one side of the brick edifice to the other.

Why would Izzy be in town if she's so afraid of Griffin? Why warn me and then stay close by?

Griffin assured me this morning that no one could scare me into running away from him. He wouldn't let that happen...Did I tell him that I was fearful of that?

I casually walk past the cleaner's, peering through my peripheral inside as I keep my pace. No one is in the front area. No one. This shop doesn't offer tailoring, so customers don't step foot into the back room. I saw her walk inside. She should be in there.

I pivot and walk back again, being less discreet as I focus my attention directly in the window, confirming there is no one in front of or behind the counter. There's no one to ask if they saw a woman walk in and through their shop.

Irritation fires through me as I yank the door open and step inside the dry cleaning business. The bells on the door are a dead giveaway that someone else has entered. Still, no one comes out from the back room.

The fresh scent of laundered linen, lilac and a hint of vanilla, don't set the stage for an instance where I should be sneaking into the back area of someone else's business.

Regardless of my morals, I move around the counter and between the round metal racks hanging from the ceiling. The shirts, suits, and dresses are usually gliding along the moving conveyor, dangling in unison.

I poke my head into the back room, a space the same size as my back room but less cluttered, and very little inventory. The machinery is all evenly situated on the far-left side in a row, making the task of dry-cleaning look like a simple step-by-step process. I'm sure the machines don't work without an operator, though.

A shriek stuns my ears, forcing me to spin around and gasp.

"Dear God! You scared me half to death! Jessica?"

Mrs. Glover just stepped out of the small bathroom, holding an upside-down broom in her hand, ready to whack someone.

"Someone was just inside. I saw them," I told her.

"It's you," she bemoans, flustered. Mrs. Glover must be in her mid-to-late eighties now and I probably just took a year off her life, scaring her like this.

"No, someone came through just before me. There's a woman parked in one of your spots out back. I saw her walk right into the back room, but now I don't see her anywhere." I sound more concerned over a parking spot than most might be.

"You young mothers with your rampant schedules, sleepless nights, and endeavors to run businesses with your imaginary third limb is what causes these moments of delusion. You're imagining things, Jessica. You need to get some rest. You listen to me. I know best."

"You're probably right, Mrs. Glover. I'm so sorry for startling you." I keep looking at the back door, wishing I could see through it to where that woman might be standing.

"You don't want to rot your brain at such an early age. Before you know it, your kids will be off on their own and you'll be left mindless." I'm not sure she understands what she's saying or realizes that most mothers in this generation don't have the choice but to do everything all at once, but I know better than to fight with a sweet, older lady.

"You're absolutely right, Mrs. Glover. I will take your advice to heart."

"Good. I hope you do."

"Have a good day," I tell her, leaving the way I came in.

Filled with frustration, I make my way down to the end of the block and around the building to my car, finding that woman's white sedan is still parked where it shouldn't be.

I shouldn't care this much. I wouldn't if something about her wasn't making me feel crazy right now. She's probably sitting in her car scoping out the scene from behind her tinted window.

With a heavy step off the curb, I rush toward my car door, but halt in my tracks when I spot a folded note stuck to the window.

I spin around to look at the illegally parked car, wondering if she can see me staring back at her. She could be no one, but someone left me a note. I reach for it, my hand shaking. I can't steady my fingers no matter how hard I try. My muscles cramp as I try to separate the edges. Everything is a struggle and all I want to know is what's inside.

Finally unfolded, I scan the words and momentarily forget how to breathe.

TWENTY-NINE

APRIL 2001 - TWENTY-TWO YEARS AGO

Izzy

04/18/2001

Dear Diary,

It's been two of the most amazing weeks of my life with Romeo.

Holy cow...I didn't think guys like him existed. Well, not in real life. Every romance movie I've ever watched has left me wondering if the story is based on true life. I've been confident that anything seeming too good to be true is a fantasy to dream about.

But Romeo is proving that theory wrong. He is seriously the sweetest, kindest guy I've ever met.

I was unsure about him at first. But now that I've gotten to know him better, I can't seem to stop thinking about him when we're not together.

Izzy

I shove my diary under my mattress on top of the several notes I collected from Romeo before we finally met. He's so much more mature than all the guys at school. It's refreshing.

The phone rings and I dive toward the end of my bed to pick up before anyone else does. As I put the receiver up to my ear, I hear, "Yeah, hold on a sec. Izzy!"

"Hannah, hang up!" I shout.

"Why can't I talk too?" She continues talking as if the call is for her.

"Because no one called for you," I tell her.

"Mom!" Hannah shouts. "Izzy is being mean!"

A crash from Hannah's phone tells me she's hung up on the other end and I can finally talk privately. "I'm here," I say.

"Izzy, is that you?" Jess jokes down the line.

"It's not Hannah," I joke.

"She's just a little sister, being a little sister," Jess says. "I'll borrow her anytime."

"No, you don't need to borrow her," I say.

"Well, my best friend has been too busy to take my calls at night this week, so Hannah isn't sounding too bad right now..."

"Oh, come on," I whine. "You did the same thing when you were dating Kyle, then Nick too."

"Ew, please don't remind me of either," she says. "Lazy jerks." I can hear her snarl, recalling her lapse in judgment during those periods. Kyle had one goal in mind, and he planned to achieve that goal in record time for bragging rights. Jess thought he was in love with her until she caught him making out with Kristy Towner in the girls' bathroom during lunch. Then Nick pulled the plug just like she thought he would because he's heading to California for college and doesn't want to be attached to anyone at home when he leaves.

"Fine, I won't remind you." I sigh.

"Natalie and I are going to the Confection Shed for ice

cream—dinner of champions. We want you to come and refuse to take no for an answer. She told me to say that last part."

I glance down at my clock radio. It's only seven and Romeo has dinner plans with his aunt and uncle tonight, so he won't be home until later.

"Sure. I just finished dinner. I can join you. But did you not eat dinner?"

"Dinner? Ice cream *is* dinner, and I need to get to the grocery store still. I haven't had time this week. Ice cream is a perfectly suitable meal, though," she says. "Sometimes ya just need to live a little!" She hoots into the phone, forcing me to pull the receiver away from my ear. "But wait! Back up the train a little...Did you just agree to go out with us tonight?" Jess seems surprised at my response. "Will lover boy approve?" She's only teasing, but I notice a slight bit of resentment in her tone. Although the resentment might be because she hasn't eaten dinner and I have. She knows she's always welcome to eat with us, but she comes over less lately.

"I don't need his approval," I say with laughter. "Is Natalie picking us up?"

"Well, duh. She'll be here soon—"

"Izzy, there's a package at the door for you," Hannah shouts into the phone from another room, garbling over whatever Jess was saying.

"Hannah! Hang up!" I shout back. "Stop eavesdropping on my calls!"

When the silence returns, Jess continues. "She'll be here in ten minutes," she says with a chuckle.

"See ya."

I open my bedroom, finding Mom down the hall going through a pile of mail. "Is there really a package for me?"

"No, only a letter," she says, holding it out in front of her as she continues to shuffle through the others.

I grab the letter. "Thanks. Oh, I'm going out for ice cream with the girls."

"Can I go too?" Hannah jumps out of her bedroom with praying hands waving in the air. "Please, please, please?"

Mom gives me a long look, silently asking me to bring Hannah along. I glance back at her, still silently pleading.

"I can see if the other two mind."

"Yes, yes, yes!"

No, no, no, I'm whining to myself.

"Hannah, how about I take you to get milkshakes at the diner tonight?" Mom asks her.

Milkshakes are Hannah's weak spot.

"Okay!" she agrees. "Now you can go talk about boys all you want." Hannah sticks her tongue at me and jets back into her bedroom.

"Thank you," I whisper to Mom.

"I'm aware your senior year is coming to an end. It's good to spend time with your friends." Mom pauses as if there's something else to say, but I think she's just sad. She keeps telling me how much she's going to miss me in the fall when I leave for school. I know it's getting to her. "Are you going with just Jess and Natalie?"

"Yes," I reply.

"No Romeo tonight?" Dad asks, walking through the kitchen toward the living room.

"He's busy."

"Well, we'd like to meet him before the two of you go out again. Okay?"

I nod before verbally agreeing. "I'll let him know." He's shy and nervous to meet my family. He's also anxious about introducing me to his parents even though they apparently know all about me. It's only been a couple of weeks, but I'm sure he'd be up to meeting Mom and Dad at this point.

"Thank you," Dad says as I make my way back to my bedroom.

I slip my feet into my canvas sneakers and tear open the letter addressed to me. No return address.

As soon as I unfold the paper, I find a typed note with old-fashioned typewriter font. A smile unfurls across my lips and my cheeks warm.

Izzy,

People don't get good mail much these days, do they? It's either junk or bills. Or so say my parents. I don't get much mail, but I always look through it to see if anyone has sent me something. Since we can't see each other today, I figured I'd slip a good old-fashioned letter in your mailbox. I'm hoping it might put a smile on your face.

So here it is. A good old-fashioned letter.

And of course, a few words that came to me after I dropped you off last night...

In the dead of night, I brood over you
Your smile possesses me, an infatuated grin

Eyes, dark oceans of the soul, I see our tangled fate
By protecting every beat of your heart, sealing off an undying end

I'm always here, reposing as shadows you cast
A thrilling whisper in the wind, my presence you'll feel

If you're ever alone and seeking my hand
I'll be there, everywhere and anywhere forever and for all time

-R

Goosebumps line my arms. The words feel dark today, or maybe it's because I haven't gotten a note from him since we started spending time together. He's happy when we're together, so it must be the artist in him that toys with the more dramatic words. He's truly talented but denies the compliment.

The poetic words linger in my mind as I make my way outside. The music is louder than the car's engine but can't drown out my thoughts. I hold the note tightly in my hand and climb into the back seat. "I'm so happy you're coming with us tonight," Natalie says, grabbing my arm from the front seat. "I've missed you."

"I've missed you guys too. Although we do see each other at school every day, so I haven't exactly left the planet..."

"But it's senior year, and we are supposed to be having fun every night until graduation. We made a pact after Christmas break," Jess says. "Fun 'til we're done. No regrets allowed."

"You're making me feel bad," I tell them. I wasn't trying to ditch them these last couple of weeks. I'm preoccupied more than usual. A lot more than usual, I guess.

"No, no, don't be silly," Jess says. "In truth, we want to meet this guy. We should all hang out together. Invite him along. We want to know him."

"Yeah, I'll see what he thinks," I say.

"Good!" Jess says, turning around to face me in the back seat. "Whatcha got in your hand?"

I forgot I was still holding on to the note. "Oh, nothing. I meant to leave it inside." I clutch my hand tighter.

She pounces on me, her butt crashing into the roof of the car. "I want to see!" She manages to grab the note from my squeeze and plops back down in her seat to read.

Natalie pulls away from the curb and heads down the street while Jess turns the volume of the radio down.

"Izz...what is this?" Jess's few words trickle off her tongue, a strange tone lacing them.

"What do you mean?" I ask.

"I'm always here, reposing as shadows you cast," Jess highlights the line. "That's intense."

"He's just passionate with his words," I say, defending his innocence.

"What do you think '*A thrilling whisper in the wind, my presence you'll feel*' means?"

I catch Natalie throwing a quick glance over at Jess, her eyes widening with surprise. "I think it just means I'll be able to hear his poetic words whenever I think about them."

"Does he still come by your window at night?" Natalie asks.

I shouldn't have mentioned that. "You don't know him like I do..."

"Are you sure you truly know him like you think you do?" Jess asks. My heart squeezes in response.

THIRTY

Locked inside my car, staring at the note I took from my windshield, I struggle to catch my breath. My hands shake so hard as I scrutinize the paper. I'm still positive whoever wrote it is sitting in that white car just staring at me. I can feel it.

There are only a few words, written clearly in large letters.

I believe you're the one who once said:
'Are you sure you truly know him like you think you do?'
The past is like a locked box full of secrets—one you don't have the key to...How will we ever know if history might repeat itself?

I crumple the paper into a ball and throw it against the dashboard before storming out of my car toward Spring Hill Cleaner's reserved parking spaces. With adrenaline raging through me, I knock on the window of the white sedan. My heart races as I tell myself it's impossible that the woman is Izzy. But my heart pounds as I wonder who else would leave me a note that only Izzy would leave me. I want to know who the hell is screwing with me.

The longer I stand here, waiting to see if someone will open the window or door, the more sweat forms along my forehead.

Birds peep around me as if staring down and watching from power lines.

It kills me to step away when I feel so close to an answer.

I stare at the door to the coffee shop, knowing I should go back. I have a business to run.

But I can't.

I have to go home. I don't know whether someone's chasing me or I'm chasing something that can't be found.

Like Izzy.

Sometimes at night, I can still hear the shrill of my voice, screaming for Izzy while running wildly through the woods, searching for her.

It was past midnight when her mom called, asking if I knew where she was and why she hadn't come home. Izzy had never been late for her eleven o'clock curfew.

Her mom wanted to ask me if I knew where she might be. Izzy ran off from the bonfire. I had no clue where she'd gone. We figured she was with her so-called Romeo, but we didn't know where he lived, only that it was out of town.

I called Natalie's house and told her half-asleep dad that Izzy hadn't come home. Within the hour, half the town was out looking for her. There were flashlights everywhere, people walking up and down the roads calling out her name.

She sometimes rode her bike through a path in the woods. I went in that direction first, Dad following in my footsteps. Up and down mountainous boulders, around the river and past the iconic steep waterfall within the encasing tree line of our town, there wasn't a person in sight. And nowhere else to go.

Miles of thickly wooded forests, mountains, and a one-lane highway separate us from the other surrounding towns.

Izzy's parents must have called my house a dozen times throughout the next few days, asking if we had found any trace of their daughter. Izzy's mom knew we would have called her, told her right away had we found Izzy. We were all grasping at straws, praying she would turn up.

Police would come by to ask me questions about Izzy, looking for more insight, but I felt helpless, knowing so little about where she could be. As her best friend, I should have known where her boyfriend lived. I should have known his real name, what he looked like.

I didn't. I failed her.

I fly into my driveway, recalling the way I sped away from the house only a couple of hours ago, desperate to get away from the tapping on the windows and the blood on the wooden floorboards.

JJ is okay. We're okay. Everything is fine.

I still scope out the front lawn and stare through the trees on the left side of the house, making sure I don't spot any movement. *Everything is quiet and still.*

I rush inside, locking myself in. I take a minute to wipe up the dry blood I left behind earlier and toss the pink-stained paper towels away in the kitchen.

As I wash my hands, my gaze floats up toward the knife block, wondering what JJ was thinking would happen to him if he didn't sleep with a knife last night. I hate that I've read about a kid's intuition being stronger than an adult's.

That note left on my windshield, it's a threat. *History repeating itself...*Am I supposed to think Griffin is going to chase me off the face of this earth too? Am I next on his list? What message am I supposed to take from that? Whoever left it must know about the emails—or maybe it's all the same person. Whoever is doing this wants to push me away from Griffin. The woman he only appeared to be hugging in the parking lot—the woman Abby was sure looked like Izzy based off a photo.

I have no sources of information, nothing to ease my concerns other than Natalie's vote of confidence that Griffin is the sweet man he appears to be. What if she's wrong? What if he's hiding something from the past?

Those boxes. The letters. What else can I go by to reassure myself that Griffin isn't this person I'm manifesting in my head?

I charge for the basement door. With a flick of the light switch, the hanging bulb illuminates the stairs and cement floor below. I'm less afraid of the basement and more afraid of the secrets it's holding now.

Griffin's box of old belongings that I knocked over yesterday is still in the same spot. I dump it on its side, ready to shovel out the contents. I need to know everything about his past. I thought I knew it all, but can anyone ever know someone's entire past when they've only been around for two years? Those notes must have something more in them, something that will highlight facts I didn't know about Griffin before we met. Or I could find nothing. I'm desperate. I remove the shoebox with the letters and set it to the side. An Anchoren high school sweatshirt, a yearbook, banners from colleges he's never spoken about, medals without engraved details, mix tapes, and broken glass.

Blood pools on the tip of my little finger from a thin sliver stuck in my flesh. I tug the glass out, watching another blood bubble form, then drip over my knuckle. I squeeze my other hand around my finger. I scoot closer to the center of the box's opening, spotting a shimmer from the rest of the broken glass. A jagged edge, shallow cylinder encasing a long candlestick. The wick is black, wax dried into beveled streaks along the sides. It's a vigil candle.

I had the same one with the glass cylinder and a note card dangling from a piece of twine. I remember the words as I read them again now:

Together, we must pray that our beloved Isobel finds her way back home.

Griffin said he didn't know her. He asked if she was a friend of Abby's. But he was at her vigil. Only family and close friends had the vigil candles with the note cards attached. Yet, he has one. And he kept the candle. He lied to me.

I peel my hands apart, the unwounded one with drying blood smeared over my palm, and the other with my pinkie, stained red. I carefully toss everything back inside the box, pinching each object with only my fingertips so it doesn't touch the blood. I keep the shoebox out and fold it under my arm, then set the box upright before heading upstairs.

After turning the light back off, I kick the basement door closed while squeezing my hand around my little finger once more to avoid making another trail of blood in the house today.

Once bandaged and clean, I drop the shoebox on our bed and remove the lid.

These old letters from the box in the basement could be from anyone. Yet, they were alongside the vigil candle. And now that note on my windshield...I can't convince myself it's not related to the emails. Or the texts...

I remove the cover from the shoebox of letters and dump the contents out so I can scatter them across my navy-blue quilt. These could be unrelated, just an overview of a moment in the past, but there could be more. One of the envelopes is larger than the others and I pluck it from the pile.

A greeting card rests inside, the glue on the flap of the envelope dry and crumbled. I slide it out and open the birthday card, accented with a glitter birthday cake and the number twenty-one.

The same handwriting as the letters matches the words inside.

To my favorite person, Griffin,

I'm wishing YOU the happiest of birthdays with lots of love, hugs, and kisses.

They say (whoever they are) that 21 is the beginning and end of an era.

I wonder what it's like to be so old ;).

I can't wait to take this new adventure with you.

Just the two of us, leaving the rest of the world behind as we find our future together.

And I already know what you're going to say when you open this box:

'I'm not a watch kinda guy.'

Maybe you wouldn't say that to me. I just know it's true.

BUT, this one is different...

This watch is frozen in time.

The hands will never move forward...

Giving you the moment 9:03PM to always remember.

Me

THIRTY-ONE

I tear through every envelope, searching for anything that might have Izzy's name on it or a picture of her. Anything to link Griffin to Izzy. All these puzzle pieces, scattered with edges that don't line up.

I've been sitting here for hours, reading every word of this girl's love-sick notes, and there isn't one hint at who she is. Why would Griffin say he didn't know who Izzy was when he must have been at her vigil? And do these notes have anything to do with Izzy, or are they just another example of teenage love from Griffin's youth completely unrelated to Izzy?

I push my sleeve up, checking the time. School will be over soon. He'll be going to his faculty meeting.

The faculty meeting he was thinking about before getting into the shower yesterday.

I clear off the bed, gathering the letters and envelopes to toss back into the shoebox, and slide it under the bed.

My stomach can't take much more uncertainty. I feel like I can't trust anything at all.

Downstairs, I grab my bag and check to make sure I have

everything before leaving. *My phone isn't inside.* That thing is beginning to burn a hole into my life. It's no wonder I keep forgetting it. I spot it on the dining room table and grab it before heading out the door.

I need to talk to Griffin, ask him about the vigil candle. Tell him about the note on my car. I need to see if this meeting is real or just an excuse for something else. This can't wait and I'm sure he has a few minutes' break between school ending and the meeting beginning.

Driving as quickly as the law allows, I pull into the school parking lot and find a spot between two minivans where I can wait. I send him a text he'll hopefully see just after the kids leave.

> Me: *If you have a minute between class and the meeting, could you let me know? I need to talk to you about something.*

I'm sure he won't respond for a few minutes still, so I just need to wait. My fingers tap relentlessly against the steering wheel, watching the clock on my dashboard. Each minute closer to three, my muscles tighten more. I'll be stone by the time the buses pass through.

One by one the school buses line up along the curb out front of the school. The administrator sends lines of children outside per their bus number in order in which the buses arrived.

I've kept my focus on the rearview mirror as children pile into their seats, staring at Griffin's car. He bought it before we got married last year. It still has a faint new car smell. He traded in his truck because he claimed an SUV would be more suitable to help with carpooling the kids if need be. To a single mom, it was the most loving gesture.

I never asked him to be a hands-on stepdad. It's a lot to expect from someone who isn't their father. Griffin jumped into action, always happy to help. He has been nothing but charming. Has he been too charming? There's no reason to deny knowing Izzy. Everyone in this town knew her and so many from outside the town knew about the seventeen-year-old girl who went missing from Spring Hill.

The final bus pulls away, leaving the front door of the school in view again. The looping line of cars swoops in to pick up the kids who don't take a bus and move along until the last car leaves the lot.

I pick up my phone, waiting for Griffin to respond. Then I see a handful of teachers walk out from the front doors, their coats draped over their arms, a shoulder bag dangling from the other.

I'd think all teachers are considered faculty and would need to be at this meeting. Yet, they're leaving. My stomach falls.

One by one or two by two, teachers continue to leave. I haven't seen Griffin yet.

"Incoming call from...Griffin Adler." The alarming alert pipes the car speakers. I jump to grab my phone from the cupholder, tapping the Bluetooth button to remove the call from the speaker.

"Hey, honey," I say, slinking down in my chair.

"Hi, I just saw your text. What's going on? Is everything okay?" he asks.

"Yeah, I was just hoping you had a free minute to chat. I'm at—" before I can tell him I'm in the parking lot, I see him walk out of the school, glancing around, his phone pinned to his ear. I slouch in my seat. I'm not sure why I'm hiding from him.

"Sorry, you cut out. Are you at work?" he asks.

"Uh—It's been a day," I say, watching him walk in the direction of his car. "You have your faculty meeting now, right?"

Tell me the meeting's canceled and you're on your way home. Don't lie. Don't add to this mess.

"My day was fine. I just finished monitoring the end of parent-pick-up outside and heading back in for the meeting as we speak," he says with a sigh. "Nothing quite like sitting in a stuffy auditorium for three hours, listening to policy changes and debates."

He's passed my row of cars, so I sit up higher in my seat to get a clear view out my rear mirror. "They should at least give you a short break to unwind after the day." I want to cry into the phone and ask him why he's lied to me. I'm losing every ounce of strength I have to keep this conversation going. Acting as if everything is truly the way he's saying it is.

"No such luck," he says. "I've got five minutes until the feedback from the microphone slices through my ears." He laughs, following his exact portrayal of any school meeting in the auditorium. "What did you want to talk about?"

Something that will take way longer than five minutes.

"It can wait. No big deal," I say, trying to sound casual as a knot forms in my throat.

"Thanks, baby. Love you. I'll be home just after six."

I disconnect the call and drop my phone back into the cupholder. Tears fall from my eyes as I watch his car back out of the parking spot.

I pull out of my spot too, reaching the end of the row as Griffin takes a right out of the lot.

Three cars exit after he does, and I make the decision to follow him without a second thought. Only because the other three cars also take a right.

Nothing good can come out of this direction we're heading. The entrance to the thickly wooded area that begins an ascent up Mount Marston. There's a neighborhood just a minute up the road, but past that, there are sharp turns and long winding roads to hiking trails and nothing else.

Just as I feared, the three cars veer off into the aging development of houses. I follow them, fearing Griffin might notice me in his rearview mirror. I do a quick U-turn and watch him continue down the road.

Once he takes the first sharp corner, I pull back out of the housing development. I keep my foot over the brake, ensuring I leave enough space between us to stay out of view. Is he meeting someone on a hiking trail? In his work clothes?

With the distance between us, it's hard to be sure I'm still following him, aside from the fact that there hasn't been a road splitting away from this one. There's nowhere else to go.

An opening in the trees catches my attention up ahead. Red lights blink through the trees, so I slow down again, not wanting to pass the opening. A dirt road declines over a shallow hill, where the glow from the lights continue to blink in an offset, uncertain pattern. I open the right window, listening for a motor, tires moving over rubble, anything that can tell me how long this unmarked road might be. The glow of the taillights disappears.

A squeal from the brakes echoes between trees. And a car door opens and closes.

It isn't a long road.

With my gear in reverse, I back up enough to bury my car in a divot on the side of the road, beneath a tall pine. I creep forward until there's some brush concealing the side of my car.

Once out, I weave through the trees to the side of the dirt road, spotting Griffin's car at the end, in front of a log house camouflaged against the trees.

I stop, watching to see what he does. My hands stiffen around the trunk of a narrow tree, the bark scraping against my sweating palms.

Griffin walks up the front steps toward the door, his phone clutched in his hand. He knocks once before letting himself inside. The storm door crashes behind him, followed by the front door closing.

The sunlight beaming in between an opening in the trees illuminates the interior, allowing me to see Griffin moving toward the back of the house. I keel forward, wrapping my arms around my stomach. Nausea rolls through me, threatening to purge at any moment.

It's clear he's much more than an unexpected guest.

THIRTY-TWO

My conscience tells me to go back to my car. Leave. Confront him later. It also tells me to see if he's left his GPS locator on, allowing me to find him here at this log house off the road should I have happened to look.

With one quick glance at my phone, I realize I have no signal. I shouldn't be surprised. We're in the middle of nowhere. Even if nowhere is within minutes of the place I've always lived. I tap the camera icon and tap the record button, taking a panoramic view of Griffin's car at this house. If it's the only evidence I have, it'll be something.

If this has something to do with Izzy, I need to know. I have no choice but to confront him.

My knees shake with every step I take closer to the house, keeping my eyes set on the window. There's no one in the front room, though decorated like any common living room. I didn't know anyone lived out in this part of town. It's so secluded.

I wipe my palms on my pants and reach for the storm door. Laughter echoes from inside. Griffin's laughter. An interior door closes. That's it? He just walks into this house and makes his way into a room? How long has this been going on? How stupid could I be? Again.

With the storm door open enough for me to squeeze through, I try my chance at the front door, finding it unlocked and easy to open. I almost wish it were locked so I had no choice but to run away. It's too late to unsee what I've seen, though.

I ease the storm door closed so it doesn't make a sound and do the same with the front door.

Griffin is talking, but I can't make out what he's saying. A woman replies, laughter following.

Her voice. I recognize her voice. This can't be possible. I've told myself this for so long. This isn't possible.

I tread carefully down the hallway, making my way to the door between the two of them and me.

"I can't even believe—" she says. "My God."

I tell myself to go in. To barge into the room right now. Confront them. I have to. I'm a fool if I just allow this to happen to me.

My hand is shaking so hard as I reach for the doorknob. I gaze up at the wall, preparing myself to get through this. To be tough. I can handle this. I've done it once. I can do it again.

A hanging framed portrait of a couple embracing stares squarely at me before I can reach the doorknob. The girl facing the camera—short brown hair. Freckles covering her nose and rosy cheeks. It's Izzy. It's her. I'm almost sure of it. My breath catches in my throat as if she's alive in this photo. But the picture is aged. She has her arms looped around a guy, the focus only on his back and bleached blonde shaggy hair with a backwards baby-blue cap on, the same cap I saw in the picture I found in Griffin's shoebox of letters.

Written in black script along the corner of the glass reads: *When forever isn't long enough.*

I'm breathing so hard, they must be able to hear me on the

other side of the door, but their muffled conversation has continued. Again inaudible.

I grab the portrait and lift it off the nail. The back slides out of the frame and falls to the ground, leaving me with half the frame, the glass, and the photo in my hand.

"What's that?" Griffin asks, panic lacing his voice.

Feet are stomping toward me, and I make a run for it in fear of them catching *me*.

I whip open the door and run, convincing myself Griffin can't see me with how quick I've made it outside. I head right for the trees to the left of the dirt road and run as far as I can out of sight from the house, but toward my car.

"Hey!" he shouts from the front door. "Get back here!"

THIRTY-THREE

I'm not sure if Griffin saw me through the trees or caught a glimpse of my car. I didn't see him anywhere when I made a sharp U-turn to speed back toward town.

The picture I stole is lying face up on the passenger seat.

The minute I make it back to Main Street, I turn off onto a side road, then two more in case Griffin jumped into his car to chase me. Or whoever he thinks was in that house.

He was in that house. I shouldn't be running from him. I should have stayed. He'd have to look me in the eyes and confess to whatever is going on.

I keep glancing at the photo. That girl with the white strand of hair, same haircut, in this town...how could it not be Izzy? The photo is old. I can tell by the low resolution and lack of vibrant colors. Everyone in town knew her. I haven't forgotten that fact, but she only ever had the one boyfriend—the mysterious Romeo. That must be him with her in the photo.

My muscles ache from twitching and shaking. It worsens as I grip the steering wheel.

What am I going to do?

I grab my phone and fumble with the letters, trying to retrieve Natalie's contact.

The call connects to Bluetooth and rings. Again, and again. *Please pick up.* And again. "Hi, you've reached the voicemail of Natalie—"

I end the call. There's nothing I can say over voicemail.

Thumbing through my contacts, my finger hovers over Dad's name. I haven't talked to him in a couple of weeks. I'm surprised he hasn't called me with all the free time he has now that he's retired, but he's finding ways to keep himself busy.

The call connects and rings through the speaker.

"Jessica? What's wrong?" I can see why he'd answer my phone call like that. "Are the kids okay?"

"Yeah, we're fine. Well, no...Dad, I don't know what to do." My voice trails off into a high-pitched whine. I won't give him my tears. Not Griffin. Not Jack. Not Dad.

"Sweetie, tell me what's going on. I can't help you if you don't talk to me." I could remind him of all the times he didn't help me when I did try to talk to him. There's no time for that now.

"I got this terrifying email from—"

"From whom?" he questions before I can finish my statement.

"Iz—Izzy. She was warning me about Griffin being the reason she's been missing all these years." The words burn across my tongue.

"Jessica, this doesn't sound right. You know better than to believe some email. Griffin didn't have anything to do with Izzy. You know this. And you know Izzy isn't with us anymore. You were doing so well. You can't let an email bring you back to that place." He doesn't know Griffin as well as he would if I allowed him to be a part of my life. He knows him well enough to see what everyone else sees, though. A schoolteacher, animated, lively, and charming.

"It all seems so real," I utter through my breath.

His sigh from not being able to make sense of this is loud and clear. "Where are you right now?"

I peer out my window, down the narrow side street with two small houses on each side. "In my car, on a side street off Main."

"Where are the kids?"

"With Jack."

"Good. Good." Dad still admires Jack, finds him to be an upstanding man because Dad also doesn't know about the affair. Sometimes, I feel like I'm going for sainthood by keeping this secret.

"What if—"

"Jessica. Stop," Dad scolds me.

"There's someone walking around town who looks like her."

"That's not possible. We've all moved on. Haven't we?" he asks, more for his sake than mine.

"I guess I haven't."

"Do you want to come home? We can talk more. I'm worried about you."

"That's okay. I'll keep you in the loop on how things turn out."

"Jessica. Wait," he says.

"Dad, I—I'll call you back soon. I love you."

I end the call, wishing I'd never started it. A text from Natalie comes in at the same moment.

4:12PM

Natalie: *Sorry I missed your call. I've been stuck in a meeting. I should be out in a few. You at the coffee shop? I'll stop by.*

4:14PM

Me: *No worries. I'll be there.*

The town's borders are constricting, trapping every one of

us in like a caged rat. There's no other way but to turn back into the parking lot behind the shop. At least the mysterious white sedan is gone. I grab my things and make a quick run for the door. I haven't done a stitch of inventory, put in new orders, or done anything to keep the place running this week. We close in forty minutes.

I grab the clipboard hanging from a nail next to the door and peek out into the shop, finding it quiet. As expected at this hour. Sam is polishing the sterling steam frother and Rachel is cashing out the drawer.

"Hey, boss, where have you been all day?" Sam asks.

I never come in late or leave early unless there's an emergency, so I'm sure they're wondering what's going on. "It's just a hectic week. Did you have any issues while I was gone?"

"Nope. We've got it all under control here," Rachel says, giving Sam a look from the corner of her eye.

"What was that? I saw a look. What's going on?" I ask, sounding as paranoid as I am.

"There was no look," Rachel says, drying one same spot of the metal cylinder.

"Guys, whatever is going on, just say it. I can't take any more surprises today." The words spill from my mouth, ones I wish I could put back in.

"Surprises?" Rachel asks.

I have my hand in front of my face and close my eyes. "Look, just...tell me what the look was for. Please."

THIRTY-FOUR

Rachel drops the drying rag by her side and her gaze follows. "Someone came in looking for you earlier. They wouldn't leave a name or tell us what they needed. She seemed upset or angry. She said it was important that she talk to you right away. We tried to—"

"What did she look like?" My words feel sticky in my throat.

Rachel closes her eyes and waves her hands around like she's trying to recall details but can't grasp them. "Uh. She, uh..."

"Brown hair, fair skin. On the shorter side, petite. A pretty woman," Sam says.

"What was she wearing? Did she have any distinguishing features? Anything about her hair?" I press.

They look at each other and shrug. "Uh, she had on red pants!" Rachel shouts as if she's playing a timed trivia game.

"Anything else? A white streak in her hair, framing her face?"

"I—I'm not sure I studied her hair that well. Nothing else stood out," Sam says. "Do you know who she might be?"

"Did you give her my phone number?" I keep firing questions back to their questions. They don't need the answers. I do.

They both seem taken aback by my question this time. "No. She was skittish and in a rush. She said she was meeting someone at 3:15 and couldn't stick around."

She's been here. She'll come back.

"Your favorite customer has arrived," Natalie exclaims, walking through the door.

"Ah—" Sam glances between my frazzled appearance and Natalie's contrasting cheerful glow. "Yes, you are! Can I get you a large chai, non-fat milk, and honey?" Sam offers, buying me a minute to collect myself.

Natalie steps up to the counter and pulls her wallet out. Her focus is on the menu above our heads—not me. "Yes, that sounds perfect. You're a sweetheart."

I step out from around the counter, taking Natalie to the farthest bistro table from where Rachel and Sam are.

As soon as she takes one look at my face, she can't seem to look away, even as she takes her seat. "Um, yeah, you look terrible," she says.

"Can't be worse than how I feel," I reply. "I can't stop questioning if that email is real. The parts about Griffin. I'm not sure he's always been completely honest with me." I can't answer my own question, and I don't know why.

"Wait, where is this coming from all of a sudden?" Natalie asks, pressing her hands into the tabletop. "Why do you think he isn't being honest with you? About what? This can't be a thing, Jess. It can't. This is crazy."

I wrap my hands around the back of my neck, squeezing at the tension. "I'm just—something isn't right." I debate what to divulge. If I say what I'm thinking, I can't take it back. "He's been acting weird. He lied to me about what he was doing after work today. I watched him go into someone's house on the town border. I don't even know who lives there. He's been hiding text messages from me and changed his phone password. Although he's had reasonable excuses and all...it's just—it's a lot. He's never lied to me before. At least not that I'm aware of."

Natalie tries to close her mouth that fell wide open over the last thirty seconds. She presses her palms down to the table and closes her eyes. "No. Mmhhm. There are explanations. I'm sure of it. It might have something to do with work?" Natalie says, her words saying one thing, her expression telling me I'm right to be concerned.

What would she say if I told her about Abby spotting him hugging a woman in a parking lot, one who looked like Izzy? Would she brush that off too? She'd tell me her daughter, Bella, exaggerates all the time. It's never malicious. She just has a wild imagination. We've had this conversation before. If I told her JJ was sleeping with a butcher knife last night, she'd tell me to bring him to a therapist immediately or ask what I've been allowing him to watch on YouTube.

And the note on my car. None of this can be chalked up to coincidences. Something is going on and I can't make sense of anything.

"A work thing, yeah could be," I respond to the simple explanation. I do wonder what she would consider to be a work thing. Is going into someone's house, one I've never met, appropriate and easily categorized under a work thing? "And to make things more stressful..." I lower my voice. "I might be genuinely going insane because I'm pretty sure I also saw Izzy walking through the parking lot out at the back of the shop earlier today."

As if her name alone has summoned it, a shadow spills over the table, followed by a crowd mumbling outside on the curb. My heart races as I clutch my hands on top of the table. The group of people shuffles past the shop window, all taking a quick glance inside. So quick...it's like they'd rather not, yet can't stop themselves, peek in. I watch them, trying to figure out why they don't look familiar. The window is too thin, separating me from anyone on the curb. *They're just teens. Probably heading down to Pizza Stone.*

Natalie slams back into her chair, her mouth hanging open again, and I remember what I just said. "Izzy? How can this be possible? Where?" she yelps. I peer over at Rachel and Sam, hoping they can't hear our conversation. "Sorry. I don't understand any of this..." She combs her fingers through her hair and huffs. "Did you do what I said yesterday? Write back to that email and see if she knows something only Izzy would?"

My chest deflates, realizing I hadn't updated Natalie about the email exchanges. "Yeah. She couldn't answer the question I asked but told me she remembered me telling her that she needed some space from Romeo. If it's not Izzy on the other side of that email, who would know something like that?"

Natalie reaches across the table and places her hands on top of mine. "Jess, I'm getting worried about you. You have a lot on your plate. You've taken on too much. It could explain some of this, couldn't it?"

I study the look in my friend's eyes, wondering if she's questioning me instead of what's going on. "What are you saying?"

Natalie's head tilts to the side, a grimace tugging on her lips. "Sweetie, Izzy's disappearance traumatized you, and I think you've been triggered by this email. You're going back to that frame of mind you were in twenty-two years ago."

Anger warms my face as I stare dumbfounded at Natalie. "You were there too. Why is this just me?"

Am I going crazy? Is nothing what it seems? Why am I alone in all of this?

Her lips purse and she hushes me. "I'm not invalidating any of this. But you should consider talking to someone. It could help."

"I'm talking to *you*," I snap back. "I thought that would help. But you're discounting the fact that Griffin is off doing God knows what and that he lied to me, all while I've been reading emails telling me to get away from him because he's not who I think he is."

"You're right," Natalie says, lifting her hands from mine. "It's a lot all at once."

"Yeah, it is," I agree.

She takes in a deep breath and pauses. "Where was this house Griffin went to?"

"Past the new development toward Nettle."

"Hmm," she says, quirking her lips to the side.

The pain resurfaces in my chest and tears fill my eyes again. I press my lips together, trying to keep my composure. But I can't. "Griffin's going to be home soon. I need to close up and—"

"I have your tea," Rachel calls out to Natalie from the counter.

"Thanks, girl. I'll grab it in a second," Natalie says, shifting her moods more flawlessly than I can. She leans across the table. "You should go home and have a talk with Griffin. He's a good guy, Jess. Don't let all that crap in the email get to you. Whoever sent it wanted you to react this way."

I clench my fists, feeling every one of her words ache through my bones. "Yeah, maybe."

The bells on the front door jingle. I didn't switch the sign to say: closed. I should have before I sat down. There's a wooden beam blocking my view and Natalie is staring at me, waiting to see if I recognize who's walked in since she can't see whoever it is from her angle either.

It all happens at once.

My heart falls to the pit of my stomach.

My pulse throbs in both ears.

Sweat beads across my neck.

I can't breathe. I'm in complete panic mode.

"There you are. I've been looking for you."

THIRTY-FIVE

I jump from my seat, shoving it into the table. The legs scream across the floor, and the chair wobbles from side to side. My heart thrusts into my throat.

My voice cracks as I struggle to speak. "I—I—uh, was just on my way home." The words come tumbling out. I sound like Abby, when catching her doing something she shouldn't.

Griffin narrows his eyes, staring with concern. "I got out of my meeting early. Tried to find you, but your phone mustn't be working again," he says, posture rigid.

In a frenzy, I snatch my phone from the table and shove it into my pocket. My nerves are fraying with what I've discovered, the confrontation within reach.

"My phone's fine. I've gotten calls," I say, avoiding his stare. He should be the one unable to look me in the eyes.

"Hey, Nat." Griffin shifts his weight nonchalantly, peeking around me to greet Natalie with a wave and a warm smile. He's so calm, oblivious to my racing heart.

Natalie clears her throat, a sign of awkward discomfort. "Hey," she says. "I didn't realize what time it was. I need to get home. But, uh—do you need any more help with inventory?"

Feeling robbed of security and a sense of control, I turn to face Natalie's pained expression. "No, but thanks for coming by. It was nice catching up," I say through gritted teeth, my words strained, my distress obvious.

"Is JJ in the back room?" Griffin's question cuts through the silence of Natalie slipping on her light coat. He has no clue what I've been through today on top of finding out he's deceived me.

"No, JJ wanted to stay with Jack too. He's much better today."

"Jack?" Natalie asks, tugging her purse up over her shoulder.

"Everything's fine," I assure her with a poor attempt at a smile. "His blood pressure is acting up."

"Okay. Well, if you need anything, you know where to find me." She gives me a quick hug and whispers, "Be strong," into my ear.

"We're all cashed out. So, we'll see you tomorrow," Sam says. "I'm walking Rachel to her car."

They're both staring at us with wide eyes, waiting for me to say something other than, "Okay." I don't want to question the need to walk Rachel to her car. In this town, that's laughable. What's got their hackles up? Is it the same thing that's getting to me too?

"Walk her to the car? Did something happen here?" Griffin asks, taking his hands out of his pockets. His stance is less nonchalant now.

"No," Rachel says, quicker than anyone would typically respond. "My car has been making a weird noise."

"I was going to pop the hood and take a look," Sam says, shifting his weight uneasily. The two of them don't have a clue as to what's going on, yet they clearly know something's up.

They might have overheard my conversation with Natalie. I hope not.

No one wants to be here. The tension in the air is suffocating.

As the shop empties out, Griffin stares at me with suspicion. He knows something is off, but I don't know what danger I'll be facing when I confess. If he is what "Izzy" has accused...she's told me to run. But I'm here, alone with him.

"I know how to clear a room. What have you told them about me?" Griffin tries to make light of the situation when we're in the middle of a very dark place.

"Yeah. I'm not sure they know a whole lot about you." Just like me.

"Are we picking up the kids tonight?" The casual question is jarring against my mindset. *JJ was sleeping with a butcher knife last night.* Nothing is okay.

"No," I say, my one word spoken with clear defiance. "I don't think that's a good idea."

Griffin cups his hand around the back of his neck and squeezes. "Is there something else you aren't telling me?" he asks, his voice deep and intense.

I shake my head. "I think that's the question I should be asking you." My voice is full of fear.

He holds his hands out to the side, confused. "What are you talking about?" He arches an eyebrow.

I hesitate, knowing what will come out of my mouth. My chin quivers and I want it to stop.

Griffin steps toward me with his arms out for a hug. "Hey, hey, it's okay. Come here."

"Stop," I shout, stepping away. "Tell me where you've been since school got out, because I know you weren't at the school." Before he can answer, my body starts to tremble.

His cheeks redden and he lowers his head. I'm not sure what he'll say. "I—I, it's not what you think. I shouldn't have lied to you..." he says so quickly, he might as well have taken out a knife and stabbed me without hesitation.

Everything I've been afraid of happening again is true. I don't trust my husband. And this familiar ache in my heart is something I can't live through again. My skin burns with rage as I try to keep control of my emotions.

"How do you know what I'm thinking?"

He steps in closer. I want to run.

I step back, knowing there's nowhere to go. There's a wall behind me.

"Don't come any closer," I growl.

"Jess, come on, honey. I was just helping a colleague with something."

That's the best he's got?

"A colleague?"

"Yes..." He's looking at me like I'm crazy.

I turn toward the counter and begin to pace, clenching my hands, releasing them, clenching again...Then pivot and repeat.

I can't breathe. I need more air.

"I had to go to Ms. Flannagan's house, she's the floating teacher's aide. You've met her. I was helping her put together the commemoration display to give Principal Baker on her last day. It's a gift on behalf of the teachers."

I'm aware there's a teacher's aide, but the name isn't ringing familiar, and I don't recall meeting her. Regardless, whoever she is and whatever they were doing, is a secret—something he was purposely keeping from me. A lie.

"You told me you were going to a meeting in the auditorium. People don't lie unless they're hiding something."

Griffin clasps his hands together and rests his fists on his chest. "Jess, the last thing I want to do is hurt you."

"I'm all too familiar with this pain. So, I'm not sure how you were *trying* to avoid that." Griffin and I have never had a serious argument before. We're in uncharted territory.

"If I told you I had to go to Ms. Flannagan's house to help

with this thing, you would have been uncomfortable with the thought of me being at some woman's house."

"No. Griffin, she's a colleague. I've never questioned the extracurricular parts of your position before. Why would you assume I'd be uncomfortable? But did you consider how I'd feel if I found out you were lying to me? You're so concerned with my feelings, yet that didn't cross your mind?

He lowers his head in shame. "You're right. I was wrong. I see that now. I couldn't have been more wrong. But the lie was only because I love you and didn't want to stress you out over something silly and insignificant. I know what you've been through in the past and I was just trying to protect you."

If I've learned anything in life, it's that people don't just lie once. "Love and lies are the beginning and end," I utter, knowing this was more than just a side-trip to a teacher's house.

"You still don't believe me." His gaze falls as he takes a shuddering breath.

"Do you hear what you're saying?" I ask him. "You just admitted to lying. I'm supposed to just believe whatever comes out of your mouth now?"

"It wasn't preplanned. Ms. Flannagan was supposed to bring the display to school this morning, but she couldn't fit the glass pieces into her car. We were all supposed to work on it at the school—all the faculty. It was the reason for our meeting. I was going to tell you about the last-minute change when I called, but—I was flustered and a lie came out instead, hoping to spare you more stress." It's like he can't get all his words out at once, but he's trying. He wants me to hear every word.

There's nothing worse than a lie than having an excuse for the act.

"I don't know what to say, Griff...I followed you to the house."

He recoils, his brows furrow together. "You followed me?"

I scoff because he sounds angrier than I am. "Yes, of course I did. You lied about where you were, and I wanted to know why you went there."

"But how could you have followed me?"

"I was at the school when you called in return to my text message. I was hoping you'd have a second to come talk to me outside of the school before your meeting, but I watched you walk outside and lie to me. For the life of me, I couldn't understand why you'd lie, especially since this was school-related, as you say."

"It *was* school-related," he says, sticking to his story. Griffin shuffles his weight from foot to foot, digging his hands into his back pockets. He chews on his lip and peers up at me. "Jess, did—did something else happen today? Another one of those emails?" He's trying to distract me from the issue at hand. But the mention of the emails reminds me of the other lie.

"Why'd you tell me you didn't know who Izzy was?"

"What? I don't..."

Lie. Lie. Lie.

"I need you to leave so I can lock up the shop. Please—just go," I tell him.

He takes in a deep, shuddering breath and presses his hands to his hips. "Jess, we need to talk about this," he says. "Whatever it is your upset about, I want to talk it through. I want to fix things, and—"

"I don't want any more lies, Griffin."

"No more lies. I was never trying to hurt you. I swear."

"But it does hurt. And I deserve the truth about Izzy."

His nostrils flare. His lips stay shut. He doesn't deny knowing her, but he doesn't admit it either. "I'm going to follow you home so we can talk, okay?"

THIRTY-SIX

I need more time before we talk. I'm angry, assuming a lot of variants to what's going on between us, and I'm not sure I can handle a calm conversation about why he thought it would be okay to lie to me at least twice today.

Despite what I need or don't need, Griffin follows behind me, each road I take until I finally concede to the direction of our house.

In the darkness of the night, the sheen from the photo on the seat beside me catches my eye at each streetlamp I pass. Flannagan. I haven't heard that name before. The female voice was vaguely familiar, but no one I could put a name to.

The photo from that woman's wall doesn't fit into this mess, but there has to be some relevance because she seems to know Izzy. Yet, I don't know anyone who lives in that house. My life intertwined with Izzy's. I knew her family and extended family. She didn't know anyone who lived in that end of the town.

I veer off to the side of the street before our driveway, allowing him to pull in first. He's hesitant to do so but after a moment continues past me and up the driveway. I drive in behind him.

By the time I put the gear in park, he's already made his way into the house, giving me the time and space I need. I'm still not ready to talk yet.

I grab my phone and open my inbox, scrolling down to the last email exchange between Izzy and me. I promised myself I wasn't going to continue talking with this person, but I'm not sure I have much to lose at this point. I tap the reply button.

To: IzzyBee83isMe@aol.com
From: Jessica Peterson
Subject: Re: Re: Re: Hey you...It's me.

Izzy,

You must want me to think you're here in town. Why is that? Do you want me to question my sanity, wondering how it's possible to see someone who looks just like you wandering around outside my shop?

Even my staff told me someone came in looking for me—a description mirroring the woman I saw—your lookalike.

Then I found the note on my car today, repeating words only the two of us have shared.

Griffin says he doesn't know who you are. He's never heard your name.

Maybe you're confusing him with someone else...

Jess

I click send, not sure if she'll respond or if she does, what the response will be.

Griffin storms out of the house and toward my car, a metal baseball bat dangling from his hand. He opens my door and I flinch, scooting into the corner of my seat. He's breathless, covered in sweat, his veins pulsating across his forehead.

"Someone's been in the house. Stay out here. I'm calling the police."

I clutch my neck. "Wh-What did you find?"

"Just take a breath. It's OK," he says. "I'm here."

"What happened?" I demand.

"There's a broken window. Butcher knife on the sofa. Blood splattered on the wall. Framed photos pulled down. All smashed. There's glass everywhere."

I lock my focus on the dashboard, the green neon symbols burning my eyes into a blur. My chest tightens as I try to take in a breath to calm the incoming stream of internal questions. I don't understand what's happening. The tapping on the window earlier...Someone must have been out there. Panic zings through me, leaving me with a cold sweat and light-headed. "Why would someone do this to us?"

"After I call the police," Griffin says, holding his phone in the palm of his hand.

"Yeah, yes. Call."

"What is that on your seat?" he asks, reaching over me to grab the photo.

My arms become limp, my legs too. I can't swallow. "A photo of Izzy and—" The answer comes out in a whisper.

"Who?" he asserts, straightening his posture outside of the car.

I shrug. "It could be you. It's hard to tell, but I'm certain that's Izzy."

Griffin slaps his free hand down on top of the car, engulfing me in a metal echo. He twists the picture around from side to side. "You think this is me? How could you think this was me?

This guy is only a bit taller than the girl, and she doesn't look very tall. And besides that, where did you get this?"

"I'm surprised you didn't recognize it from the inside of Ms. Flannagan's house," I snap. "I snagged it off her wall."

Griffin jolts his head back, shocked. "Wait, was that you inside her house? We heard someone and..."

"Yeah, it was me," I utter with a heavy breath.

"You came in to find me and took a photo off the wall," he says, clearing up the story for what must be his sake. "Why would you run? What—I don't understand...Jess, this is crazy."

"I took the picture because I saw Izzy's face. I would know who lived there if they had a picture of her hanging on their wall. And I don't know who lives there. Some random person has a photo of her hanging up. You're in their house. I just can't even figure out what to make of any of this. My gut told me to run, so I did."

"Your gut told you to run away from your husband?" he asks.

It did.

"Yeah. I felt incredibly betrayed by you at that moment, and I ran." No one knows how they'll react when they find their husband in some woman's house and at the same time find a photo of a friend who's been missing for over twenty years casually hanging on the wall. However, I assume I might not be the only person to just run.

Griffin drums his fingers heavily against the metal roof. The sound reverberates through my spine as I feel like the car frame is shrinking over me. "I don't even know what to say." He holds the picture steady in his hand for another long look. "The girl isn't even in complete focus. How can you be sure this is Izzy?"

"I just am," I say. "It's her. I'm positive."

He drops the hand holding the photo down by his side. "God, Jess, I've done so much to show you who I am, to be open and honest, but it's clear no matter how much I try to prove my devotion to you, you'll never believe it. And even when I'm trying to protect your feelings, like I did today, I'm just hurting you more."

"I'm not this delicate little flower that will disintegrate under the sun. Yes, I have a past. I also have trust issues, but I've never questioned where you're going or what you're doing until now, because I trusted you. Today, you gave me a reason not to."

"I understand," he says. "I need to call the police. We need to get someone over here to check out the house. Can we table this discussion for a few?"

"Yeah." What choice do I have? My life is one distraction after the other, pushing me farther and farther away from finding out why the past is chasing me down.

Griffin drops his hands down from the top of the car and releases his fist from around the photo, holding it under the dash light. "You must have seen pictures of me when I was younger at my parents' house and stuff. I looked nothing like that kid."

"I haven't seen many pictures of you from when you were younger."

Griffin steps back and dials a number on his phone.

"Yes, I'd like to report a break-in at my house. I live at 23 Holbrook Road." He swings his hand around, the photo dangling from his fingers as he circles the perimeter of the driveway. "A broken window. There's some blood stains. I'm not sure if they stole anything." An animal squeals in the distance, making me jump. Griffin stares toward where the sound came from but loses interest quicker than I do. "Great. Thank you."

When the call ends, he leans down, pressing his hands to his knees. "What did they say?" I ask.

"They're sending someone down."

"Good."

"Jess, I want you to be honest with me. Has someone ever physically hurt you?"

I dig my fingernails into the sides of my legs, needing to focus on the pinch rather than his subtle accusation. "Why would you ask that?" I ask, staring past him toward the dark lawn.

"The way you startle, flinch, jerk away, as if you're always in some kind of danger..."

THIRTY-SEVEN

MAY 2001 – TWENTY-TWO YEARS AGO

Izzy

The nerve-wracking statement, "We need to have a talk" coming from a parent never gets easier to hear, even at almost eighteen. I don't know what I could have done, but the tone in Mom's voice says I've done something wrong.

She even closes the door after walking into my bedroom, ensuring Hannah doesn't hear our conversation. There's no other reason for the privacy since there are no secrets between her and Dad. Not that I know of anyway.

Mom tugs my desk chair out and faces it to where I'm perched on my bed with my physics binder notes. On the bright side, this will be a break from studying for the upcoming final.

"What's wrong?" I ask.

She folds her hands on top of her lap and twists her mouth to the side, delaying her response. "Jessica called earlier."

I sit up straighter, wondering why we'd need to have a talk about Jess calling. "Is everything okay?"

Mom drops her head and sighs. "She's worried about you."

"What? I'm right here. What's there to worry about?" She'd tell me something like this. She wouldn't go to Mom.

"Romeo," Mom says, his name its own sentence because there's no need to say any more. "When are you going to introduce him to your friends? They feel like you're hiding something from them and it's making them think Romeo isn't a good person."

"But he is a good person," I slash back defensively. "You know he's a good person."

"Yes, but I am curious about why you are keeping him separate from Jessica and Natalie. There must be a reason. The three of you are like sisters. What's going on?"

I have a sister. Hannah is enough of a handful. "I don't know," I say with a shrug. "Sometimes, when things feel too good to be true, I just want to selfishly keep it that way for as long as I can. Plus, I don't want to flaunt any more of my life in front of Jess when she's already struggling with everyone going in different directions next year. All she talks about is being alone. I feel bad." That's not the entire truth, but I'd rather keep this lecture as short as possible.

"Well, she seems more concerned with you and your well-being than being alone next year, if you ask me. Jessica said she thinks Romeo has been stalking you and watching you through the windows at night. Why would she be thinking something like that?"

I can't believe Jess said all of this to Mom. I told her this in confidence. "Well, that's ridiculous. Why would my boyfriend be stalking me? And worse, watching me through a window at night. That's sick."

Mom shrugs. "I'm not sure. Some boys show their feelings in big ways at this age, and I can see he cares about you deeply. However, sometimes emotions can grow to an unhealthy level, though. Do you understand what I mean by that?"

"Yes, but there's nothing unhealthy about our relationship,"

I assure her. "Jess just over-worries about everything. She acts like an overprotective mom to compensate for not having one. She means well."

Mom kneads the skin over her knuckles, clenching her hands together. "I see. Well, regardless of all these assumptions and explanations, your father would like to talk to Romeo just to make sure we all know our boundaries for a relationship at seventeen years old."

"That's completely unnecessary, Mom. Holy cow, this is so embarrassing. Romeo hasn't done anything to cross any of these boundaries you're talking about. Please don't let Dad corner him into one of his lectures. If I were worried about something, I would tell you. I would come to you. But there's nothing wrong with the way things are between the two of us. I promise."

"Okay, okay, let's calm down," she says, untangling her hands and gently flapping them at me. "Why would Jessica think he's stalking you or watching you through windows at night?"

"I don't know." My words come out too quickly. Mom's head falls to the side, calling me out on my eager response. "I don't. But no one is outside my window at night and like I said... he's my boyfriend. How could that make him a stalker too?"

Mom's shoulders roll forward and she leans her elbows into her lap. "Sweetie, he likes to spend a lot of time with you. More time than you've been spending with anyone else. He calls constantly and—"

"We're in a relationship and enjoy each other's company. I wouldn't define that as something crazy," I argue.

"Okay. Well, if you could do me a favor and make sure you close your curtains at night, and promise you'll tell me if you ever feel like Romeo is overwhelming you. Also, don't forget about your friends. Jessica might be having a hard time right now, and she would be even if she was leaving for school too.

You're like family to her. It's a lot of change all happening at once. I don't want you to have regrets, sweetie, okay?"

"Yup," I say, peering down at my chipped nail polish, then pick at it some more.

"I know you make good choices. I just wanted to make sure everything was okay."

"Okay," I tell her, feeling the anger burn through me while wondering why Jess would call my mom to exaggerate stories I've told her.

Mom stands up from my chair, replaces it beneath my writing desk and comes over to give me a kiss on my forehead. "I love you, Izzy. That's why I wanted to talk."

"Love you too," I utter.

Every bone in my body is telling me to storm outside and across the street to confront Jess, but I know angry words never help anything, so the silent treatment is my next best choice.

I never thought I'd ever go a week without talking to Jess. We've been friends for as long as I can remember and I'd never dream of avoiding her, but she must know why I haven't been talking to her, and neither of us have said anything about her calling Mom. So now things are just awkward between us.

She completely crossed a line.

She doesn't even know him, but thinks he has other motives. I watch as Jess stands up from the table in the cafeteria, tosses out the remainder of her lunch, and heads for the bathroom.

I take the opportunity to talk to Natalie, still sitting at the table but now alone.

"Hi!" she squeaks as I sit down, placing my tray in front of me. "Where've you been at lunch this week? We've missed you."

"Oh, just studying at a back table. I have a big test and my grades have slipped."

"Bummer," Natalie says. "You've always had the highest grades of all of us." I should have come up with a different reason.

"The last calculus unit is a killer," I say, giving my excuse merit.

"Which is why I didn't take the class," she says with a giggle. Natalie tilts her head from side to side as if inspecting me. "Hey, did you change your hair or something? What's different?"

"Oh, yeah, I put in some blonde highlights and cut back on the makeup. I'm trying to go for a more natural look. Does it look bad?"

"You braided back your white streak of hair. It's hardly noticeable now. That's what it is. Why are you hiding it? That's like your Cindy Crawford mark."

"Oh, yeah. I just wanted a change,' I say, sweeping my fingers over the thin halo-style braid.

"Well, I love it all. It's very chic."

I twiddle with a silver ring on my thumb, spinning it in circles while thinking of a way to ask about Jess. "So..."

"So..." she echoes.

"Is Jess mad at me or something?"

"Jess? Mad at you?" She laughs. "She thinks you're mad at her."

I'm not happy about what she did, but it's not worth losing my friend over. "No, I mean—my parents drilled me with questions all week, but everything's fine. I'm not mad or anything." Even though I still am a bit, but I'm not one to hold grudges.

"Well, good. How about the three of us go to the movies tonight? We were debating between *Pearl Harbor* and *Moulin Rouge*."

I pick up a carrot stick from my half-eaten lunch and snap a bite off. "Actually, I've already seen both...with Romeo. Plus, we have plans tonight."

"You two have plans every night, huh? Things must be getting serious?" she asks, fanning herself. "That good, huh?"

I can't help the smile growing across my face. I shrug at her question. I'm not sure what she considers serious. "I mean, I love spending time with him. He makes me happy."

"You're in love," she sings, flapping her hand at me.

My cheeks burn from embarrassment. "I don't know."

"So, why won't you let us meet him?" she adds. "We want to love him too. We still don't even have a clue what he looks like. Not even a picture. We're dying to know him."

I take another bite of the carrot stick. "He has shaggy, bleach-blonde hair, about a head taller than me, and dresses like he lives in the mountains," I say with a laugh, keeping the description general for the common guy around our age. "Yeah, he's just really—"

Natalie leans across the table, lowering her voice. "Shy. Yes, you've told us. But, dude, we don't bite." She jiggles her eyebrows. "Not like he evidently does." I adjust my pink silk scarf to re-cover what I didn't mean for her to see. Natalie has had her fair share of hickeys. Same with Jess. I was just a prude until now.

"It's nothing," I say with a sigh.

"Yikes. Well, that's not nothing. And neither is that," she says, pointing to my wrist. "What did you do to yourself?" Her eyes are glued to the stupid bruise I got yesterday.

I almost forgot about it.

"Oh," I laugh. "I tripped going up my front step yesterday. I'm such a klutz."

She grabs my hand to take a closer look at my wrist, but I notice people staring at us, so I tug away. I regret coming over here. "People are staring at us," I utter.

She takes the hint and pulls back. "Sorry. So...ask Romeo if we could give it a shot, okay? We can do something with the three of us. It could be super casual. Hang at the bonfire or the falls." It's the same question every time I'm with them. It's like there's nothing else going on except for me having a boyfriend.

"Yeah, I'll ask him again. Last time, he said it would stress him out."

Natalie's jaw drops. "Rude. He doesn't know us. How could he be sure we'd stress him out?"

"Well, I've told him you both have lots of energy and talk a lot," I say with a shrug. "It's not an insult to you. It just might be a lot for someone who is of the quieter type, ya know?"

"Well, I'm sure we can make an effort to tone things down," Natalie says.

It's not just toning things down. Natalie must know Jess is like an overprotective sister. Natalie can be calm and mirror another person's level of socialization but Jess, not so much. Plus, from the beginning when Romeo sent those first letters to me before we even met, Jess has been expressing her concerns about him. I can't imagine what she might say if given the chance to meet him.

"I also kind of told him what Jess did and said to my mom. It just came out. It was upsetting me, and he asked what was wrong." It would be nice for him to meet my friends, but I can't blame him now.

"Yeah but Jess loves you, Izzy. A couple of those poems were a little heavy and then the other parts about someone tapping on your windows, and watching you from the dark... That would kind of scare me."

"I don't think the intent was to scare me," I argue. "I told him I'm infatuated with the idea of chivalry. Isn't that what all girls want?" Someone to idolize them. A guy who doesn't want to share his girl with anyone. Says he can't imagine ever loving anyone the way he loves me. That we'll be together forever because his heart says so.

Natalie gives me a long, hard stare just as the bell rings. Lunch is over. Without another word from her, we're ushered out of the cafeteria like a herd of sheep.

The world is turning against me.

THIRTY-EIGHT

Since Griffin questioned if someone had hurt me in the past, I've been staring out the windshield toward the house lights.

"I—I don't know what classifies as someone hurting me, okay?" I utter. "I'm sensitive. That's all."

"Did Jack—"

"I—can we just not go there?"

Griffin rolls his shoulders and stretches his neck from side to side. "The kids are with him all the time. If he hurt you—"

"Please stop. I would never put my kids in danger." The police are minutes away from invading our house, probing us with questions, and God only knows what will follow. Recalling more of my past isn't on my current agenda. "I don't have a short and quick answer to give you."

"Jess," Griffin says, releasing a lungful of air. "I haven't done anything to betray you. I promise."

Those words are easy to speak.

Flashing lights round the corner at the end of the street and Griffin heads toward the edge of the driveway to greet the police. I should join him, but I can't move from my seat.

Blood. A broken window. Shattered glass. That's what

happened to Izzy's house two days before the senior bonfire party. It seems like only yesterday that she came running to me, scared out of her mind.

* * *

I can't help but think Izzy needs an intervention. However, I'm not sure how well it would work, knowing she's head over heels for this poisonous, mysterious Romeo guy. Natalie and I have had to sit back and watch Izzy fall into a trap of control and unhinged behaviors by a man we don't know for almost three months now.

I've questioned how I'd act if I were in her shoes—what I'd do if she and Natalie confronted me with their concerns. Would I push them away or listen? Everyone wants the sort of attention that makes them feel constantly desired, adored, and like they're the only person who matters. It's just not realistic.

Natalie told me about the conversation she had with Izzy at lunch the other day, so I'm waiting on a bench in front of school so I can catch Izzy on the way in. I wish she still needed a ride to school in the mornings. We'd have more time to talk. But she doesn't need us now, since Romeo drops her at the student parking lot. She gave up on saving money to get her car fixed because he insists on driving her everywhere.

I spot Izzy walking up the sidewalk, her new oversized Dior sunglasses concealing half her face. I make my way toward her, arms open. A hug will be the best way to fix what's broken.

She takes the embrace without question. A moment of silence passes, when I feel a shuddering breath tremble up her back. "Are you okay?" I ask. She shakes her head, then nods, confusing me. "Talk to me. What's wrong?"

Small gasps of air precede her words. "I think you were right about Romeo," she says, her voice squeaking.

My heart pounds and I curl my knuckles into my fist, feeling a pop, pop, pop. "What do you mean? Did something happen? Did he hurt you?"

I wrap my arm around her and lead her off the path, toward a tree large enough to give us a bit of privacy as other kids pile into the school. We step into the shade of the overhanging branches, and I notice her cheeks are red.

"Yes. I'm not sure what to think or do...I had a group meeting at the library last night for my astronomy report. I was gone for a few hours. Mom took Hannah shopping at the outlets in Nettle. So, they were gone until even later than me." Izzy sniffles and runs her sleeve-covered fist beneath her nose. "When I got home, I found that someone had broken in through my bedroom window. The photo collage I had covering my wall was torn down. Each picture was in pieces. The stuffed bear my grandfather gave me before he died...My diary was out and open on my bed to the first entry I made about Romeo. I've never left it out. It's always been under my mattress."

"They hurt Grizzly?" I ask.

"Yeah, it was torn at the seam. All the stuffing pulled out. The plastic eyes were torn off and in their places were black marker-drawn circles. Blood stains covered everything in my room, from my comforter, the teddy bear, and photos. Whoever broke in must have caught themselves on the glass."

"Whoever?" I ask her, wondering how she could question who did this. "Who do you think it was?"

She swallows hard as if something is lodged in her throat. "I don't know who would—"

"Oh—Izzy. What did the police say?" I don't want to ask her if she thinks it was him. I'm scared she'll run from me. I don't know what's going through her mind. She needs me to just listen. I can do that.

"You think it was him, don't you?" I can't help wondering if this is a trick question. She runs her finger beneath her glasses, wiping up tears.

"Do you?" I turn the question back on her.

"He seemed disappointed that I had to go to the library last night. I think he was mad that I went."

"Did you call the police?" I lose my patience, trying to err on the side of caution with her feelings. I'm too terrified of what this guy has done to punish her spending a night without him.

"No," she whimpers. "I cleaned up the mess before Mom got home. I got the blood stains out so it didn't look like anything happened in my room."

"The broken window?" I ask, my words sharp and direct.

"I had an old baseball, so I told my mom one of the neighbor kids on the street must have accidentally hit a baseball against the window, hard enough to shatter it and I found the baseball in my room as proof. I don't want to put Romeo in jail. You understand that right?"

Not exactly. My muscles all tense in response to her statements. I'd be terrified out of my mind if I were her. How can she not be? "Izzy, he can't act like that. That's criminal behavior. He could hurt you. Guys who act like that are the type to do something awful later. You don't want to wait until it's too late."

"I'm not sure what to do," she cries. "I'm so scared."

I hate understanding how forgiving love can make someone. "You should tell your parents the truth." It isn't my place to give her advice and I don't want to tell her to do something that will cause her more problems.

"I could be overreacting," she says, sniffling again. She shakes her head as if brushing away the concerns. "But I don't want to feel scared anymore. I need to get away...This has to stop."

"It will. I promise. Talk to your guidance counselor. Ask them what you should do. Don't let this go. You can't."

With one last shuddering breath, she loops her arms around my neck. "I'll figure it out. I don't want to be late for class." Her words, a hoarse whisper. "Thanks for listening."

* * *

"Mrs. Adler, one of our detectives would like to ask you a few questions. Will that be all right?" A police officer stands by my car door, distracting me from the memory of what Izzy went through.

"Yes, of course."

"Would you mind stepping out of your vehicle?" he asks.

In a moment of distress, I search for my bag, forgetting I placed it on the floor in front of the passenger seat. Once retrieved, I drop my phone into the outer pocket and yank the keys from the ignition. The officer takes a step back to give me space and I follow.

"Mrs. Adler, I'm Detective Baker." She's wearing a white blouse, dark dress pants and a matching unbuttoned jacket. A badge hangs from a thin chain down the center of her chest. The detective appears a bit younger than me, my height, blonde hair pulled back into a braid, and completely unfamiliar. She reaches out to shake my hand.

I reciprocate the handshake, spotting Griffin in a conversation on the front step with a man dressed like Detective Baker. She leads me down the driveway, out of sight from Griffin, but within the light of her vehicle parked on the street. "Mrs. Adler, is there anyone you can think of that might have had a motive to break into your house?"

"I—" Ms. Flannagan's name is the first I want to spit out. Whoever she really is. "I'm—this is just so unexpected. I don't know who would do this to us—"

"Detective Baker," the other officer shouts down the driveway. "Could I see you for a moment?"

"Wait here, please," she says.

THIRTY-NINE

Two neighbors have driven by, rolling slowly by the driveway, staring at me as if I'm a leper under the flashing lights. Word will start spiraling around town tomorrow that there were multiple cruisers at our house. Everyone will want information about what's going on in our sleepy town.

Detective Baker said she'd be right back, but it's been at least ten minutes. My phone has buzzed in my bag twice and I'm not sure if it's okay to take a call, but it could be one of the kids. I reach in and grab my phone, finding Jack's name on display. I turn my back to the house and answer the call.

"Jess, what's going on? I heard a dispatch call go through for your address over the police scanner. Is everyone okay?" He's whispering into the phone, hopefully keeping this conversation quiet from the kids. I forgot Jack has a radio that picks up the police scanner frequency. It used to drive me nuts when he'd listen to reports coming in, but he claims to have a right to know what's going on in the small town we live in.

"Someone broke into the house. I don't want the kids to find out. We're fine." Fine is a broad description.

"What happened to the cameras we had installed?" *We. In the past.*

"Griffin took them down because the batteries kept dying within a week of changing them out. We hadn't gotten around to replacing them yet."

He huffs, likely frustrated because of all the work he put into keeping this house secure. Now it sounds like I just let it all fall to the wayside. There's been a lot of needed maintenance and we're keeping up the best we can. The house was newer when he was living here. "Who would do something like this?"

"I don't know."

"I don't want the kids back in that house until the cameras are up and working again. What about the security system?"

This must be when my ex tells me I've earned a mother-of-the-year award. "It wasn't working correctly either. Griffin just ordered a new one."

A deep throaty growl rumbles against my ear. "Jess, after everything you've seen over the years, I'd thought you'd be a little more vigilant about your safety in the house."

Cameras outside my house don't do much for me if I'm living with the person I need to keep out.

It's always the people I let into my life who end up hurting me the most, and for some reason, I never see it coming.

"Mrs. Adler?" Detective Baker calls out, walking down the driveway in my direction.

"I have to go, Jack. I'll keep you updated. Tell the kids I love them. Don't tell them anything else, please." I end the call and shove my phone into the side pocket of my bag.

"Yes, ma'am," I reply.

"Your husband says there isn't anywhere else for the two of you to stay tonight. We've gone ahead and cleared the house, and we're going to keep an officer on watch tonight."

"What about the broken window and the blood..."

"Your husband is boarding up the window. We've collected

samples of the blood. The injury was likely superficial from the act of breaking in, but the DNA could help us with a lead. In the meantime, keep the doors locked, and call us if you have reason to believe someone is attempting to break in again."

"That's it then?"

They asked me dozens of questions separately to Griffin. I thought that indicated they were speculating about a possible domestic dispute. I didn't have answers to most of their questions aside from the break-in happening later in the afternoon since everything was in one piece when I left just before three. They ensured me they would have an officer pass by the house routinely throughout the night and to call them if we have any more information. Griffin must have had even fewer answers since he was gone all day.

"Until we have more evidence, a DNA sample that matches someone in our system, our hands are tied. All we can do is keep watch to see if whoever broke in the first time, makes a second attempt. I wish there was more we could do for you."

What if I said I don't feel comfortable staying here with my husband? I should say so. Or would I be incriminating him with coincidental evidence?

"Thank you, detective." She gives me a quick nod and moves past me to her car.

I can't stay here. There's blood on the goddamn floor. I pull my phone back out and type out a quick message to Natalie.

7:45PM

Me: *Hey. Is there any chance I could crash on your couch for the night?*

I watch the display, waiting for the message to be tagged as "read", but it remains as only "delivered". After everything that happened today, I'm not sure I'd respond to me either. She has a kid too. I shouldn't have asked. Jack's apartment isn't a choice because Griffin would know where to find me and the kids if he was upset enough to come looking.

I pass the other detective on the way up the driveway. "Have a good night, Mrs. Adler."

"Thank you. You too." My response couldn't sound any more deflated.

The other police disperse, each giving me a passing nod on the way out of my house.

The hammering of nails pelts through my head like a bag of rocks. The sound grows louder as I reach the front door. "Don't worry. I'm not going to sleep until I hook up the new security system. I'm putting those old cameras back up until we get new ones," Griffin says, making his way toward the back porch where one of the cameras had originally been installed.

"I don't want to stay here tonight," I tell him, spotting the butcher knife on the couch. Griffin mentioned the knife before calling the police, but why didn't they take it as evidence?

"Where else are we going to go?" he mumbles with a nail pressed between his lips.

"I don't know, but..." I spot a newspaper insert under the stack of mail on the coffee table, grab it and wrap it around the knife. I'll have to bring this down to the police station, I guess.

"I'm scared too, but I won't let anything happen to you. I promise," he calls out from the porch. His confidence seems surreal.

My phone buzzes, giving me hope Natalie is responding. If Griffin is so persistent on staying here, he shouldn't care if I go to Natalie's. One less person for him to protect.

Upon looking at my phone, I'm disappointed there's no reply to my text. Only a new email in my inbox.

The drill Griffin's now using might as well be screwing a hole against the side of my head rather than the wall as I click into the email.

To: JessPetersonXoXo@aol.com
From: Izzy Lester
Subject: Re: Re: Re: Re: Hey you…It's me.

Jess,

I'm not in town. I'm nowhere close, trust me. I'm not sure who you saw that resembled me, but I assure you, it isn't me.

As for the note on your car, I'd venture to guess Griffin might have something to do with it. Maybe he suspects you're onto him after reading my emails. That's why I told you to get away from him. He's a very intuitive man. More than I gave him credit for.

I'm sure it must be hard to see him in a new light. Trust me, I get it.

Once he had me where he wanted, trapped, he warned me… if I ever had the chance to report him to the police, he'd make sure my family paid the price. He'd take away the people I love so I'd always know what it feels like to be a betrayer. I wouldn't question what he's capable of. It's been easier to just erase myself from society. People like him want what they want and if they can't have it, no one can.

I can't tell you where to go. Just don't let this happen to you too.

Izzy

I drop the paper-wrapped knife in my bag and run up the stairs as Griffin continues setting up parts for the alarm system. I want the notes from the shoebox.

While moving between each corner of the house in his installation process, Griffin spots me returning down the stairs. "What's that?"

"Questions I want you to answer."

"Right now?" The boards are secure. He's just adding more nails at this point.

"Yes." I drop the box on the coffee table and open the thread of emails from Izzy. "Go ahead and read these letters, then the emails. After, I want you to honestly tell me...that if you were me right now, you'd still want to sleep in the same house as you tonight."

My words are sharper than the point of a knife and I'm sure I'm slicing through him, but he is way too calm right now for what we're going through and there must be a reason. I can't stop shaking. Or take in a full breath. No alarm, boarded windows, or camera is going to make the reality inside of this house go away.

Griffin doesn't seem as interested in the notes from the shoebox as he is with the emails I've been receiving.

I watch in suspense as he scrolls through the words. He runs his hand up and down the side of his face and behind his neck. His jaw drops. He recoils when reading certain lines.

Tears fill his eyes.

He drops to his knees and presses his hands over his face, muffling a soft cry.

All I can do is stare, wondering if he's about to confess the truth.

A cold sweat drapes over me. A dizzy spell anchors me toward the couch.

"Why—why are you crying?" I ask, my words raspy, lacking confidence.

"This is all too much," he cries out. "No matter what I say or do, this bullshit is just following you—us, and it's not going to stop, is it?"

I stand back up from the couch, trying to keep myself upright through the fear pulsating through my veins. I take steps backward, toward the door, needing a way out.

"You can tell me this is all some sick joke, but you've already lied twice today. I'd be a fool to take your word for much right now," I say.

"What do you want me to tell you?" he groans.

"Tell me you knew Izzy. Tell me the whole truth. You have the vigil candle. You were there. And yet, from out of town. Therefore, you must have had more of a reason for being there than the rest of us in Spring Hill."

"I—I don't know where—"

I pull out the blurry picture from the box. He kept it for a reason. It must mean something to him. He'd know who was in the photo even if I'm not sure. "That's you and her. Isn't it?"

He stares at the picture, a tear falling from his eye.

FORTY

MAY 2001 – TWENTY-TWO YEARS AGO

Izzy

I open my diary, wanting to add a new excerpt or two, three... Before I touch my pen to the paper, I reread the entry I wrote yesterday after school.

Holy cow, I was so naïve yesterday.

May 16th, 2001

Dear Diary,

All I can do is stare at the wooden boards Mom nailed up to my broken window. She said it's going to take a few weeks before she can buy a replacement. They're expensive, I guess.

I've been cleaning up the mess from last night for hours, mostly trying to put the pieces of photos back together. I still have a ways to go but needed a break.

Everything is terrifyingly surreal. I've questioned the definition of love and jealousy. I've tried to understand what triggers a happy person to become someone completely different. It's impossible to accept the truth of what I need to come to terms with. I'm just not sure how it will turn out.

Izzy

I'm not so naïve today as I bear the weight of my anger against my pen, screaming at the diary that's done nothing to deserve this wrath.

I take up pages, just purging words, wishing they would make me feel better.

They don't.

The next time I open my diary and read what I'm writing, I'll feel smarter than I do right now. I'll recognize that I've grown after having to learn this screwed-up life lesson.

I scoot off my bed and make my way over to my open closet door. My desk chair is the only way I can reach the ceiling panel that opens into the attic's crawlspace. Hannah and I don't use this space for anything and have no desire to investigate what may be up there aside from layers of insulation. Plus, Dad has always told us mice have a village up here. Whether he's right or not, it's the best place to hide my diary now. No one can find this again, or ever see the things I've written inside.

I shove it between the plastic covered layers of pink insulation. I move my chair back to my desk and tell myself my secrets are secure once again.

I wring my hands together, stress nagging at my stomach.

"Izzy, Jess and Natalie are here!" Mom calls from down the hall.

I grab my backpack and slip into my sneakers. "I'll be home later," I say, passing Mom and Dad on the way to the door.

"The bonfire, right?" she confirms.

"Yes, it's senior night. My class is going to be there. It's even on the school calendar." The class president and administration figured if they sponsored a bonfire night, they could prevent the seniors from having their own, which is known to turn into a booze-fest.

"I'm just—"

"Being my overprotective mom," I finish her sentence and give her a kiss on the cheek.

"Curfew is still at eleven. Don't forget," Dad says.

"I won't be a minute late," I promise.

"You never have been. I'm just saying it for my own sanity," he replies.

Jess's car is bouncing with loud music and the two of them are dancing around. "Who's ready for the best night ever?" I shout. I'm not usually the party starter, but I intend to enjoy myself tonight. I don't want to regret missing out on these last high school memories.

"Our Izzy-belle is back and ready to part-ay!" Jess hollers.

Natalie hops into the back seat, allowing me to ride shotgun. "Thank God you're coming tonight. I'd have dragged you out of wherever you were and forced you to be with us. I got like four disposable cameras. Memories for everyone," she exclaims.

"I've got a couple too!" I say. I need to replace a lot of pictures I had hanging up. Thankfully, I still have the negatives to most of the destroyed ones.

"You seem so much happier today, Izzy. Are you feeling better?" Jess asks.

"I am."

"You're doing the right thing."

"Ditto," Natalie says. "What's the right thing, again?"

"She's breaking up with crazy pants."

"Oh, duh." Natalie giggles, then hiccups.

"Did you two already start drinking?"

They echo each other with a "yes" and a "no." Thankfully, Jess said no seeing as she's driving.

The sun is about to dip below the horizon by the time we turn down the narrow opening between the trees where everyone parks. The school must have insisted on parking cones tonight. I'm pretty sure this isn't a public parking area, but I'm sure the school administration warned the police department of what was going on here tonight.

Music weaves through the trees, guiding us toward the rocky path we take down to the clearing around the bonfire. Tables are set up with snacks and drinks. Red and white streamers are dangling from trees embracing the theme of our school colors.

And balloons. There are dozens of balloons branded with the Class of '01 tied to branches. I'm sure my classmates will suck all the helium out of them by the end of the night, a promise of my entire class sounding like a gaggle of drunk aliens.

The principal, vice principal, and a few teachers are standing behind metal grills, preparing food. They've gone all out for this. I'm impressed.

Less than an hour goes by before I see flashing spots every time I blink. So many people are taking pictures, and in the dark, we'll all be blind by morning. The music brings everyone together around the fire, songs with words we've all memorized, and dances we'll never live down if caught on camera. It's the best.

A hand on my arm tugs me away from the circle and spins me around to face the back of a black hooded sweatshirt. I try to pull my arm away, but Romeo peeks over his shoulder, grins and purses his lips together to shush me. We step over the fencing logs into the woods, out of view from the rest of the class. "You're here," I say.

"Of course I am," he says, taking my hands into his.

I nod. "Yeah, our senior night is in full swing..."

He clears his throat. "I just want to talk for a minute and show you something. Then you can get back to the event, okay?" he says.

"I'm nervous," I utter, staring into his shimmering eyes.

"Don't be," he says.

"Okay," I whisper.

"Izzy?" Jess calls out above the music. "Where'd you go?"

Romeo presses his finger against his lips and tugs me ahead. I look back and forth between where we're heading and what I'm leaving behind, feeling torn.

The walk is less than a minute from where I was. I can still hear the music through the trees. Along the ledge of the falls, he pulls me in between three waist-high rocks and drops down. He takes a garden shovel out of his pocket and digs a shallow hole before sticking his hands in to comb through the dirt. "Has anyone ever told you what's buried here?"

The smell of firewood and musty leaves stirs around me. "No. We're in the middle of the woods. How do you know what's in there?"

"Because," he says with a smirk.

A twig snaps behind us, and I spin around to see if someone is nearby, but I don't see anyone. Chills slice up my arms and another twig snaps. I take in a deep breath, catching Romeo's eyes as he searches through the darkness too.

"Are you cold?"

"No," I say, peering around again. I feel like there's a spotlight on us.

"What's wrong? Something's wrong. I can tell," he says.

"I—I owe you an explanation for why I didn't answer your calls yesterday."

"Oh," he says. "I'm sure you had a good reason. It's okay."

The leaves behind me rustle and my nerves fray.

Everything is wrong with this moment.

"No, it's not okay. I didn't answer because...What you did the night before scared me. The break-in—everything you destroyed in my room. You went way too far, and I'm not sure I can get over it. I just don't understand why you'd do it."

Romeo pulls his hood down, his brows furrowed with confusion. "Izzy...I—I..."

"I already told you...when we're not together doing our own things, and you show up and leave traces of your existence behind...it freaks me out. But the other night, breaking into my bedroom, destroying one of my cherished stuffed animals, destroying my photos, and reading my diary..."

Romeo takes a step back and runs his fingers through his chin-length bleached hair. "You honestly think I broke into your house?"

I drop my gaze to the black dirt beneath us, spotting white gauze wrapped around his hand.

"Then what's that? What did you do? You look hurt, and there was blood all over my room."

Romeo's eyes widen and he takes a step back. "I was skateboarding this morning and wiped out..." he says. "Back up a minute. You said there was blood all over your room? Did you call the police?"

"No, of course I didn't. What would I tell them? Someone broke into my room. You'd be the first person they question. You're the first person *I* questioned."

"Izzy, I didn't do this," he says, his words firm and pointed. "All these things you've accused me of lately—following you around when we're not together and tapping on your windows at night...none of it is true. How do I get you to believe me?"

I swallow against my dry throat. "I just want it all to stop," I whisper.

Romeo holds me to his chest and wraps his arms around me. He presses a kiss on the top of my head. "Me too."

"But you—"

"I know what you think," he says, taking my hand into his. "But I have something for you—something to make you realize how much you mean to me."

"No. You have to stop. We can't—"

"Please, just give me a minute," he begs.

"No," I say, my voice croaking.

"Please...as an early twenty-first birthday present?"

"Your birthday isn't until tomorrow," I remind him.

"Shh," he says with a chuckle. With the sharp end of his shovel, he taps inside the hole. "Hear that?"

"Yeah..."

"It's pyrite, 'fool's gold' some call it. It can be hard to find unless you know exactly where to look." He retrieves a small silver ring with a piece of metal tied in a loop. He chips off a piece of the rock and frames it between the thin metal. "I want this to be a reminder of my promise to always protect you." Romeo places the handmade ring in the palm of my hand, the golden rock glistening with a metallic coating.

"It's—it's really something," I say, breathing heavily as I slip it onto my index finger. "But...what about—"

"Things are still new between us and we're just figuring each other out more and more every day. But whenever we're together, I feel like I'm living in some dream. I've fallen in love with you, Izzy."

"Oh," I say, placing my hand over my mouth. "Holy cow..." I clench my eyes and groan.

He chuckles softly, knowing I've been trying so hard to stop saying "holy cow" to everything. "You're adorable, and for the record, so are your, 'holy cows.' But you don't have to tell me you love me or anything. I wanted to tell you how I feel." Romeo brushes the dirt off his knees and sighs—a sound full of frayed nerves. "And...I also want to ask you if you would like to take a cross-country road trip with me this summer before school starts in the fall? Like an adventure between adventures?" He chuckles through his strained apprehension.

"I don't—I'm not sure what to say..." I know what I want to say but not here in the middle of the dark woods.

"Holy cow?" he asks jokingly.

I snicker and shake my head.

"But seriously, you don't have to say anything. You can think about it. Take all the time you need. Ask your parents too, obviously." His words don't match the clear disappointment clouding his face.

"Romeo—I—I," I struggle to get the words out. "I can't do this." A sob garbles in my throat as I turn to run back to the bonfire.

"Wait—" he shouts after me.

My reappearance doesn't garner much attention with everyone still caught up in their song and dance. But Jess spots me and runs to my side. "Did he show up? Romeo?" she asks.

I nod and sniffle. "It wasn't anything bad, but—" a hard cry comes out and I can't catch my breath. I slide the pyrite ring off my finger and put it into Jess's palm. "He gave me this..." I say breathlessly. "He wants me to leave with him for a road trip this summer."

"What? Izzy, no, you can't! You'll end up in a ditch somewhere. You have to get away from him," Jess says.

I look around frantically as if he'll pop up at any second. "I told him I can't go, and I left." I start to cry.

"It's okay. It's okay. I'm here," she says, folding me into her arms.

"No, you don't get it," I whimper. "It's my fault. I should have told him the truth sooner."

"What truth?" she asks, sweeping my hair off my face.

"He loves me. And now I'm running away from him. I let this go on for too long. You were right. I should have listened sooner."

Jess shakes her head, her eyes bulging with anger and fury. "You shouldn't feel bad because he loves you. He's dangerous. He's been brainwashing you. You know how much *we* all love you. Please, listen to me. Let me take you home."

"No—I just hurt him. I've broken his heart. It's over." I try to take the ring back out of her hand, but she's holding it clenched between her fingers.

"Izzy. No. This isn't about a broken heart. You obviously need to get away from him. He's obsessed with you. It's too much. Time will make everything better. I promise."

"You're right. I need to just get away right now. I can't be here. I want to be alone. I'm sorry," I say, running toward the line of parked cars. I live less than a mile from here and I need to leave.

"Izzy, come back," Jess shouts.

Tears from the fear of my decision stream down my face, whisking over my ears with how fast I'm running away. Through the car-lined wooded area and onto the pavement. I gasp for breath, even though I feel like the world might be out of air to offer me.

I haven't gained much distance before a car turns onto the road from behind me, the headlights holding me in its spotlight. I veer off to the left into the dirt, out of the light to allow whoever it is to pass by.

The engine grinds and growls, warning of a growing speed. Rocks are spitting out from beneath the tires, raining along the pavement like hail. The headlights bleed over me again and I can't figure out why when I'm off the road, steps away from trees. I continue running but twist my head over my shoulder to—

The impact of the car against my body is like a swinging wrecking ball, catapulting me over the deadly ledge above the jagged falls. The moment of impact—a stabbing by a million knives all at once. Then, like rubber, I bounce until I'm again falling, and falling, and—it's endless until the hungry mouth of ice-cold river water devours my body. But it also numbs the pain.

Now I know.

This is how my short life ends.

FORTY-ONE

Griffin pushes himself back up from his knees, making a slow lunge for the couch before he opens his mouth to speak. He's been staring at the photo of Izzy for endless minutes. "I—I..." he gasps.

"Don't bother. The white streak of hair beneath that glare... You won't convince me that isn't Izzy. And this is you, isn't it? You had bleached-blonde hair back then. I knew at least that much about you from her."

Griffin covers his mouth, his eyes wide, unblinking. His chest constricts and shudders before he drops his hands to his lap. His bottom lip hangs. This can't be a case of shock. "I...I swear, I only knew her for a few months. It hardly even counts as knowing someone. Then she was gone."

The photo drops from my hand, drifting to the ground like a feather. "You were the guy she was dating, weren't you?"

He's grasping at his hair, gasping for breaths. "Jess, I didn't know what was going to happen to Izzy," he shouts, drawing in ragged breaths. "Whatever happened to her...wherever she went, it had nothing to do with me."

It's as if someone has kicked me in the back, my lungs

struggle to find air. I bend at the waist, doubled over, waiting for the words to form on my tongue.

Why keep this from me? Why act as though the name was completely unfamiliar? Another lie.

"What wasn't your fault?" I refuse to put answers in his head. I need the truth. "Answer me, Griffin."

"Losing her. It wasn't because of me," he says, tears still streaming down his cheeks.

I growl, backing toward the door. "You were Izzy's Romeo." My words crack into a whisper, unable to speak of such a terrifying accusation.

Griffin stands up, his eyes bloodshot, face clammy. "She was amazing, wonderful, beautiful. Perfect," he utters.

"Answer me," I demand through gritted teeth. He's taller than me by a foot. He has strength I can't win against in a physical battle. All I can think about is the email, saying Griffin is like two different people—the charmer, and the stalker. "You're Romeo?" I shout, my body trembling with fear. I need something to protect myself. He could come at me. We saw the bruises on Izzy. That email...it's all true.

Griffin gives a slight head roll, but not in a way that confirms or disagrees with my question. "Romeo is gone, Jess. So is Izzy."

"You never told her what your real name was, did you? You lied to her. You conned her into believing you were this amazing person—the same man I fell in love with two years ago."

As if his tears were running from a faucet, they stop after shutting it off. His voice deepens and his shoulders square. His switch has been flipped. "You're unbelievable, you know that?" he says, pointing at me, his finger like an arrow. "I never lied to Izzy. Ever. However, if she lied to you, I'm sure she had a reason."

I swallow the knot in my throat. *She wouldn't lie to me*. She was my best friend. At least until "Romeo" stepped into the picture.

"Do you expect me to believe this now? We all know you showed up out of nowhere and fell in love with Izzy right away. What was it about her? Why her, of all people? Was she easy to fool and manipulate?" My bravery is faltering. I'm sure it's obvious to him as I'm shaking.

He's still, very still. His arms cross over his chest, a look of comfort, complacency. "I didn't do anything you're accusing me of."

"You left her notes with these crazy obsessive poems that made you sound like you wanted to kidnap her and run away."

I've been taking slow steps around the open living room, toward the kitchen.

He lifts his hand to his chin, scratching at the shadow of hairs that have grown since this morning. "You shouldn't read notes that aren't intended for your eyes."

"Stop deflecting!" I shout, clenching my fists by my side. "Tell me what you did to her—did you take her? Torment her? Kill her? You can at least give me that."

Griffin takes a couple steps in my direction. A wall of nails might as well be closing in on me. "To understand the workings of someone's mind, it might be helpful to understand your own first. Don't you think?"

"What is that supposed to mean? Are you suggesting I'm clueless to what's going on right in front of me? Because everything in my gut is telling me to get the hell away from you as fast as I can before you do to me what you did to Izzy."

"This is exactly what I mean. I didn't do anything to Izzy. I didn't lay a hand on her. I didn't hurt her. I didn't—" he pauses and sniffles. "I didn't—" His words come out in a weak whisper. "—kill her." Griffin drops his head. "I loved her. That's it."

The way his face wallows following his statement, it jabs me in the gut. *He still loves her, even after what he did. He's sick.*

"Then why would she be gone?" I can't breathe. I've let go of the ledge I didn't realize I was holding on to. I don't know what will break my fall now. "How are you here, living with what you've done?"

His eyes bulge as he shifts his gaze from left to right. "I just said I loved her. I wasn't the one hurting her."

"Where the hell is she then?" I yell. As soon as the words come out of my mouth, the memory of college acceptance week during our senior year flashes through my head.

* * *

It's been a crap week, everyone receiving their college acceptance letters. Not me. I've gotten four rejections out of the seven I sent out. Even if I got in anywhere, I'm not sure I'd bring my letter to school to show everyone. There are people like me who are sitting on the edge of their seats in anticipation. I guess we don't all think that way. Dad has always told me no one likes an attention-seeker. Keep my business to myself. I should have asked him what's worthy of sharing? He's had no problem telling me about every raise and promotion he's gotten over the years. Merits of how much time he's invested in work rather than me.

The clatter of platform Mary Janes out of sync with a shriek echoing between the school walls, warns me it's Izzy before I can even see her face.

"Holy cow. You guys. Holy cow. You're not going to believe this," she says with a hair-raising squeak.

"What?" Natalie says before I do. "What's the news?"

By the look on her face, I can tell what she's about to say. It's the same look everyone's had on their faces this week. "I got acceptance letters to Salem State, University of New Hampshire, and—" she clears her throat. "Drum roll, please." People around us join in her excitement, rattling on lockers. "Brown University has offered me a full-ride scholarship." She covers her mouth and jumps up and down.

"Whoa," I say, my lungs searching for air. "That's absolutely amazing, Izzy!" It's been her dream to go to Brown. She's had her heart set on that school acceptance. She just knew, I guess. "We need to celebrate!"

"Yes! Major celebration is in need," Natalie follows.

We pile into Izzy's house at the end of the day. Her mom is still at work and her little sister is still at school for another hour. Izzy's future was glowing in her eyes and watching her excitement took away some of my personal disappointment. At least for the moment.

"I'm going to grab some snacks for us," she says, closing us into her bedroom.

Natalie flops onto Izzy's bed with a magazine and I drop into the checkered beanbag next to her desk, peering around for something to fiddle with.

I spot an envelope in her little pink trash bin from Brown University, but it's full of folded paper. It must be her acceptance letter. I'm sure she didn't mean for it to end up in the trash of all places. I reach for it to place it up on her desk. A small strip of paper slips out onto my lap.

REMINDER!

Wait-List Acceptance Deadline: March 10th, 2001

Please follow the instructions on your wait-list letter to secure your spot.

As mentioned in prior correspondence: From the wait list, candidates are chosen to fill available spots which may exist after the final number of currently accepted students complete their enrollment by their April 1st, 2001 deadline.

"Nat, look at this..."

She grabs the envelope and the strip of paper from my hand, reads it, and scoffs. She doesn't debate whether to take the full paper out. She just yanks it from the envelope, reads a few words and tucks it all back in. "Put it back in the trash," she says.

"Really?"

"It's Izzy. She always adds a little extra excitement to her news. A little exaggeration," she says with a quiet laugh. "Nothing new. Plus, she got into like four other colleges, so she's got options. No biggie. We love her regardless, right?"

We do. But I hate questioning what exactly she exaggerates about. This goes beyond her typical fibs about pulling an all-nighter to study, or working a ten-hour shift at the diner, which isn't possible with our school schedule...If she'd lie about this, what else would she lie about?

* * *

Griffin folds his hands together, squeezing his knuckles into a ball. "If I knew where Izzy was, dead or alive, don't you think I would have said so by now?"

"No, I don't think that. You said you didn't know who she was earlier. How can I believe a word you say?"

The line between what Izzy told us about Romeo and what I was sure I knew is becoming blurrier by the minute, and yet, I'm now accusing my husband of being the cause of her disappearance—*death*. Whoever sent those emails is accusing Griffin. That's where this started.

Griffin stares at me with a coldness I've never seen before. He leans against the dining room table as if needing support. "You didn't mention her name because of the painful memories it brought you. Why don't you just consider me to be in the same boat as you?"

"I don't know, Griffin. Misery loves company. When I mentioned her name, you'd think that would be the perfect time to say you knew her. Not only knew her but were in love with her—my best friend. Why did you say you didn't know her?" I shout.

"I don't know!" he shouts back. "It was my spontaneous reaction after hearing about that email. I was trying to ease your nerves, not give you more reason to believe what you read. I was protecting you."

"Were you also protecting Izzy when you chased after her the night at the bonfire. You chased her so far away, no one would ever see her again, didn't you?"

He narrows his eyes at me and white knuckles the top of a chair. "She didn't run away from me. I didn't chase her. I didn't abduct her or hold her hostage. I didn't torment her. That wasn't me, Jess. Was it?"

FORTY-TWO

Griffin takes a step toward me. His eyelids become heavy, the corners of his lips sink. "With all you've accused me of, I want you to tell me something now," he says.

"What?" I ask, taking a mirroring step away from him.

"When we met two years ago at the school and 'bumped' into each other, per what I've defined as 'fate,' why did you act as though you didn't know who I was?"

I'm not sure what kind of question this is. We met at a school function. Unlike most people who work in Spring Hill, he was living outside of town. Naturally, a new face was intriguing. Neither of us wore wedding bands—an invitation to exchange friendly words. I'm not sure I'd refer to our encounter as kismet.

"How would I have known you? Izzy did what she could to keep us from knowing each other."

"I don't believe that," he says.

"It's true. The only thing Izzy told us is that everything you did to and for her, was out of love for her. *Love*."

"I don't understand what that means," he says, his eyes narrowing.

"Love. You know what love means. And yet, I vividly remember the moment we exchanged the history of our past relationships. You didn't mention Izzy. So, how could you have loved her?"

"I don't recall having that discussion," he states without hesitation.

I haven't forgotten a moment of our first date—the night I felt like I was seeing life out of a new set of eyes, or just rose-colored glasses.

"Really? Because I remember it as if it were yesterday," I say, lifting my concealed left hand up to the top of the refrigerator where I moved the knife block. "You avoided the topic of former relationships. Quite smoothly, in fact."

I'm not sure how long we've been sitting here at this table covered in white linen under dim lighting, staring at each other as if our eyes are portals to an unexplored world. I have to keep reminding myself this is only our first time out together. I just feel like I've known him forever already, somehow. The others in the restaurant have closed their bills and we're one of the last remaining couples still sipping on coffee.

"Okay, here's the fun one. Past relationships," he says.

Dating at almost forty is like a game of twenty-questions with the fear of giving the wrong answer. "Well," I say.

"I was married for fifteen years. Didn't quite have a stable relationship before then because I was in high school. So, I'm afraid my relationship history is mundane. My ex and I decided on a divorce two years ago after he had an affair."

"Ouch," Griffin says, shifting around in his seat. "Nothing good can ever come from cheating. I don't get it. Either break things off and move on, or stay put and fix it, right?"

"Exactly," I say, my response coming out as a breath of fresh air. Someone understands me.

"What about you? Any serious past relationships? Marriages?"

He folds his hands over the table and juts his bottom lip out before shaking his head. "I've had some relationships, but a bad streak of luck with women who planned to move out of the area. My parents still live in Anchoren, so I'm not going anywhere too far."

"I've never met someone who wants to move out of the area," I say, knowing it's a small-town joke people share here.

"That's why we're all still here," he ends the joke. "Except for the one who—"

The waiter interrupts our conversation by placing the check on our table, calling an end to our date.

Griffin pulls his wallet out as I reach for my clutch. "Don't even think about it," he says, handing his card and the check to the waiter. "I asked you out. That's how this goes."

I'm so out of my realm but not completely out of the game, I think. "Thank you so much."

"The pleasure was all mine."

"What were you saying? The one who?"

He frowns, his lips forming a cute little pout. "Hmm. I'm not sure where I was going with that. Anyway, as I say, I don't have much of a past to speak of. I can say that with certainty."

* * *

That was Griffin's first lie and I gazed right past it.

"It doesn't matter how long we stand here, facing each other or how many more questions I ask you, because it's clear I don't know you at all, do I?" I say, slapping my hands to my sides, pinching my fingernails into my flesh.

"We've been together for two years, Jess. How could you ask me something like that?"

I'm losing the strength to stand, hovering by the kitchen counter, knowing this bit of space is the only barrier between us. "I don't think I know you," I croak, my voice breaking. "Not the real you. The person you were before we met."

"That's what the email said, so sure. I can understand why you'd assume something like that. Or think it's the right thing to say now. What I'm trying to figure out is: why would you believe an email from someone you haven't spoken to in over twenty years and at once conclude that it must be true?"

"I don't know," I shout. "As soon as that email arrived, I find you sneaking around, hiding text messages, playing with fuses in the basement because of a light bulb—one I know you didn't really switch out because we had no new light bulbs lying around. With everything that's happened in this brief time, my eyes are open wide now, and I'm seeing what's been right in front of me this whole time. Your hidden past. Your lies. Your masquerading charm."

Griffin grabs a chair from the dining room table and brings it between the pillars, just on the other side of the kitchen counter. He makes it known he's comfortable while I try to hide the tremor in my hands. His anger and frustration dissipate as if there's been a logical conclusion. "Just to focus on the email for a minute here first...If I received an email where someone told me to run away from my wife, I'd be pretty upset at whoever sent it, rather than assume the worst of my own wife."

It's not as if those thoughts didn't go through my head too. But I can't just ignore the email and act like it didn't happen, especially with his little lies percolating. I have children to protect. He has no skin in the game. "I don't want to believe anything I read, Griffin. I was angry that someone revived a sense of hope that Izzy could still be alive. Whoever wrote that email reopened all my old wounds. Then simultaneously, I find out you're not being honest with me. Of course, the email sent up warning flags in my head."

Griffin takes in a slow, deep breath and nods his head before crossing one leg over the other. Then he clasps his hands together and rests them on his knee. He looks like a therapist listening to a patient. "So, with all that said, where do you think we should go from here? You tell me what you would like to get out of this debate. Do we just call it a day and move on in separate directions?" His words are cold and heartless. He's so calm, seemingly unaffected by this conversation. We've been happy together for two years, yet without a moment to process, it appears as if he couldn't care less whether I'm in his life or not. People don't act like that when suggesting an end to their marriage. Is he toying with me?

"*Where do we go from here?* That's all you can say. God, Griffin," I huff, pressing my hand to my heart. "I must be just as disposable as Izzy, right? It's as easy as throwing out the trash. That's all I see on your face and hear in your voice."

"Believe whatever you want, Jess. It's clear I won't be convincing you of anything different," he says, his words snide and vengeful.

Tears fill my eyes as I silently question how I'm talking to the same man I've spent every day loving for so long. This person I'm staring at—it's not him. This isn't the Griffin I know. I take a shuddering breath before responding. "I guess—" I sniffle and swallow back the sob rising up my throat, "right this second, I can't be here with you." I press the back of my hand to my mouth, feeling the tears fall one by one down my hot cheeks. "I'll—I'll find somewhere to stay tonight."

Griffin coughs out a sardonic laugh and stands up—another reaction I wouldn't have imagined him having. When he drops his hands into his pockets, my heart falls into my hollow gut.

"Yeah, you're not going anywhere tonight," he says, peering over to the clock on the wall. "And step away from the refrigerator. I know where you moved the knife block." He gestures his hand toward the knives. "I'm not going to attack you." He makes a show of emphatically rolling his eyes. "I get that you have trust issues and Jack obviously hurt you in some way. I know the whole long saga about your mom leaving you when you were seven. It all ties back to that. Everyone is going to hurt you. Everyone is going to rip your heart out and stomp all over it. Most importantly, everyone is going to pay for the mistakes *she* made. Am I right?"

Neither he nor Izzy have anything to do with my mom leaving. She was just the first of many heartbreaks. "You have no clue what you're talking about," I tell him.

"Sure, I do. Your biggest fear is that everyone you love will eventually leave you."

"No one has proven that fear to be irrational," I tell him, my words wet with phlegm. "Everything my mom told me before she left has turned out to be true."

* * *

"I never wanted to be a mother. You were too lazy to make sure that didn't happen. She's seven now. I stuck it out long enough. You can figure out what to do with her." Mommy shouts at Daddy. A baby-blue canvas suitcase is in her hand, the one we use when we drive to the beach.

"She needs a mother," Dad argues, his loud voice hurts my ears. "For God's sake. She's right here, listening to you. Jessica might not understand any of what you're doing right now, but someday, she will. She'll remember you walking out of this house. You're going to ruin this poor girl's life."

Mommy shrugged. "She ruined mine. So, I guess that makes us even."

She won't even look at me. I've been brushing the purple hair on my small toy pony, over and over in the same spot. Single strands keep falling out into my hand. Mommy gets mad a lot, but then she takes a time out and everything is better for a little while.

Daddy's crying this time, though. He comes over and sits down next to me, putting his arm around my neck. "Don't listen to a word she says."

Mommy waves her free hand in the air, her keys jangling against each other. "She can't live in a world of make-believe," Mommy says. "It's better to understand that this world can be an ugly place, and no one will ever truly care about you. Everyone will eventually leave for someone or something better. And they'll never come back."

"That isn't true," Daddy says, flapping his hand at her as if she's a pesky fly.

"Jessica," Mommy says, pointing her finger at me. "You remember your daddy's words when he's busy working sixty hours a week, and you're sitting here all by yourself with no one to talk to but the wall." Mommy laughs, acting like her words are a joke. But I don't understand. When she stops laughing, she turns around and walks out the front door like she does in the mornings to get the newspaper off the driveway. Except, she slams the door behind her. The bang makes me jump in my seat.

"She'll be back, sweetie. She always comes back," Daddy says.

* * *

"You were lucky enough to have a loving father who provided for you, gave you everything you needed, made sure you wanted for nothing. Of course he had to work a lot. He was a single dad doing the best he could. Be thankful for at least having that. Some kids don't even have one good parent."

"You sound like you know what I lived through, but you don't. You still have both of your parents. I needed a mother.

She left me without a care in the world. That ate at me day after day my entire childhood. You had two parents growing up. You have no clue what it's like."

"You're right. I'm also lucky none of my prior relationships worked out so I could end up here, like this—my wife accusing me of a crime. One might think, if it were true, I'd have been accused and arrested for the things you're freely convicting me of. Yet, I'm a schoolteacher, and after several full background checks that all checked out clear."

"Great. I'm glad no one suspects you did anything to Izzy. I'm still not staying here tonight. You're not keeping me here to keep rehashing the fact you lied about knowing her."

I should have made my way to the front door rather than the kitchen, but I'm making a run for it now. Griffin doesn't move a muscle while I race myself to the door.

"Fine, but before you go, can you do me a favor?" he asks, twisting around in his chair. "Can you grab that thing out of my coat pocket? On the banister."

"What thing?" I ask, my hand squeezing around the doorknob.

"Something I came across recently. I want to see what you think about it."

The debate in my head is short-lived. I tear open the front door. "I'm done. I can't—"

"You can't drive anywhere without your keys," he says, pulling them out of his pants pocket.

I pat myself down, unsure when I dropped them.

He stands from the chair and takes slow, casual steps in my direction. I run outside and race to my car, jiggling the door handle. I left the car unlocked.

It's locked now. He's got me right where he wants me.

For two years, this has all been an act.

He's already outside and there isn't enough time to try his

door. There's no sense in even locking myself in either car because he probably has both sets of keys on him.

I head for the street, buying myself time until I figure out what to do. I'm not sure there's anything I *can* do, aside from hide in the woods and pray a bear doesn't find me before he does. He's following me, but making it seem like there's a safe distance between us. I put my phone in my bag. I hardly ever put my phone in there, the endless pit. I have nothing on me. I have no means of making it anywhere safe.

"Where are you planning to go?" he asks, still walking slowly behind me.

I make a beeline for the woods to the right side of the road, running in blind. There isn't an ounce of light beneath the thick tree coverage. I grab a hold of a tree and slide around it so I'm away from the path where I entered. The leaves lightly brush against each other above my head, a whisper of wind whistles around me, but there are no footsteps. He's not calling out for me. I slide my back against the coarse bark until I settle between two roots of the tree. I wrap my arms around my knees and bury my face.

For a second, all I can hear is the sound of my own blood rushing in my ears. But then a stick crackles. A blinding light flashes against my face. And a hand closes around my wrist, yanking me up to my feet.

"This isn't how it's going to end, Jess."

FORTY-THREE

"Let go of me," I scream, pulling my hand against his closed fist. My skin pinches and twists in his relentless grip.

"Are you out of your mind? Mrs. Turble will hear you or someone else. They'll call the police," he grumbles through ragged breaths.

"Good!"

I fight to break away from his grip, but he's holding me with more force than he's ever touched me with. My sneakers are scraping against the pavement as I skid and trip over my own feet, refusing to go back inside with him.

"How could you do this to me?" I don't care how loud I am. I hope the world hears me. I pray at least someone does.

Griffin is big enough to take complete control over my squirming body. I couldn't have imagined he'd ever handle me in this way, with such force and determination. He doesn't care if he's hurting me or if I fall. He has an agenda and that's all that matters.

I've spun in so many circles, the interior lights surprise me just before the echoing slam of the door. He tosses me onto the couch, keeping his arm stretched out, his finger pointed at me. "Don't move," he grits through his clenched jaw.

He's red, his hair wild, sticking up in every direction. Veins are pulsating across his temples, the red lines webbing through the whites of his eyes are dark and menacing. His nostrils flare as he storms toward his coat hanging from the banister.

The second his back is toward me, I glance at the door, debating my next strategy to get the hell out of here. He's slid the deadbolt. Another hurdle.

My knees bounce like rubber balls as he fiddles with whatever he's taking from his coat pocket. A small black pocket-sized notebook covered in peeling stickers.

"What is that?"

Griffin grins and moves his chair, bringing it closer to me, on the other side of the coffee table.

A muffled buzz startles the momentary silence after he takes a seat and I spot my bag hanging from the coat closet door. "It could be one of the kids," I say, standing up to run for it.

"Sit down!" he shouts. "Your kids are better off with Jack right now."

Hearing him spit out the words "your kids" as if they're foreign objects he's never met underlines the true nature of this confrontation.

"How could you say that to me," I utter, my blood rushing through my veins with fury.

Griffin makes himself comfortable in his chair as I'm standing between the closet door and the sofa. I'm afraid to move closer to my bag but refuse to give in and go back to the couch.

He seems indifferent either way as he begins to read from the small notebook:

May 9, 2001

Dear Diary,

I'm so excited to go out with Romeo tonight. By the way, his name is Griffin Roe Adler, but he doesn't like going by his first name. I can't understand why. I love it, but I guess we all love what we love.

I have a very guilty conscience after lying to Jess and Natalie today at lunch. They wanted me to hang out tonight, but I told them I had too much studying to do. They've been getting upset by all the time I spend with Romeo because they make it sound like we're all running out of time. I get it.

We're going in different directions next school year. Natalie has been in a relationship with Tristen since sophomore year so she's not so worried about splitting up her time between him and her friends. Jess doesn't have a boyfriend and I think that's half the issue she has with me spending so much time without her.

We've been besties forever. It makes sense, but Romeo isn't going to college with me, and I want to enjoy this time with him. I'm completely head over heels for him. He's so sweet, caring, compassionate, and the boy can kiss. (Sigh)

Write more later.

Love,

Izzy

"How do you have her goddamn diary? What kind of freak are you?" I say, spit flying from my mouth.

"I'm not ready to tell you yet, and I'm not done reading," Griffin snaps, turning the page.

My phone begins to buzz against the door again and my

heart plummets into my stomach. It must be Abby. She'll call until she reaches me. "I need to answer the phone."

"No."

"Or what?" I ask, my confidence wavering in my voice.

"Don't push me, or you'll find out," he says. "Sit down."

I refuse to sit down until I can make sure Abby is okay.

"On May eleventh, Izzy wrote: *Dear Diary*," Griffin begins to read.

I'm completely freaked out right now and I'm not sure what to do. Someone has been tapping on my window at night, scaring the living daylights out of me and no matter how fast I run to the window, I can't see anyone or anything. Then in the morning, I find blank notes on my car window.

I didn't tell Mom what was going on because I didn't want to freak her out. Then I was worried maybe Romeo was just playing games with me or something. So, I confronted him yesterday and told him he couldn't tap on my window like that at night anymore. And the blank notes were creeping me out.

Romeo's face became paler than a bedsheet. It was like he had the wind knocked out of him. He told me he'd never done something like that. It was mean and terrifying. He told me to tell Mom so she could call the police next time. But I was afraid she would still think it's Romeo and make it so I can't see him anymore.

Last night I did something I've never done before. I snuck Romeo into my bedroom after Mom went to bed and locked the door. I figured it would be the best way to prove the tapping and notes weren't coming from him like he said.

Shoot. I have to go.

Write more later.

Izzy

"What kind of sick game are you playing?" I cry. "It's like you think Izzy is about to walk through the front door. Why?"

"Izzy can't walk through the door, Jess. She's dead." His sentence is short and punctuated with a stinging slap.

I reel back. Of course, it's what I've been terrified to accept all these years—but hearing him say it out loud makes the contents of my stomach rise. I'm going to be sick.

"If anything about those emails were true, I wanted it to be that Izzy is still alive. But if she's dead like I thought, why would someone be writing me emails from her address, and saying the things they said about you?" I manage to heave out.

Griffin smiles, a sweet, sickening smile that belongs to a sinister being, not my husband.

"I don't know anyone who would do something like that?" he says with the slightest smirk perking at the corner of his lips.

The emails must be from him. He wanted to hurt me, and for a reason I will never understand.

"You wrote the emails. Didn't you?"

He cocks his head, looking at me coolly over steepled fingers. "I didn't say that. But we know it wasn't Izzy. She's dead. It's true. In fact, her body's just been found."

FORTY-FOUR

My lungs are burning. Nothing in my body is working the way it's supposed to—especially my brain which is tumbling and spinning into an abyss.

"I don't believe you. I would have heard about it. Natalie too."

Griffin presses his lips together and puffs out his cheeks before releasing a heavy breath. "You can believe what you want."

"What do you want from me? Or with me? Why are you even with me?" I shout. He's so insanely calm that it's making me feel like I'm going to implode.

"I'm with you because I thought I knew you, Jess. I never imagined you to be this other person—this broken, desperate or neurotic woman. You need help."

"Give me my keys, Griffin."

He clears his throat and crosses a leg over the other. "You know," he sighs. "When something is broken, as people, it's our nature to try and fix it." He takes a long breath. "You might not be fixable, though."

Tears well in my eyes, falling into the pit of grief he's digging for me. I run my fists across my cheeks, wiping away the proof of the pain I still feel over Izzy all these years later.

"Screw you," I cry out.

He chuckles and reopens Izzy's diary, flipping toward the front. "It's written right here. Clear as day just three years before she disappeared:

February 15th, 1998

Dear Diary,

How can the world be so hard on one person and give another everything? Is it perception? Do I call myself lucky because I feel lucky? Or am I truly lucky?

I was supposed to go out and celebrate Jess's birthday with her and Natalie tonight, but Dad has gone on a business trip and Mom got called in for an emergency shift at the hospital. Now I have to stay home and watch Hannah instead of going to the movie theater then the arcade. The three of us have had a countdown to the number of days left until the new Titanic *movie releases. I offered to buy the tickets as her birthday gift and wait in line early to make sure we got seats. I feel awful that I can't go, but I told the two of them to go without me. I want to make sure they celebrate Jess's birthday. She deserves it.*

When I called to tell her that I wasn't going to be able to make it tonight, she told me I was selfish, backstabbing, and didn't care how much this night meant to her. She told me 'It must be nice to have everything in the world but can't find a way to spend one night with her.' She said my mom must hate her too with the choice she made.

Mom has given Jess at least two meals a day for the last

eight years. She takes her shopping with us for clothes and school supplies. Mom has done everything she can for Jess, but if she's called into work, she doesn't get the choice to say no.

I've been sitting here in tears for an hour, wishing Jess would understand that I didn't plan for our night to end up like this. I've done everything I can to be the best friend possible to her and it never seems like enough. Hopefully, she doesn't stay mad for long.

Izzy

"This is who I unknowingly married, Jess. A narcissistic martyr—not a trait I was holding out for when looking to settle down with someone. And you know what the worst thing is about people like you?" He stands up from his chair and steps toward me. His shadow claims mine against the wall, smothering me until there's nothing left.

"You want to break me to pieces? Go right ahead," I goad him.

He won't be the first and I'm sure he won't be the last. Him and his beautiful face, perfect hair, flawless personality...just broke my heart like the rest of them with his cruelty.

"You fooled me into thinking you cared about me—that we were this perfect fit—two strangers destined to be together later in life. You were so goddamn believable too. You must not have felt a hair of remorse when making the decision to trap me. If I had any clue you were Izzy's best friend—the one she kept me away from—to protect me, as she said, I would have run as fast as I could as far away as possible from you." He brushes his hand down the side of my cheek. "You still want your keys, sweetheart?"

"Give them to me," I grunt.

"No problem. Take them." He grabs my hand, drops them

into my palm, then wraps his fingers around my wrist. "These are yours, right?"

I glance down, finding my keys—but not just my keys.

Frigid air shoots up my lungs, ice holding my body hostage. I can't move an inch.

FORTY-FIVE

"Where did you get this?" I ask him, clutching the clinking metal rings.

"Your keys?" he asks, toying with me.

"No. This mood-stone key chain." I hid this away after Mrs. Turble handed it to me the other day.

"Finders keepers..." he says with a smirk. "But here, you can have it back. Again. Even though you're the one who lost it."

"What? Mrs. Turble found it outside the other day and gave it to me. I thought I had lost it, but—I'm not sure how it ended up outside here. I hadn't seen it in years."

"Oh, geez," Griffin says. "I must have dropped it outside while carrying some of my boxes in. I guess it's easy to lose."

My face tightens with confusion. "Wait, why did you have the key chain in the first place? It was mine. How would you have even known it was mine?" The words fly out of my mouth.

"Well, I was with Izzy when she bought it for you—her mysterious best friend I couldn't meet, and when her best friend lost it, I happened to find it," he says simply.

"Where?" My question catches in my throat.

"Why don't you tell me where you lost it..."

I'm done taking part in this game. I make a run for the closet door where my bag is hanging, hoping he stays where he is so I can get out of here.

He doesn't try to jump toward me and take my bag. I hate questioning if he's going to let me leave the house as easily. I don't waste a moment more before making a lunge for the front door.

"Don't bother, Jess. This is all going to end tonight."

"Are you threatening me?" I squawk, gripping my hand around the doorknob. The lump in my throat keeps growing, making it impossible to swallow.

"Izzy refused to tell me her best friend's name, you know—your name. It wasn't just you and Natalie she concealed names from. You didn't know my name and I didn't know yours. Izzy was so worried about me meeting you because it would only cause you pain to realize there was someone new in her life. She said you didn't want anything to come between the two of you because she was all you had left. She always talked about how frail and sensitive you were, and she needed to protect you. The purpose of all her secrets were to protect you."

My eyes fill with tears. A sob breaks through my tight throat. I gasp for air, but it's not enough to smother the grief burning through me. "She called me frail and sensitive? She would never say something like that about me," I scream, fisting my hair. "And that night of my birthday, I apologized a million times for acting like that—a hormonal teenager. You're not going to judge me based off a written excerpt of a day when I was fifteen."

"You were selfish," Griffin says, unfazed.

"Don't you dare blame me," I say with a foot out the door. "You're the one who took her away from us because you needed all of her or none of her. She was so upset that night at the bonfire. You gave her no choice and took her away!"

I'm out the door, steps from my car when he follows, shouting after me.

"That's enough. Everyone might have believed you before now. Jess—the 'poor girl' who lost her best friend. But after getting a hold of Izzy's most intimate thoughts this week, I've been forced to face the truth—words as clear as confessions about you. Soon, everyone will know you have never been the victim. You're the abuser."

FORTY-SIX

My car headlights flash, the alarm beeps, disarming the car. But it wasn't me who unlocked it.

I look down at the keys in my hand, realizing that I'm holding my spare set with the dead battery. I turn back toward the front door to see Griffin with the other set of keys pointed at my car. "I said this is over tonight, Jess."

A car speeds by without a clue in the world as to what's happening here right now. The world is still moving around us, yet we've been staring at each other in silence for a long minute.

Griffin walks toward me, and I continue this tango, taking twice the number of steps backward.

"Why did you come after me, Jess? What is it you were hoping to gain?"

"I didn't come after you," I say, my words quiet, loose.

"Bullshit!" he screams. "You knew exactly who I was, and you knew I had no clue who you were. It's obvious from what I read that you always wanted what Izzy had. She wrote something along the lines of: You were so jealous that she found someone who wanted to give her the attention no one would ever give you. She never told me this stuff back then. She kept it all inside like a good friend would do. You were the lousy friend —the one who wanted her life. So, you went for it..."

My heart pounds so hard I'm breathless, digesting each word as it hits me. "Why would I seek out the man who took my best friend away?" I argue back. Three days ago, I was positive she was dead. Then I had to question everything because of the emails. Now, I have no clue what to think at all.

Griffin cackles, the sound bouncing between the surrounding trees. "Jess, she's dead, not hiding. In case you missed that part."

"Prove it!" I scream. "A missing person like that would have been on the news if they were found."

"Not if the forensic report isn't finalized," he says. "But soon. Soon, everyone will find out her true cause of death."

"I don't believe a word you're saying." I wish I could see through his eyes, the thoughts swirling around in his mind—whether deceit or just plain maliciousness. "You only know she's dead because you're the one who killed her, and you want someone else to take the blame."

Griffin bites down on his bottom lip so fiercely I wouldn't be surprised to see blood.

I make a leap toward my car, hearing the doors automatically re-lock by use of the working key fob in Griffin's hands. I struggle to manually unlock the door blindly in the dark. "Don't even think about it," he says, pointing at me, standing in the same spot he's been in at the front door. "You want to call me a killer. If you believe that, you'll do what I say."

"I have children," I cry out at him, trying my hardest to get the key into the lock. It slides in and I twist, then jolt the handle. "We can go our own ways and call this what it is. A mistake. A stupid, screwed-up mistake. Just let me go." I get into the car and shove the key into the ignition.

The car alarm stuns me, blaring in every direction. The engine won't run.

He steps back into the house only to return seconds later with the shoebox full of letters. He tosses them all out onto the lawn.

"Every single one of these letters from a lunatic who wanted me to leave my girlfriend for her...writing to me as if we were in a relationship when I had no clue who the hell wrote a single one of them. It's been over twenty years of wondering who wrote them. But when I read about what lengths you'd go to just to keep Izzy all to yourself, a light bulb went off. Not a real one. That's why I didn't need a replacement. I grabbed your grocery list off the fridge door and brought them down to the basement to match up the handwriting to those psychotic letters. That's when I realized each one of them came from you—Izzy's best friend—stated clearly in her diary as Jessica Peterson. Your handwriting hasn't changed a bit, by the way. But I want to know, Jess...was it me you wanted, or Izzy? You didn't know who I was then, or so I've assumed."

My heart thuds hard, fast, stealing my breath, making me tremble in waves of dizziness. He's not planning to let me out of here alive.

He charges toward the car, unlocks it with his key fob and tears the door open as if it was nothing but a piece of paper. I try to twist the key in the ignition again now that it's unlocked, but he shoves me into the center console. "Move over," he demands.

"Let me out now!" I try pushing him back, but he lifts me by the arm and slings me over the middle console. "Where are you taking me?"

"To turn yourself into the police," he barks at me.

"The police? For what? Caring about my best friend?" I cry out. I'll be safe there if that's where he's taking me. I can pray that's where he's taking me. Please, God.

"I'll let the police decide if these diary excerpts were written about a 'caring' friend or an obsessive psychopath clinging to her side the night she went away."

I secure my seat belt just as he peels off the driveway. The interior lights are gone. It's pitch black inside and outside aside from the digital gauges behind the steering wheel. I can see a glow on his scowl, his jaw grinding back and forth.

"Is this what you did to Izzy?" I ask in a whisper.

"Shut up, Jess."

"You probably didn't offer to take her to the police first," I say louder, clenching the fabric of my pants.

Griffin slams on the brakes, flinging us both forward to a halting stop. "If you say her name one more time, we won't need to go to the police."

FORTY-SEVEN

Griffin's turbulent driving terrifies me, but I'm more afraid to speak up. My head spins as we race down each road at three times the speed limit, the tires screeching at every sharp turn. My heart races faster.

He takes an abrupt turn away from the direction of the police station. Whipping down dark, unmarked roads.

"I thought we were going to the police station?"

The car stops short in the middle of the road, fueling my panic. He skids off to the side, gravel kicking up against the doors. Once stopped, he toys with the key chain dangling from the ignition key. "I realized I never answered you about where I found this mood-rock key chain of yours," he says, fiddling with the newly added one to my set of keys, secured in the ignition.

"Why does it matter?" Every muscle in my body is tighter than a cord of rope and all I can do is stare through the dark woods, wishing there was safety somewhere between those trees.

"Trust me. It matters," he sneers, toying with the mood-rock key chain. *My* mood-rock key chain. "I can't believe I dropped it outside the house. It was with my boxes of old stuff." He had my key chain. How? Why? "Thank goodness we always have Mrs. Turble to depend on for finding things on her morning walks. And Abby was helpful too because she told me all about the rock key chain you wouldn't let her see. She said it must have been something important and therefore in your top dresser drawer. I'm not a snooper, so I didn't know this little detail about you—one of many details I didn't know about you. But Abby was right. There it was, in your drawer—the key chain that was lost then found." I didn't want to ever lose it again after it had been missing for as long as Izzy has been gone. That's why I had it in my top drawer.

He'd had it all this time since I lost it over twenty years ago. Why would he be holding on to it?

Terror courses through me as I search for an escape I can't find.

"For twenty-two years, I hoped Izzy was still alive somewhere," he says, making it sound like he's the only one who has missed her.

He was only a part of her life for months compared to the rest of us.

He sniffles and rests his head back against the seat. "Just before she disappeared, I asked her if she would go on a cross-country road trip with me for the summer before she started college."

That was what pushed her away. His incessant need to claim her all to himself.

She didn't want to go.

"She told me she'd do anything to make that happen," he continues. "I can recall the smile beaming from ear to ear as I jumped up and down. We talked about camping under the stars, hiking, stopping at every old diner along the way to rate their French fries and milkshakes." He stops talking and takes in a shuddering breath.

"That's not what happened," I grunt.

"How would you know?" he snaps back, his voice pitched in a whine.

"I was keeping an eye on her when I saw her disappear with you at the bonfire. I watched from the woods as you asked her to go on a road trip with you after you gave her the fake golden promise ring you dug up from the ground."

Griffin laughs, a casual sound in contrast to my paralyzing thoughts of what he could be capable of. "She was right, I guess," he says, rubbing his hand up and down the side of his face.

"Ab—about wh-at?"

"That you'd be watching us."

My brows furrow as I try to decipher Griffin's contorted logic. He's shifting the blame onto me. But for what?

"All I did was keep an eye on my friend. I was worried for her safety."

"It was all a setup," Griffin says, his words cutting through me, slowly, painfully.

"Why—what purpose...what reason could there be to form a setup?"

There is nothing but stale air inside of the car. I try to open the window, but I'm not surprised he's locked them from access on the driver's side door. I open the door and scramble to unbuckle my seat belt, but he takes his foot off the brake. "Don't even think about it. Close the door."

I ignore his threats and release my seat belt despite the car speeding up. But he takes a sudden hard left, forcing my door closed before slamming on the brakes again. I catch myself on the dashboard.

"We can do this all night, Jess. We're not done talking."

"Do what? Try to kill me?" I shout.

He ignores my question and squeezes his hands around the steering wheel as the next words spill out of his mouth. "It was a setup because none of what Izzy told you was real. She wanted to make you believe she was trying to get away from me, but that wasn't the truth. It was *you* she wanted to get away from. You were smothering her, controlling everything she did, and not because you cared about her. It was because you needed her. She was your lifeline."

"You can't blame this on me, Griffin. I saw the notes you sent Izzy before you revealed your identity to her. Were those fake too? Because my gut told me something wasn't right about you. Your intentions were not all they seemed."

"What's with you and those notes? They stopped after we met. I was sharing poetry with her. It was art, not murderous warnings."

"You baited her in with beautiful words that had double meanings."

"That was all in your head, and your head alone," he says. "We were in a relationship long after those notes ended, and we had made our plans before that last night, knowing you'd be watching. It felt like you were always watching. We just didn't know why."

Izzy wouldn't have betrayed me like that. Not before she met him anyway. It's like he'd brainwashed her. How could she let that happen?

"If it felt like I was watching, it was because you felt you had something to hide. Everything you're saying right now is a well-thought-out excuse to free yourself from the blame of what happened to her that night. I have no reason to believe you," I seethe.

He pulls her little diary back out of his pocket. "It's in here. It's all in here."

I still want to know how he got his hands on that—who would have given it to him?

He opens the book to another page, and I take the free moment to make another attempt at jumping out of the car.

His hand catches on the back of my shirt, but he doesn't

have a tight enough grip to hold me back. With my bag wrapped around my arm, I race into the woods again, hoping I can find a place to hide this time.

He's quick to follow. Like a predator, I hear him chasing me, catching up. My nerves are shot and I'm numb from head to toe, running on nothing but adrenaline.

"I loved her. She loved me," he shouts from behind. "It's true. I never hurt her. I never crossed a line. You were the one who made me out to be a monster."

I reach into the side pocket of my bag for my phone, but I trip. One of the millions of roots waiting to catch my toe takes me down before I can get far enough away to have a chance. I land against the spongy dirt.

His hand wraps around my ankle. "Stop running," he demands.

"You turned my best friend against me," I tell him. "She and Natalie were all I had. And Natalie was already drifting away. You didn't need to keep her to yourself, control every minute of her life, take her away from everyone who loves her."

"I didn't," he argues. "I begged to meet her two best friends, but she refused to introduce us. She knew my friends. But you two were drifting apart and you couldn't handle it."

"That's not true," I say, yanking my foot against his relentless grip.

He climbs over me, pinning me to the ground. "You couldn't handle the thought of Izzy leaving you behind," he says again, his words more menacing.

The last time I peered into his eyes as he hovered over me must have been a moment of delusion.

* * *

"I love you so much," he says, billowing the sheets over our heads. "I've never been happier in my life." His warm lips are every-

where all at once. His hands holding my wrists against the mattress. Electrifying currents of desire blaze through me, reminding me of all the good life has given me these last two years after feeling nothing for so long.

"Promise me we'll always be just like this," I beg.

"For life," he says. "Just like this. You and me." It's taken a lifetime to believe words so sacred. But there's honesty written into his beautiful eyes. All I've ever wanted is someone to trust. To know they'll be here when I wake up in the morning. To experience a type of love that can be felt, not just spoken. Finally, it's my turn to be the lucky one.

* * *

Griffin pulls my car keys out of his pocket and dangles just the chained mood-rock over my nose. "I was with Izzy when she bought this thing for you, a birthday present she was sure you'd love. She found it in a boutique craft shop along the shore when we went away for a weekend during spring vacation," he says. "It was the weekend she told you she had to go visit her aunt in Connecticut."

How many times did she lie to me? She knew how much lies hurt me. She promised nothing would ever come between us.

"Even though she had to tell you a story to get away for a weekend with me, she spent most of that time searching for the perfect one-of-a-kind birthday present for her best friend. I couldn't understand why she cared so much about someone who didn't seem to care about what made her happy, but I helped her find the perfect gift. I wouldn't tell her who to love."

Griffin brings his face closer to mine, his breath falls in layers over my cold face. I can't breathe. I can't think straight. I can't figure out how to get out from beneath him.

"She said you loved the key chain so much because you'd

never seen a mood-rock formed out of crystal. She told me you hooked it on to your mini backpack-purse, so it went everywhere with you. Until you lost it."

My heart is pounding so hard against my rib cage, it might burst from my chest.

"You know, I couldn't figure out how that special gift—this key chain ended up on the driver's seat of my truck the very same night Izzy ran off from the bonfire. But now everything is so clear."

FORTY-EIGHT

MAY 18TH 2001 - TWENTY-TWO YEARS AGO

Jessica

The smoke from the bonfire is beginning to settle, making it harder to find where Izzy has run off to. I reach the clearing between the trees where the cars are parked and grab my small key chain flashlight, dangling from my purse. I hold it in front of my face, finding a cloud of dirt and the back of Izzy's short hair bouncing in the wind as she turns onto the main road.

No matter how many times I call out to her, she doesn't stop or turn around.

Heavy footsteps grow from behind me, but there's too many trees in that direction to see anyone.

I keep after Izzy, trying to catch up, still calling her name every few seconds.

"Hey, wait!" a man's voice shouts from behind.

I spin around with my flashlight, finding no one in my direct line of sight. There's no time to stop and look for whoever is following me. Izzy's in danger, alone and on foot, already away from the makeshift parking lot we've formed. She must be running down Purgatory Road along the cliffs and waterfall.

As I make my way between the parked cars, a set of headlights washes over me as the crunch of tires on dirt fills the air. Someone is maneuvering a three-point turn, navigating through the tight spaces. I duck behind a vehicle, aware there isn't enough space for both me and another car to pass. "*Hurry up!*" I grumble. As the car's headlights align with the exit onto Purgatory Road, I catch a clear view of the ugly teal bronco with a white hardtop over the bed. I recognize that car. The one I've seen Izzy get into countless times from a distance. There's no doubt the infamous Romeo is behind the wheel, and in pursuit of Izzy once again.

No. Not this time.

I scan the area around me, finding a rock, one small enough to throw but large enough to jolt a car if driven over. I toss it into the truck's path, hoping it does the job. I cross my fingers and squint as he approaches. *Please, please, please. Thunk.* The front tire of the truck hits the rock, tossing it back in my direction.

He slams on his brakes and jumps out. His bleached-blonde hair whipping around the sides of his backwards baseball cap. "Oh, holy cow! What was that...Everyone okay out there? Hello?" Romeo shouts with panic. *Seriously? He sounds just like her.*

The passenger side door stays open as he circles around the truck, looking for what he could have hit.

My knees ache from squatting between the parked cars and my pulse hammers through my body. *It's now or never.* I make a run for it and jump into the driver's seat, close the door and throw the gear in drive.

The rumble of the overworking engine muffles the shout behind the truck, but I can make out: "Hey, man, what the hell!" before jamming my foot against the gas pedal until it won't move any farther.

"Don't you mean, 'holy cow'?" I mutter to myself while

skidding along the dirt alley until the rubber hits pavement. At least he won't be chasing her now.

FORTY-NINE

My heart hammers, beating against the inside of my body as Griffin continues to bear his weight over me, pinning me to the wooded ground between walls of trees. I'm choking on each breath while trying to keep my composure, knowing I can't let him see the weakness within me. No one will see us in here. They'll only find what looks to be a broken-down car on the side of the road.

"Tell me why that key chain was in my truck, Jess," he demands again.

"Obviously, I don't know. Izzy must have taken it back from me when I wasn't looking. How else would you find it there? I didn't even know who you were or that you had a truck."

Griffin inhales sharply through his nostrils several times, his chest exhales heavily against mine. "Bullshit! Stop lying. Just cut the crap, Jess! You knew I had a truck. You knew who I was. You followed us around. You were the one watching Izzy through windows at night, tapping on the glass, and breaking into her house...Then you blamed me. If you could just scare her away from me, you'd have her back all to yourself, right?"

"Is this the story you've crafted to retain your innocence?" I utter.

"I'm sure you remember stealing my truck that night before ditching it on the side of the road after passing a couple of sharp bends just far enough away from the bonfire. That's when the mood-rock must have broken off your bag, falling right into the fold of the driver's seat," he says, staring through me, but enunciating each word clear as day. "I didn't find it until I went to sell the truck years later."

I don't know when I lost the key chain. I just knew it was gone, like her. It was a haunting sign I wanted to erase from my mind.

"In reality," I say, mirroring his accusation. "You double-parked and blocked Natalie's car, and also left the keys in your truck. So yeah, I took the first vehicle I could use and left to find Izzy. I didn't steal your truck. If I had, I wouldn't have left it down the road in plain sight. You shouldn't have blocked someone in at a school event you had no right being at."

"You're right. I shouldn't have been there. But I was, and yet, it still has nothing to do with what happened to Izzy that night. Tell me what happened when you tried to find her? Did you just give up and go home?" he asks.

Bugs are crawling around the base of my neck from lying on the ground in the middle of the woods. There's nothing I'm going to be able to say to get him to budge. "No. Did you try to find her?"

"Let's stop the back and forth," he says, his arms trembling from holding his weight over me for so long. "I know you wrote me those notes when Izzy and I were together—the ones you found in my box. You were the love-sick mystery girl, acting as though you and I knew each other when I had no clue who was holding the pen. Yet, you knew I had a girlfriend, and you were determined to make yourself sound like a better fit for me even though we had never met. I never responded to one of your letters. Not that I could, since they had no return address. But if I could have responded, I would have told you to leave me the hell alone. You must have hoped that the notes would drive a nail between Izzy and me. But they didn't. I told her about them. I was honest with her and said I had no clue who was sending them. She believed me. She wasn't worried I'd respond, because she knew me well enough. We figured they'd eventually stop. Except then I received a greeting card and a gift box two days after Izzy disappeared. I buried them away, refusing to pay any attention to them, wondering if Izzy worried more about the letters than she told me. All I knew was, I wasn't going to read anything more from her—I mean—you." He tsks his tongue against the roof of his mouth and shakes his head at me as if I've been a misbehaved child. "It's easy to see now after reading everything she wrote about you. You were obsessed with her. And her life. She had the perfect family, a boyfriend who made her happy. A future with open doors. She had it all. And that's what you wanted."

"You've made a lot of assumptions tonight—none of which make sense or will solve the one question everyone in this town wants an answer to...No one knows where Izzy is or where she went."

Griffin swallows hard and grinds his jaw from side to side. "That's not true. I already told you her remains have turned up. You must have figured twenty-two years was a long enough time for the thought of Izzy to be left behind. That's why you swooped into my life, acting like a stranger—someone completely unrelated to my past. You fooled me. You tricked me. I thought you were someone special—someone I could be happy with and spend the rest of my life loving. No one had made me feel much of anything after I lost Izzy, and now I know you were just toying with my heart. But for what purpose?"

The fear inside of me thaws. A moment of clarity expels the words dancing on my tongue. "I wanted to be loved by someone like she was. I wanted the chance to feel love for the first time. It wasn't a crime. I didn't know you were living in Spring Hill. It wasn't until I saw you at the school, knew you were unfamiliar, yet also, vaguely familiar. I heard someone call your name—a name I came to learn through town gossip while everyone was on the hunt for Izzy. In that moment, I knew exactly what Izzy had seen in you—why she'd wanted to spend all her time with you, and how magnetizing your personality was. After all I've been through, I felt like the universe had brought us together for a reason. We were side effects of Izzy's loss. I thought, together, we could find happiness we both deserve."

"We weren't a side effect of Izzy's loss. You're the reason she's gone, aren't you? She didn't want to introduce me to you because she knew it would hurt you as you had craved that same type of happiness. But I'm seeing now, it was more than that. You wanted it to be your turn to feel happiness twenty-two years ago, so you tortured your best friend and put her through hell," he says.

I was the one going through hell. No one will ever understand this.

"I didn't put her through anything."

"You did. Now, I know you were the one who convinced her I was a stalker. You made it look like I was the one breaking into her house, following her, writing her deranged poetry—because the thought of her being that happy meant you'd be more miserable. It all makes sense." There's no anger left in his voice. "But as I just read in her words: she knew the truth. She knew it was you trying to scare her all along."

My lungs are collapsing. There's nowhere for me to run, no more words to fall back on. His confidence is oozing out of him. He knows too much even with my lack of admission.

"I never truly fell in love with anyone until you came around. I was a lonely teenage girl, trying to hold on to the few things I had left in my life." My words are raw and unfiltered.

"Being honest isn't so easy, is it?"

"Honest? You know about my past with my family and then the psychological abuse I endured from Jack to add to it all. I told you I had baggage when we began to date," I whisper. I didn't specify how much baggage, but that's a moot point.

"What now, Jess? Do you want to turn yourself in to the police or are you going to make me do that for you?"

"What would I turn myself in for? Being a jealous teenager who put a couple of ideas into my friend's head? You were the one who ran off with her. That reality is clear as day in those emails I got."

Griffin sweeps my hair off my face and brushes his knuckles gently down my cheek. I could forget why we're here like this if he'd let me. "Jess, come on. You know that's not true. Tell me what happened to Izzy that night of the bonfire. I won't tell anyone. It'll stay between us. I just need closure before the details in the forensic report are final and plastered all over the news. Can you do me that favor?"

I glance past Griffin, up into the dark trees with the hint of moonlight casting a glow on just a few hovering branches.

Some things are better left a mystery.

As if my response has been stuck inside a pressure filled bottle for years, the words shoot out.

I take in a lungful of air and continue. "I pulled out onto the road and took the first sharp bend. Your truck's headlights illuminated the path ahead, capturing the sight of Izzy running along the outskirts of the trees. She made it farther than I thought she would have. It didn't take long to catch up to her."

"What happened when you caught up?" he asks, sounding as if he's holding his breath as his words crackle.

"I gripped the steering wheel tightly as I headed toward her. I remember holding on as if I might somehow fall out of the truck at the speed I was going. She was running along the most dangerous ledge on that road. I needed to stop her before something happened."

"Jess...you probably scared the hell out of her..."

If I could shrug under his weight, I would, but all I can do is stare past him up into the wavering leaf-covered branches. "Izzy's last words kept playing in my head over and over as I got closer to her. She said: '*I just hurt him. I've broken his heart. It's over.*' Except now I know it was all a lie."

"You left her no choice," Griffin says, a breath hitching in his throat.

"I left her no choice but to leave me here to rot so she could disappear into the night like she did..."

Griffin's hand squeezes around my wrist, his rising level of anger clear.

"Izzy loved *you*, not me. I knew her tears weren't real that night. She had done nothing but lie to me over and over since we were kids."

"She wouldn't lie to you. But from what I've read it looks like you gave her no choice," Griffin says, his words pinched into a whine.

"That's not true." I huff a laugh. "She would say things like: '*Your life will turn out to be just perfect. You don't need a mom for that.*' But she has the perfect mother. She couldn't know otherwise. And she'd say things like, '*Your dad works so many hours because he loves you more than anything and wants to give you the world.*' I didn't need the world. I just didn't want to be alone all the time. She said: '*My parents will always be here to help when your dad can't.*' I needed a mother's love, not just someone who would listen to me. She knew all this. She went as far as telling me: '*We're like sisters.*' Izzy had a sister, Hannah. She didn't need me but promised: '*Nothing can tear us apart.*' It turned out our friendship might as well been made from cheap tissue paper. It was irreparable."

"She did love you. She worried about you constantly. She

didn't know how to help you more than she had. How could you not recognize that?" Griffin asks, his eyes narrowing at me as if I'm some kind of deviant.

Lies. Lies. And more lies.

Izzy only felt sorry for me. Her mom told her to feel sorry for me. Everyone felt sorry for me. My dad didn't even want to be around me because he felt so sorry for me. I know what he thinks: *even her mother didn't want to be around her. Poor kid.*

I didn't choose this life. No one expected me to turn out right. People did so little to conceal their whispers around town. I've heard it all. I even heard it from Izzy's mom once, too, at the general store. She didn't know I was on the other side of the canned foods wall. But I heard her loud and clear: "*Poor Jessica...Of course, I'm sure you know her mother abandoned her...The woman made it clear she never wanted a baby.* I just don't understand *why'd she kept her in the first place...You know what they say about a daughter who doesn't have any female influence...She'll end up just like her mom someday. It's so sad...*"

"People will say my mom loved me too. She didn't. But at least she left me with advice to live by. The last thing she said to me was: '*No one will ever truly care about you. Everyone will eventually leave for someone or something better. And they'll never come back.*'"

"That's a ridiculous comment that came from an obviously unhinged woman," Griffin argues. "Goddammit, Jess. What the hell happened to Izzy that night? Tell me. Just tell me now." He punches his fist into the spongy ground next to my head.

"I had no say over anything that happened in my past, but for once, I was finally in the driver's seat. So, I took back the control. I would decide who would love me then leave me." I close my eyes, visualizing that night all over again. "The headlights formed a yellow hue along Izzy's back, her auburn hair glowed red with dust angelically sparkling around her. *So perfect. Always just so perfect.* No one is that perfect. No one! I pressed my foot on the gas pedal until it wouldn't go any further. Gravel was catching in the treads of the tires as traction and speed built up. That's when I heard my mother's words in my head saying: 'Everyone eventually leaves for someone or something better. And they never come back.' Izzy wouldn't do that to me if she couldn't come back. If I made the decision for her, she'd never have to hurt me."

"Wait," Griffin says, pushing himself up on his shaking arms. "What—what are you saying right now...what does this mean?" His eyes fill with tears, one falls free, landing on my neck.

"I closed my eyes just before the truck crashed into Izzy's petite frame. The quiet thud against the iron-grill covered-bumper jolted me in my seat, and I slammed on the brakes. I opened my eyes just in time to watch Izzy fly forward just before falling over the side of the ledge. Then, I glanced at the clock on the dashboard. It was 9:03PM—the moment Izzy's life would forever be frozen in time."

* * *

She didn't even scream. I quickly shove the gear into park and jump out of the truck until I'm standing between the headlights shining against the trees by the jagged cliff's ledge.

The headlights do little to help me see the black river below, though. I can't help but wonder the actual distance of the fall versus what Izzy must have felt like while plummeting. This river is one the few up north that will usher anything in its hold all the way to the Atlantic Ocean. Izzy wanted to travel. Now she can see the world.

I take a few small steps closer to the dangerous edge, overlooking the steep roaring waterfall that hammers against the dark hole of choppy river rapids.

I clench my hands to my heart, staring out into the darkness. A cold wet breeze lodges in my lungs, burns, strangles me.

"Izzy?" My voice is so weak. What is there to say now? "Holy cow!" I mock her repetitive whiny words. "Can you hear me?" I call out over the ledge, my words evaporating into the mist. "Why were you running so close to the edge? There's no barrier here, just ledge. One wrong step and—I know. You didn't take a wrong step. You're too smart to do something like that? Your parents raised you correctly. Your mother raised you with love." I cup my hand over my mouth, continuing to stare down into the abyss. "I wasn't given that opportunity. That's the difference between you and me. It was me in the truck, even though your last thought might have assumed it was Romeo. You might have thought the brakes stopped working. You'd give someone the benefit of the doubt. That's just who you've always been. But the truth is, it was me. I chose to hit you. I chose to make you go away so you wouldn't have to make the decision to leave me. I saved us both from that pain."

* * *

Griffin's breath shudders as if he's suddenly freezing. He could be, but I can't feel much now. "You—you killed her..." he gasps for air. "You drove her off the side of the cliff with my truck... After reading through her diary, I didn't want my suspicions to be true. I wanted to be wrong. I wanted to be wrong so badly."

"It—it was an accident," I say, my words coming out in a stutter.

"No, Jess. No, it wasn't an accident. You hit her with my damn truck!"

Griffin falls to his side, freeing me from his caged arms and legs. Sobs buck through him as he holds his wrist up to his face, trying to read the time on his watch. He squints and turns his hand in several directions before catching a thread of light from the moon. "9:03PM," he says. "That's what the birthday card said too. The one in your handwriting that I didn't open until last week. What the hell—"

"I know," I utter. "I set the time and removed the battery. I thought it was the right thing to do since she bought it for you as a birthday gift. But she said you made a comment about disliking watches, so she was going to return it. She just never had the chance. I thought you might still want it as a memory of her."

"What is wrong with you?" Griffin cries out. "Why would you do this? Any of this?"

"I don't know," I howl. "And I don't know what to do now. I was so stupid back then." My words are full of remorse, hoping he can see how sorry I am through this one and only confession to the horror I live through day after day. I know I was a monster and can never undo the things I did.

"I—I—" he says through a wheeze. "I don't know," he says, peering back at the watch. "Just, how, Jess?"

"I have kids. They need me. They need their mother. I don't want them to turn out like me. If I could take it all back, I would. You have to believe me." I struggle through the nerve pain reeling through my body, pushing myself upright. I dry my tears against my sleeves.

"Okay, okay—let's—wait," he says. His hands shake as he brings them to his face. His eyes bulge as he stares over my shoulder toward to the tree. Another cry bellows from deep in his throat. "Jess, you—you killed her," he says, as if the reality has stunned him again. His words are quiet and drift along the passing breeze. "She's really dead."

Griffin realigns his stare onto me, his eyes glossy with disbelief, a hollow form of despair. His mouth parts and his brows crinkle. He takes in a breath to speak but words don't form on his tongue.

"You already knew she was dead," I utter. "You said she was found...You knew she..."

His chin trembles and struggles to swallow against the dry air. "I lied. No one has found Izzy," he whispers. He drops his head into his hands and rocks back and forth, breathing heavily. Blood dribbles down his fist. He must have caught himself on something when he punched the ground.

I feel around for my bag that fell beside me. I reach inside, searching for something to clean up his wound. He's crying so hard, the sound echoes between the surrounding trees. "You—you—you, need...you—need to turn—turn—yourself i—in..." he chokes out, still holding clutching his face between his hands.

I grab a hold of his arm. "Please, no," I beg.

He jerks away, keeping his hands glued to his face.

"Griffin, please listen—"

"No," he shouts.

"Okay," I whisper before grabbing him by the back of his head, grasping at his full head of tousled golden-brown hair. I'm grateful for something to hold on to. Though he whips his head back from the shock of me grabbing him, he has very little fight left in him. "Let go! What—what are you—" he groans.

"Just let me fix the pain..." I guess we can learn a lot from our kids.

The sharp blade of the butcher knife glides smoothly across his throat, grazing bone. Blood gushes from the seam as I release my grip around his hair. His body thuds heavily against the ground. His face still staring in my direction with unblinking eyes, wide with shock.

"I wish you could have loved me like you loved her. I know you never will," I whisper.

Everyone will eventually leave for someone or something better. And they'll never come back.

It would have been helpful if Mom had told me there would

be times when I had to make sure for myself that they never came back.

FIFTY

MAY 18TH 2001 - TWENTY-TWO YEARS AGO

Jessica

I turn back toward the direction of the bonfire, prepared to abandon Romeo's truck at the clean crime scene. It's funny to think I'm less of a stranger to this truck than Romeo after all this time. At least I don't have much of a reason for sticking meddling love notes between his wiper blade and windshield anytime I see the ugly teal thing parked somewhere in town now.

He wouldn't even drive up to Izzy's house. She'd meet him at the end of our road. I'll probably never know why he was such a secret.

While walking along the edge of the trees, I spot a figure heading in my direction. It must be him. Romeo. I'm sure he wants to know why someone took his truck too. No one even knew him at the bonfire. This will be a suitable time to ask him why he refused to meet Izzy's best friend.

Then I'll tell him what happened to her. How I was trying to save Izzy when I found her taking her life. I couldn't get to her in time. There isn't a hint of evidence on his iron-bar caged bumper, but I wiped it down with my sweatshirt just in case.

My hands splay across my neck, my nails digging against my skin. I drop to my knees, crying out like a howling wolf. The figure picks up his pace, running faster in my direction, a flashlight wavering with each step. The headlights are still blaring from the truck, giving me enough light to see the person as he approaches.

He's not who I was expecting. This isn't Romeo. I may not have met Romeo up close, but I've seen him from a distance—his yellowy-bleached hair is hard to miss. This guy looks nothing like him.

"Are you okay?" he asks, breathless as he reaches my side.

"No," I cry out. "No—my best friend— she—"

He stretches out his hand out and helps me up to my feet. "She what?" he asks, panic weaving through his words.

"She jumped," I say, my voice squeaking before going silent. "She took her life."

"Did she?" he asks, his question too calm. He leaves me with a long pause that drives panic through my veins. "Life can be hard when we fall into the shadows of others. Some of us never get noticed, are never listened to, and just simply never matter. But others...seem to have all the luck, don't they?"

I study at him, cogs spinning. What does he know? "Hey, I remember you. We were friends before junior high, right? It's been a while since we've spoken."

He shrugs. "People come and go."

I just blink at him.

"You know what I think?" he asks.

"What's that?" I reply, trying not to let my tears get the best of me. "Maybe, if two people who are never noticed, never listened to, and have never mattered, find each other...neither will ever have to be lonely again."

"What do you mean?" I ask him.

He turns around, scoping out the area behind him, waving a flashlight around. "Don't worry. No one else saw. I'm the only other one walking along the dark trees at this hour. No one else needs to know," he says. "I've noticed you. You've noticed me. We can share that. Forever. We can stick together, and never have to worry about finding that place of loneliness again. Plus, we would each have too much to lose if we left each other's side after what we both know just happened."

"Jack, it's not what you think—" I start.

"It's what I know," he says. "Jess, let's walk away before that pretty boy who was screaming about his truck being stolen figures out where it is—where his girlfriend is..."

"Where is he—that guy?" I ask, fearful of when he'll show up.

"Scuffing along the road, grumbling."

I glance back in the direction of the bonfire, grateful for the hill masking our presence. "He didn't see anything?" I confirm.

"No. It's only me here. I saw you running after Izzy. The editor of the school newspaper needs to know what's happening before everyone else. I just wish I had gotten a picture before it was too late."

"But you just said..." I'm wheezing desperately, wondering if Jack is going to report whatever it is he saw happen.

"I said if you stick with me, no one will ever know what happened." He takes my hand. "Let's get out of here before others show up. I parked down the road so I wouldn't get stuck trying to get out. We can just call it fate tonight, if you like."

FIFTY-ONE

My body is convulsing from aftershock of what I've done, and the cold is biting through the air. My stomach gurgles every time I look at Griffin's severed body.

What did I do?

Oh God.

What did I do?

What was I thinking?

Self-defense. That's what it was. He was going to hurt me. I think.

He would turn me in.

My kids wouldn't have a mother, like me.

I had no choice.

My hands shake uncontrollably as I empty his pockets, take the diary, his wallet, phone, and keys, shoving them all in my purse. Then I remove the battery-less watch and add that to his things. It's still *timeless,* marking the minute and hour of Izzy's last breath. I'm the one who sent it to him after Izzy "disappeared." An anonymous condolence of sorts. He only started wearing it again after he found her damn diary—wherever the hell it came from. It was a warning I didn't see coming.

Now Griffin and Izzy can *be frozen in time* together.

I can't catch my breath as I make every attempt to clean the knife's blade and the handle with the loose material from Griffin's shirt, leaving it without my fingerprints. I pluck a few large leaves from the tree branches within reach and wrap them around the knife to transfer the handle to his hand.

"You didn't have to do this, Griffin. I could have gotten you help. You know this wasn't the answer," I cry out. "I'll get help. Stay here," I tell his lifeless body. "I'll be back soon. Don't worry."

My gut bounces around in my hollow body as I run toward the hint of streetlights. My tears are thick and heavy, and I can hardly see straight when I stumble out of the woods. It takes a minute to find where we left my car, unsure of how far and in what direction we ran. I stagger along the side of the road to the mile marker, counting my steps from where I exited the woods.

Mile marker 331 and fifty-two steps south.

I'm shivering when I slide into the driver's seat of my car. I turn the key in the ignition, drop my bag on the seat beside me and crank up the heat. I stretch my foot for the brake, finding that Griffin adjusted my seat to his height. He knew how much I hated when he did that.

It doesn't take me long before I turn into the parking lot of Jack's apartment. My hands are still shaking as I grapple with the center console, searching for wet-wipes or disinfectant wipes—anything to get the splatter of blood off my hands and arms.

I scrub my skin until it's raw, using the flashlight on my phone to check every part of my body for evidence. Thankfully, I'm wearing black clothes.

I collect the wipes and toss them in the dumpster in the corner of the parking lot.

There's no such thing as relief in my life—just hurdles I have to keep clearing.

I take a few deep breaths before approaching the main apartment door with my jingling keys in hand. I try to sort through the dozen I have to find the right one to his front door. I've had it in case of an emergency, but I've tried to be respectful of his privacy when I drop the kids off. "Too many keys," I groan to myself. After a long minute, I find it and let myself inside, then tread lightly up the stairs. I tap my knuckles on the door, trying to be just loud enough for him to hear me but not so loud I wake anyone. Hopefully, he's not asleep. If I know Jack, he's sitting on his recliner watching live streams of police chases.

Jack only had one quality I was interested in—the ability to keep a secret. We got together because he loved me, and I loved knowing the past wouldn't come back to haunt me. Life was comfortable, survivable. I guess it was too comfortable.

The floor creaks and something scratches up against the door between me and the inside of his apartment. He's checking the peephole. The chain link falls, the deadbolt releases, and the door squelches as it opens in toward him. "What are you doing here?"

"I need your help," I whisper, walking into the open living room area of his apartment.

Jack's complexion becomes pale, and he runs his hand over his glistening bald head. "What the hell did you do?"

I lift my left hand and twist my wedding band back and forth.

Jack drops his head back and makes his way toward his outstretched recliner. He leans forward, resting his hands on the arm rest. "This isn't part of the divorce decree," he says. "I agreed to the custody term, left you the house, and promised to keep our mutual respect of silence for the past. I didn't agree to be at your beck and call if you ever screwed up again. If it doesn't involve the kids' well-being—I'm not..."

"It does. Are they asleep?"

"Yes, why..."

"I can't risk anyone finding him."

"Jesus Christ. How? What is it?"

"He's—" I drag my finger across my throat. "I had no choice. He was trying to smoke me out. He said he lied about Izzy's remains turning up, but what if he wasn't lying?"

"So what? She jumped off a cliff?"

"No, she didn't," I say, my words blunt.

"So, you're worried they'll find previous trauma? At this point? I doubt it, but...This really just came up all of a sudden? You've been together two years. He never mentioned her name once. Then this week, he's somehow got dirt on you?"

"Yeah—I—I don't know what to believe. What's true? What's a lie? He somehow got hold of her diary too, and there was a lot written in there."

"Well, where did he get it from?"

I shake my head so hard it throbs. "I—I don't," I gasp, "I don't know. He wouldn't tell me. He could have had it all this time and just decided to read it. I don't know. If someone else had it...they would have read it, right?"

Jack's face burns a fiery red and I worry what I'm doing to him now. "Jessica, where is the diary?"

"In—it's uh—in my bag," I say, glancing at it dangling from my shoulder. "I'm sorry. I don't want you to get stressed out. I don't want to hurt you—"

Jack lowers his gaze to my side, spotting my bag now pinched under my arm. "Stop. Jessica, where is Griffin?"

I swallow hard, my throat is like sandpaper. "In—um—in the woods."

"Jesus Christ, Jess. What woods?"

I press my fingers to my temples, gasping for air. "It's—I—I counted. Well, it's mile-marker 331, fifty-two steps south and straight into the woods—" I say, gasping for another breath. "About—um—a thirty-second walk."

"That's a good fifteen-minute walk to the falls over the river. Are you out of your mind? No. Jess. No." Jack's ears are turning burgundy, and I need to—I shouldn't have come here. What was I thinking?

"I'll go handle it. I'm sorry. I'm sorry," I cry out. "I didn't pick the place. I thought he was going to kill me. I think he was. I don't know."

"No. Just—I need to think. Christ," he grunts under his breath. "You're not going back there alone, and we aren't leaving the kids."

"I just didn't know what to do. I wasn't coming here to ask you to—"

"Get rid of his body?" he asks in a breathy whisper.

"Yeah," I utter.

"You're not going to be able to do that." Jack paces back and forth, blowing air out of his nose forcefully. He sounds out of breath. It's my fault. "I'll handle it. We're still in this life together whether married or not. If you go down, we both go down, and I won't let that happen to our kids."

I didn't deserve Jack when we were married, and I don't deserve him now.

Jack huffs and puffs as he makes his way over to the coat closet. He grabs a backpack, then moves into the small kitchen, reaching up into the top cabinet for supplies. He drops them into his bag so fast I hardly see anything more than a can of some kind of spray. "Jack—" I don't even know what to say. I don't know what other choice we have.

"Just stay here with the kids. I'll be back." Jack rests his hand on my shoulder on the way out the door. It's the first time he's touched me since he moved out of the house three years ago. I never noticed his touch until it was gone.

* * *

I knew never to be shocked when this day came. Our relationship, then marriage, has been anything but normal. Meeting at the scene of a murder forms an unexplainable bond, but not one that promises a happy ending. Jack loved me. He wanted to marry me. He wanted to give me a good life. I wanted the same, but not from him. If I denied his proposal, he'd be a flight risk. If I left him at the altar. I had to wait until he no longer wanted to be with me. Then I'd become the risk to his immoral decision of withholding the truth about Izzy.

"My heart is breaking, Jess," he says, hanging his head to avoid looking me in the eyes.

"It shouldn't have to be," I utter. "This was your decision to make, not mine."

"I want something you can't seem to give me. I wasn't looking for it—for her. It just happened. Like us, you know?"

"Yeah, I know," I say.

"Why couldn't you love me the way I loved you, Jess?"

Under different circumstances, things could have been different. If I didn't fear what would happen if I broke his heart. If we found each other and built our relationship off a solid foundation rather than toothpicks bridging a gap. "It wasn't a choice I made. I'm not a whole person. I'm broken, and unfixable."

"I tried to help," he says.

"I know. You did. You gave me comfort, a home, a family." It wasn't enough for him. If we don't end things amicably now, I'm not sure what the future will hold. "What will happen to me after we do this?" I ask, the words speaking out my biggest fear. Will he go and report me to authorities so he can have the life he's always deserved? I wouldn't be able to blame him.

His head falls to the side. "Come on." He points over to the living room couch where the kids are snuggled up in blankets watching a movie. They're oblivious to what we're about to tell them, making this much harder. "I will never jeopardize their innocence by letting them watch their mother go to prison," he says. "And their father for being an accessory to the crime. If you go down, I go down. There's no denying that."

I didn't exactly ask that he show up at that exact moment. It just happened. He wanted me and I had to give myself to him. "I know this isn't the life you expected to have with me," I tell him. He thought I'd eventually love him the way he loved me.

"I have no regrets, Jess."

We've always been honest with each other. That came with many ups and downs. Especially when he told me he was falling for his secretary. I told him to go be with her. He told me he couldn't do that to me. "You've been a good husband."

"You've been the perfect wife, even if you've never loved me —not with the type of love a married couple should have for each other. You can't force that onto someone. I was still happy to be with you. We played our roles. We had two beautiful kids."

He sees the life we've had as a prize, and I've seen it as a hiding place.

"You deserve to be loved. That's why I want you to go."

"I'd stay if you said so. I'd fire her and forget she exists."

"I know," I tell him. "I might not be able to love you but setting you free is the best I can do."

I'm not sure why this hurts so much. I'm losing my peace of mind, my sanity, my normal. And I'm agreeing to put our kids through this divorce with us, knowing they might hate us for it after.

"You can always rely on me; you know that right? Whether we're married or not. I'm not going anywhere. If you need something, I'll be there."

He pulls me in and wraps his arms around my neck, stroking his fingers through my hair. "You're my best friend, Jack. Always."

"Mine too. Just don't murder anyone else, okay?"

* * *

He held up to his end of the bargain. I didn't hold up mine. Once we were divorced, his secretary didn't want anything to do with him. The appeal of an affair was gone.

Then I found Griffin.

I knew who he was, of course.

I had watched Izzy and Griffin more times than I'd like to admit—enough to know exactly what he looked like. I wanted to be with him as soon as I saw the way he looked at her. When he opened a door or pulled out a chair. The way he just listened to her talk about nothing and seemed like it was the most fascinating thing in the world.

And then there he was, twenty-two years later in the same room as me, not married, no strings attached, no Izzy.

Jack told me it was a bad idea. He told me to stay away, not to swat at a bee's nest. I didn't listen. I was convinced Griffin was the safest person to end up with because if anyone would try to figure out who was in his truck that night, it would be him. He wouldn't question the woman he loves.

Jack said it wouldn't end well. I told him to trust me.

God, I let him down.

I fall asleep in Jack's chair. I have no clue how long I've been asleep when the click of the door jolts me awake. Jack bursts into his apartment, breathing heavily as if he ran all the way from the woods. "What happened?" I ask, keeping my voice down. I stumble out of his chair, rushing to him to grab his shoulders. He looks like he's about to keel over.

His complexion is pale, verging on a green hue I've never seen before.

His lips clamp shut, and he waves a hand at me, gesturing for me to keep quiet.

"You're scaring me, Jack."

He swallows hard and takes in a deep breath. "The scene is —it was a massacre—inhumane, Jess. There were body parts everywhere, his clothes torn to shreds. Bones scattered around. His hair was the only decipherable feature I spotted." Jack shudders. "It's something I wish I could unsee."

FIFTY-TWO

I'm staring at Jack, mindless, incapable of predicting what could be worse than the situation he was already resolving.

"What's going on?" Abby says, poking her head out of the bedroom she and JJ share. "Mom, what are you doing here?"

"Shh," I tell her, hoping JJ doesn't wake up too. "Everything's fine. Go back to bed."

She stares at me as if I'm covered in blood. I know I'm not. "Are you kidding? You both look like you're about to have heart attacks or something. Where have you been? Where's—"

I press my hands together, pleading she'll stop. "Please, go back to bed. I need to talk to your father alone. We'll talk in the morning, I promise."

She doesn't argue, which surprises me. Whatever look she's deciphering on my face must be enough to scare her back into the room.

"Something got to him, Jess."

"What? What does that mean?" My body is hollow with air floating around like helium in a tank.

"I don't know. A bear, a coyote. He was ravaged. I disposed of the remains so no one would go hunting for the animal."

The animal. I'm the animal, except for the ravaging part.

"Romeo is finally reunited with his Juliet, tragic ending and all," Jack whispers.

My imagination is doing me no favors, picturing the scene I forced Jack to handle. "I'm sorry."

"Who else knows about those emails and who the hell broke into your house tonight?"

The police investigation.

If they reach back out to us for an update, they'll want to know where Griffin is.

"The kids know about the emails. Natalie. I mentioned it to my dad too, but he brushed off the topic." I need to come up with something to tell Natalie. I left her a message, asking to stay with her tonight. Then Griffin disappeared. "Griffin must have been the one writing me those emails, pretending to be Izzy. I think he wanted me to confess about Izzy."

"Did he set up the house break-in too?" Jack asks.

"I wouldn't be surprised. His intention was clear—he wanted me to confess what I know about Izzy. Everything that happened this week must have been part of his plan."

"Your dad brushed off the topic?" Jack presses.

"He didn't want to hear anything about Izzy."

Jack holds his hands out. "Well, can you blame the guy? You're his daughter. He knows you...And you know his silence has been your alibi all these years, Jess. Don't hold it against him."

* * *

Jack, my newfound counterpart, dropped me off at home just an hour ago, which was still thirty minutes past Izzy's curfew. From the moment I walked into the house, I was waiting for the phone to ring. Mrs. Lester would want to know where Izzy was and why she hasn't come home yet. I wasn't sure if she'd call my house or Natalie's first.

It was mine.

"I'm so sorry, Mrs. Lester. She left without saying a word. I can help you look. I'll have my dad bring me back to the bonfire. We'll find her, don't worry," I assure her.

I hang up the phone, keeping my gaze on the receiver as I place it back into its cradle.

"What's going on?" Dad asks, walking into the kitchen with tired eyes and messy hair—his common appearance after falling asleep in front of the TV every night.

"Izzy's missing," I tell Dad, staring at him through tear-filled eyes after hanging up the phone. "That was Mrs. Lester. They can't find her. She never came home. I have to go help look for her."

"She was with you tonight at the bonfire with the rest of the class, wasn't she?" Dad asks, scratching the back of his neck. He seems half asleep still, trying to collect his thoughts.

"Yes, but she left because she was upset about this boy she's been seeing." I leave out the part that I went running after her. "I thought she just needed a minute to pull herself together. When she didn't come back, I assumed someone gave her a ride home."

"Natalie was supposed to drive you both home," he says. He never seems to know as much as he appears to right now. With the hours he spends at the office, I'm always left to my own decisions on where I go and when. I must have told him the plan at some point.

"Yeah, it was the plan, but—" I should have told him she took off without us when I got home tonight.

"Who else would she have gotten a ride from?" Dad presses.

"That guy. Romeo. Her boyfriend. I don't know. I've been telling her he's no good. He's bad news. I kept thinking he'd lock her up somewhere. What if that's what he's done?"

"Okay, okay. Calm down. Let's not jump to conclusions. Do

you know this guy's phone number? Can you call to make sure they're together?"

"No. I don't have his phone number or his real name. I don't even know where he lives. Izzy wouldn't tell us."

Dad runs his hands through his thinning hair. "This isn't good."

"We need to go look for her!" I tell him.

"Okay, okay. I'm getting my keys. Grab a flashlight. Meet me in the car. The police will be looking for her too. We need to make sure you tell them exactly what you just told me about this Romeo guy."

There are dozens of people with flashlights, forging through the woods, calling out Izzy's name. I can't believe what I'm hearing or that this is real. The police are everywhere, questioning all of us. I told them about Romeo and my concerns, but I'm not sure it's enough to help. No one knows his real name or anything about him.

"Jess, we've gone in a circle around the same group of trees a dozen times. Let's keep moving," Dad says.

"Do you think he did run off with her?" I ask him.

Dad stops in front of me, breathless from running circles. "Jessica, if you have a reason to think that's what happened, I need to know."

"I don't know, Dad. I would have already told you."

The image of Izzy's body falling over the ledge flashes through my mind. My stomach burns and I fall to my knees, purging everything I've ingested today.

I clench my eyes, questioning why I did what I did, knowing there's no way to undo it or take it back. Tears fall and I gasp for air.

Dad reels me up to my feet. "Are you okay?"

"No. She's gone," I cry softly.

"No, we just need to find her. Standing here isn't helping."

"She's gone," I sob. "She was going to leave me anyway. I didn't want to feel that way again."

"What the hell are you talking about?" Dad says, grabbing me by the shoulders and yanking me around.

"I don't know," I say through broken sobs.

"Did you—" he says, stopping himself. "Why do you think she's gone?"

More stomach acid wreaks havoc, folding me in half until I fall to my knees, purging again. I struggle for air after vomit suffocates me. I grasp at dry leaves, clenching them as if they're something to hold on to.

"You can't force people to stay in your life. We've gone over this so many times," Dad says. It's as if his reminder can help this situation now.

"I know. I'm the one who decides who stays and who goes," I croak out.

"No. You're not," he argues.

"I want to go home."

Dad's pacing around me. He pulls a handkerchief from his pocket and pats his face dry. "Are you sure she's not out here?"

I nod. "I'm sure."

"I—dear God. I don't know what to—" He helps me up by my elbow again and shines the flashlight in the direction of where we entered the woods.

"I'm sorry," I whisper.

* * *

Jack and I never talked about that night with my dad again. Dad's silence was my cue to never say another word about Izzy. But I was dying inside. Holding everything inside of me just made things so much worse. I'm obviously crazy like my mother. I must have inherited that. Living like this has never been a choice I wanted to make.

"Okay. Let's not go back down this road again right now," he says with a hush. "Where's the diary now? You have it, right?"

"Yeah. I have it." I walk over to where I dropped my purse and reach inside. The small book burns like a blue flame against my hand as I retrieve it. "Good, we need to burn that thing."

I flip through the pages, finding thick black marker scribbles across blank pages with:

May 18th, 2001 – Part 1

Jessica Peterson, my ex-best friend, is the demonic stalker!

Holy cow! That girl is ruining my life!

I just figured out she's been writing Griffin anonymous, sick notes, trying to get him to break up with me. She thought I wouldn't see them or recognize her annoying bubbly handwriting with a crooked heart above every i. I didn't want to believe it was true until I spotted her leaving a note on his car in the center of town today. I haven't told him yet. I'm going to be so embarrassed to tell him she's the person I've been calling my best friend.

May 18th, 2001 – Part 2

And while I'm writing out confessions in bold ink: Jessica Peterson was the one who broke into my room and destroyed everything I love. I've loved her like a sister. And she has absolutely broken my heart, trust, and anything else that can keep a friendship together.

I found a piece of her pink baby-doll T-shirt she had on yesterday stuck to a piece of glass under my bed.

She's also the one who read my diary, left it open on my bed to the page where I confessed Griffin's real name. She knows who he is now. It all makes sense. But why? Why would she do this to me?

Her plan was to make me think Griffin broke in.

Even worse, she's been the one staring through my window at night and tapping on my glass. I caught her the night Romeo stayed over. He had already fallen asleep, but I was waiting for the tapping to happen like it does every night. As soon as I heard it, I was relieved to know it wasn't Romeo, but when I got to the window and shined my flashlight outside, I couldn't believe my eyes when I saw Jess running across the street into her house. I bet she was the one who wrote that last letter that was supposedly from Romeo. He said he didn't write it, and I believe him. It was too dark and twisted to be from him and he said he doesn't have a typewriter. Who does that??? Why would Jess be doing all of this to me?

May 18th, 2001 – Part 3

Also...

Jessica Peterson is just like her mother. There, I said it. It's true.

She's selfish and jealous despite how much I have tried to be the best kind of friend I could be to her. Clearly, it's never been enough.

It's so obvious she doesn't care about anyone but herself.

May 18th, 2001 – Part 4

This is the last thing I have to say...And I need to stop taking up so many pages with my hateful words but...I'm not that person. I'm a good person.

Jess is not. She's not a good person. She might not have one good bone in her body, in fact. If something ever happens to me, Jessica Peterson is to blame.

I don't think she's going to stop ruining my life until she has everything she wants. Including Griffin Adler.

October 09, 2023

JESSICA WILL GET WHAT'S COMING TO HER...

The last entry is written with a date from last week, but I know that's not Griffin's handwriting. Whoever wrote that is the one who gave him the diary.

"Izzy knew it was me who broke into her room," I mutter. "She never confronted me."

"I'm not sure she had the chance," Jack says.

I close the book, letting the words simmer. "Yeah."

Just like her mother...How could I be like someone I hardly know?

"Look, why don't you take my bed? I'll sleep on the recliner. I have some whiskey if that'll help," Jack says.

Griffin was going to kill me when he got the chance. What else could that last entry mean? It was self-defense tonight. I knew something bad was going to happen.

He left me no choice.

FIFTY-THREE

Natalie texted me several times before I was able to peel my eyes open this morning. I might have slept another hour before I felt Abby's cold, hard stare spiking through my half-closed eyelids.

I'm up.

"Mom!" she whisper-shouts. "You're still here! I've been worried about you." She runs to my side and wraps her arms around me, squeezing the air out of my lungs. I hold her tightly, pressing my cheek against hers.

"I'm sorry, sweetie. I had to handle a couple of things. Everything is okay now, though."

"I told you Mom was okay, Abbs," Jack says.

Abby peers up at Jack with the doll-like eyes she's used on him since she was a toddler. "I know, but you had a weird look in your eyes. I understand more than you give me credit for sometimes."

"I know, kiddo," he says.

"Mom!" JJ shouts after racing into the room, making a running lean for the bed.

"Well, what happened?" Abby presses as they both snuggle into my sides.

A long sigh expels from my mouth, and I drop my head, staring down at my lap to make sense of everything that's happened while thinking up a simple explanation. "Well, Griffin left me last night. I know it seems sudden, but it wasn't meant to be between us. I'm sorry I dragged the both of you into a new life with him. I wouldn't have if I had known this would be the outcome."

Abby's eyes widen in shock and confusion, a tug-of-war in her mind as I watch her thoughts percolate. She takes a seat next to me on the bed. "Was it all true? What those emails said?"

She'll never trust me again if I tell her we've been living with this crazy stalker all this time. "The emails just made us realize we don't know each other as well as we thought. Life can get complicated when people settle down with someone new at my age. We've both lived so much of our lives already that it's hard to completely know someone after just a couple of years."

"Oh," Abby says. I know I didn't answer her question or settle her concerns, but I don't want to say much else.

"We'll be okay," I say, wrapping my arm around her.

"So, that's it?" Abby confirms.

"That's it." The end of a very long chapter in my life. It's hard to understand how I could have thought I needed one thing, person, to make me happy—only to find out I was completely wrong. I know now, my kids are all I need. That's the one answer I'm sure about. That's what Mom taught me.

"I'm sorry, I think. I assume it's for the best," Abby says with shrug.

"Yeah," I tell her.

She rests her head on my shoulder as if I'm a source of comfort. After everything I've done, despite her awareness, she still finds me to be her safe place. That's the difference between my mom and me. She was never a source of comfort.

"You know...there was something a little too perfect about him. It's hard to put my finger on. I think it was the hair. Men your age don't have hair like that," she says with a chuckle.

Jack and I exchange a quick glance as I try to push away the description of what he found in the woods.

"Wait...Griffin's gone?" JJ asks as realization settles into his head.

"Yes, buddy."

"I didn't get to say goodbye," JJ says, pouting. "What about school? Is he still going to teach?"

"Son," Jack says from the doorway. "I think Griffin's left town. Some people have a tough time deciding what they want in life, and if you don't go looking for it, you may never find out what that is. I'm sure he'll find whatever that might be."

"Oh," JJ says. He pauses and stares at the dark flat screen TV hanging on the wall across from the bed. "Does that mean we can watch *SpongeBob* in bed?"

A sigh of relief is the only sound I can muster, thankful the mind of a seven-year-old skips from one topic to the next within seconds.

"Give your mom a few minutes to get up, JJ. Come on and eat your breakfast. Abby, you too," Jack says, corralling them out of the bedroom.

I grab my phone and look at Natalie's messages:

6:05AM

Natalie: *Jess, I am so sorry I didn't see your messages last night. OMG. I hope everything's okay? Call me right away.*

6:55AM

Natalie: *It's almost 7:00AM. You've never slept this late. Please text me.*

7:15AM

Natalie: *Jess…*

7:30AM

Me: *Things aren't great. It's a long story, but Griffin left me last night. I don't even know where he went, but he said things are over between us. I'll call you when I can pull myself together.*

7:31AM

Natalie: *So, that bastard was having an affair?*

An affair. I wish. That would have been easier to handle than blackmail. The heaviness in my head pulls me back to the pillow. I reach over to Jack's nightstand to place my phone back down, but it buzzes just before I release it.

What now?

A new email notification pops up with my daily spam. I tap the icon, wanting to empty my inbox. I wish I could so easily do the same for my head.

My eyes glaze over the list of marketing promotions, settling directly on the last incoming message.

Re: Re: Re: Re: Re: Re: IzzyBee83isMe@aol.com: Hey you… It's me…

My heart pounds, heat prickling down my spine. If Griffin was the one sending the emails, posing as Izzy…how has this just arrived in my inbox?

There's no physical warning before the bile in my stomach forces its way up my throat. I drop off the side of the bed, grasping for the small trash can in the corner before my insides spew out of me in a blaze. I stare at the rim of the metal trash can, gripping my stomach in pain. My veins pulse. All of them. My muscles all strain from the pounding of my heart and a cold sweat weighs me to the ground.

FIFTY-FOUR

Smoke from burning toast settles over me. Distant laughter between the kids reminds me of an innocence I only knew at an early age. Time can't rewind.

I gaze up at the bed, knowing the phone is resting on the comforter. The email is a door to another dark hallway with no exit. Once inside, I'll feel trapped again. I know this, and yet, I have no choice but to turn the knob.

My body is twice as heavy as it should be, and it takes every bit of energy I have left to reach up to the bed. I slink around blindly with my hands out in front of me until I run my fingers over the device, scraping my finger over the cracked screen.

I pull it down, wishing my hands would steady. My bones feel like they're attached by loose screws, and it takes too long to open the daunting email. Before reading the first word, another wave of nausea strikes. With slow breaths in and out of my nose, I will myself to avoid vomiting again.

To: JessPetersonXoXo@aol.com

From: Izzy Lester

Subject: Re: Re: Re: Re: Re: Hey you...It's me.

Hey Jess,

Did you make someone else "disappear"?

You've read all my emails, asked questions, and wanted to talk in person. I didn't give in to anything you asked, yet you trusted my word. You believed me when I said Griffin was my stalker.

You'd think you'd know someone before you marry them, right? By the time you settle down together, you know each other's strengths and weaknesses, flaws, and skills.

Best friends are the same. We knew everything about each other, didn't we? We didn't keep secrets.

Well, that isn't exactly true. We did have our secrets. You, yours. Me, mine.

Yet, I suspect you might be asking yourself if you imagined everything the night I disappeared? Was Griffin really the crazy stalker you wanted me to think he was? Or was it you who couldn't handle the fact that I was spending time with someone other than you? You know the answer. And so do I.

We both know this was never about Griffin or your need for control. It's about your insecurities and fear of getting hurt again, after what your mother did to you.

But I want to make one thing clear—the people in your life are not just characters in your story. You can't erase us when it suits your narrative.

Izzy

FIFTY-FIVE

A WEEK AGO

Mrs. Flanagan

I scribble my name, Hannah, on the side of my box, so I remember to set it aside later. The packing tape howls as I tear another piece over the top flaps, a reminder of the empty space surrounding me. This house was no longer a home after we lost Izzy. Mom and Dad have been renting out the place for so long that I didn't realize how much we'd left behind for the renters to use. The furniture has seen better days and I'm waiting for the Salvation Army to come by and pick up the pieces we're donating.

The last of our belongings are in boxes now. The moving truck is half-full and will be packed to the brim by time Mason, my husband, returns after work.

I peer up and down the long hallway of the one floor dwelling, wishing I felt any type of attachment to this house. So many memories will be left here. Times with the four of us. Growing up with Izzy, always looking up to my big sister. It still hurts to recollect that life.

I was such an annoying little sister. All little sisters are annoying, though. Even though I'd argue she was more annoying than me, I never once thought those bickering moments between us wouldn't last forever.

A sister is for life.

Hers was just much shorter than mine, or so we're supposed to believe. I wish I could believe she's still alive somewhere. There's a void, regardless. Dead or missing—she's not in my life, and it still hurts.

Following Izzy's disappearance, there were only dark days. Mom couldn't get out of bed. Dad barely spoke. It was like living at a never-ending funeral.

I had to take care of the two of them myself.

I couldn't blame them.

I understood.

I felt the same but at a young age. The only difference was, I had energy to power through more than I can imagine now.

I drag my pencil down the long checklist of areas to clean out, saving the worst for last. The attic.

When Izzy and I were kids, Dad told us there were villages of mice living in the attic. He just didn't want us up there. I believed his scary warnings then. We both did. Neither of us went up there. Dad's sure there's nothing up here, but Mom thinks she might have stored a few things from time to time near the ceiling access in Izzy's bedroom closet.

This will be the first and last time I take a flashlight up there.

I remove the ceiling panel, dust snows over my head. I wave away the debris and sweep it off my head. I pull the wooden desk chair over and climb up, my hands shaking a bit as I switch on the flashlight.

Wooden framing beams and unfinished flooring part the plastic covered insulation—one path between this opening and the one in the small closet of our family room. I shine the flashlight in every angle ensuring there are no bats or rats. I'm not so worried about goblins at thirty-five.

I don't see much of anything. Mom thinks she might have left something on the other end.

I hoist myself up, trying to keep my balance on the wooden beams before reaching the solid flooring. Just before I reach the flank, my knee slips off the beam and a sharp edge jabs me. *Crap!* I move carefully, terrified I'll fall through the ceiling. Whatever stabbed my knee slides out onto the ledge of the opening in the ceiling. I wave my flashlight over to the object, finding a small book.

No way. I open the top flap, finding: This diary belongs to Isobel Lester.

It's her handwriting. I couldn't forget her neat, prim and proper handwriting that made mine look like a little child's. How could I not have known she had a diary? I snooped in her room more than I'd care to admit, but never found this.

I shove the book into my sweatshirt pocket and continue crawling along the wooden panels. It takes me less than a minute to make my way from one side to the other where the other detachable ceiling panel is. There are a couple tubes of Christmas wrapping paper and gift labels that have Santa's name scripted in perfect penmanship. This must have been the wrapping paper Mom used to give us gifts from Santa when we believed. It makes sense she would hide the evidence up here.

As soon as my feet re-touch the ground in Izzy's closet, the feeling of bugs crawling all over me gives me the shivers. I close the attic ceiling panel and replace the chair.

I force myself to look around the room once more, feeling nothing but a sense of detachment.

I lug the last of the boxes out of the house, stacking them up to make it easier to load onto the truck when Mason arrives.

The front stone-covered step, a place I used to sit and read, welcomes me. A warm spot beneath the sun.

The corner of Izzy's diary jabs me in the stomach as I lean forward and I take the book out, debating whether to open it. There's still a part of me that wants to believe she's alive somewhere, but the realist I am, knows better than to have such hope.

I flip through the pages, finding dark, angry, short notes across entire pages, landing on the last of them.

My heart flounders and my stomach tenses as I begin to read.

The blatant, blunt truth of what Izzy was going through before she did...

May 18th, 2001

If something happens to me, Jessica Peterson is to blame.

She won't stop ruining my life until she has everything she wants.

Including Griffin Adler.

She disappeared on May 18th, 2001. Never came home that night from the senior bonfire party.

No one knew where she went. Except we heard two different stories. One from Jessica, and one from Griffin.

Jessica told us Izzy was terrified of Romeo and he wanted to take her away and leave the state.

Griffin told us he and Izzy had a plan to make Jessica believe they were breaking up so they could enjoy their relationship privately, without the worry and concern coming from Jessica all the time. He also said Izzy wouldn't tell Jessica his real name or him Jessica or Natalie's names. She was insistent on keeping them separate in her life. The bits and pieces of his story led us to what we already knew about Jessica. She was frail and held on tightly to those she loved. She was terrified of losing anyone else. Her sensitivity was sometimes hard on her friends, which led to them doing what they felt was necessary to protect her feelings.

We weren't surprised that Izzy kept Griffin separate from Jessica and Natalie. Despite her concern for Jessica's sensitive feelings, this town had been a little too small at times. Secrets and privacy are understandable.

In the end, both Griffin and Jessica's stories aligned with Izzy disappearing along the perimeter of the woods that night.

Izzy never told us about the issues she had with Jess. The thought wouldn't have crossed our minds. They were together every day. But reading the truth in her diary—it's gutting. The farther I flip backward through the pages, the more shocking, and disturbing comments I find about Jess.

I drop the book onto my lap and press my hands over my face. It's been over twenty years and never knew how Jessica behaved toward Izzy. Why would Izzy protect her so dearly? It's clear Jessica was trying to destroy her life, and Izzy let it happen. She must not have thought Jessica was capable of doing more than she had already done. But it seems easy to think otherwise now.

To know these tidbits of facts have been sitting in that godforsaken attic this whole time causes fury to drive through me. Adrenaline spikes. I want to charge into Jessica's house and ask her what the hell she did with my sister. Accusatory or not, my gut tells me she knows exactly what happened to Izzy.

I know it can't be that simple, though.

A car horn pulses, a gentle hello as Mason pulls up the long driveway, parking behind the moving truck.

It doesn't take long for him to spot me on the front step next to the stacks of boxes. "Sweetie, are you okay? You're flush," he says, making his way toward me in a jog.

"No."

"What—what's going on? Are you hurt?" He's breathless by the time he reaches me. "What is that? On your lap?"

I open my eyes and glance down at the sticker covered book. "Izzy's diary. I found it in the attic."

Mason covers his mouth, his eyes growing wide. "Did you find something?"

I gasp a shuddering breath. "Not an answer, but something."

Mason takes the book from my lap and fans through the pages, stopping in the same place I did. He tosses his head back with defeat. "I—I don't even—I don't know what to say right now."

"Griffin should know about this diary," Mason says.

"I don't know if I want to open his old wounds." Not like mine. Mom's. This is twenty-two years ago all over again. That stabbing pain in my chest, it's as fierce as ever.

"He'd want to know," Mason says. "I would."

"Does your stepmom still work with him at the school?"

"Yeah, Carol's still there. I'll ask her if he is too."

Mason wastes no time taking his phone out of his back pocket and making a call. "Hey," he says when she picks up the call. "Yeah, yeah, of course. Everything is fine." Mason doesn't call her very often. He'll call his dad to talk, but their whole family seems to carry on well, post-divorce. "I was just wondering...do you still work with Griffin Adler?" He pauses, locking his gaze onto mine, listening to whatever she's saying.

"What's she saying?" I whisper.

Mason holds up his index finger. "Oh yeah? That's great. Glad to hear he's doing well. No kidding?" Mason's eyes become vacant; his pupils grow. "Do you have his phone number by any chance?" Mason refocuses on me, gesturing his hand into a scribble, looking for a pen or something. I open the notepad app on my phone and hand it over. He types in the number, then hands the phone back to me. "I appreciate it. No problem. I'll give you guys a call later." I hear her mumbling but can't make out what she's saying. "Okay, love you too. Bye now."

Mason ends the call and scoots in next to me on the step. "What's going on? You're making me nervous."

"You said Griffin and Jessica Peterson never knew each other, right? Izzy kept them away from each other?"

My heart resounds with an answer before I can form a word. "Right."

"Well, apparently, Jessica Peterson and Griffin Adler got married last year."

If I hadn't just read Izzy's dark inked words in her diary, I'd think common miseries could bring two people together.

I wonder if Griffin knows who he's living with, or what his wife has done.

I'm surprised he agrees to meet us. I haven't seen Griffin in over seventeen years. I was only twelve when Izzy went missing and fifteen when I saw him last. We stayed in touch with Griffin for a while, but distance eventually grew between us.

I haven't been to this lonely diner between the hills of three neighboring towns since Izzy worked here. Back then, I'd visit during her shifts with friends and blow straw wrappers at her when she walked by. It was always just to annoy her—a little sister's job in life.

I recognize Griffin as soon as he walks through the door. He still has the perfect hair Izzy always gushed about. Lucky man to keep all that past the age of thirty.

Mason stands up first to shake his hand. "Thanks for coming to meet us, man. We appreciate it."

I slide out of the booth and do the only thing that seems right and give him a hug. His chest thuds as if he has the hiccups, but I know that's not the case. He stares up at the ceiling and gasps for air. "My God, Hannah, you look just like your sister. Still after all this time."

"I get that a lot," I tell him, my words breaking. "Especially since I keep my hair short. And the white strand—" I point to the small section of my hair I color. "It's my way of keeping Izzy with me. That sounds weird—"

"No, not at all. It's perfect," Griffin says, tears filling his eyes, contrasting the smile growing across his lips.

We take a seat and release more breaths than we can hold within our lungs. "So, what did you want to talk about?" Griffin asks, drumming his fingers against the tabletop, his nerves clear. My gaze settles on the gold wedding band encircling his ring finger. *How could she?*

I pull Izzy's small diary out of my purse and slide it across the table. "I—I, ah—I found this in the attic of our old house the other day. I was doing a final sweep because we're finally selling the place."

Griffin's gaze locks on the diary, his forehead crinkling with sharp lines. "What is it?"

"Izzy's diary."

He stares at me for a long minute before taking the book into his hand. "Her diary? She had a diary?"

"Yeah. I didn't know either. None of us did," I say. He flips through the pages, one by one until flipping forward to the few pages I'd bookmarked. Izzy started writing in this diary when she was fourteen, sporadically at first, then more often in 2001. The first couple of entries I marked are mostly Izzy gushing about her Romeo, introducing him and the real name that he didn't like back then. But it's the bold-inked entries that catch Griffin's attention. The proof that Jessica was responsible for far more than any of us knew.

His face pales at once and a sheen of sweat swells across his forehead. "Jessica Peterson," he mumbles.

"Jessica was Izzy's best friend," I tell him, trying to keep my words gentle while the truth strikes like lightning. "They grew up together—best friends since kindergarten. Jess was at our house all the time. Sometimes, it felt like she was there so often she lived with us. But something changed during their senior year of high school, and it was hard to know what that change was."

Griffin's bottom lip falls and he places the diary down before wrapping his hand behind his reddening neck. His entire face becomes red too—the heat rising with every unfurling revelation.

"I—I don't under—Jess has never mentioned Izzy's name. Not once."

"Guilt will do that to someone." This is something more than guilt. This is sick.

"Are you sure there isn't more than one Jessica Peterson?" Griffin asks. I'm sure he knows the likelihood of there being two Jessica Petersons in this small town is near impossible.

"This photo was stuck between a couple of pages in the diary," I say, removing it from my bag and handing it to him.

Griffin's chin trembles as he glances down, finding Jessica, Natalie, and Izzy posing in front of the school on their first day of senior year. Griffin gasps for a breath and presses his lips together, turning them white. He hands the photo back. "My God."

He stares between Mason and me, then toward the back of the diner. Shock paints webs of bloodshot veins across the whites of his eyes and his brows furrow.

"I know this is a lot to take in all at once," I say. "Trust me. I know."

Griffin slides his hand down the side of his face, the scruff scratching across his dry palm. I know he's searching for a clear thought. I went through the same motions. "But do you think—" he says, pressing his fingertips against his throat.

"We don't know anything more than you do," Mason says. "This diary just sheds more light on a reality we weren't aware of at the time."

"Do you think Jess knows where Izzy could be?" Griffin asks.

I shrug. "How could she, and not tell us?" She didn't even tell her husband she was friends with Izzy.

Griffin lifts the diary back up, his hand shaking as he flips through a couple more pages. "I knew so little about her friends except Natalie. Not even Natalie has mentioned Izzy's name." It's painful. That part I can understand. Keeping a history like this from one's husband, I can't wrap my head around. "I need to think. I'm—I'm married to this woman," he says, stating the words as if they're a question rather than a fact. "Jess has kids from her previous marriage. I—" He lets out a heavy exhale.

"I know," Mason says.

I pull my phone out and open a browser, searching for AOL. If there's one thing a little sister's good at, it's knowing their big sister's passwords. She used the same one for everything. I've checked her inbox daily for over twenty years, hoping I'd see an outgoing email from her. I've kept her inbox clean from spam and even sent myself an email here and there to keep her account active. I haven't been able to give up hope that we'll find her. I tap the new email button.

"I'm confident Jessica had something to do with Izzy disappearing, or...worse," I say. "And I'm going to find out."

Griffin reaches his hand across the table. "Wait—what do you mean? How are you going to do that?" Griffin asks, glancing back and forth between Mason and me.

"Izzy must have told you one of her friends was trying to convince her that you—her 'Romeo' —were a crazy stalker or obsessed with her, and that she needed to get away from you. That's why you staged your breakup the night she went missing, right? You knew her so-called 'best friend' would be eavesdropping on you in the woods. You wanted her to think you weren't together anymore, so she'd stop bugging Izzy about you?"

The blood drains from Griffin's cheeks. "How do you know all of this?" he asks.

"I was bored, twelve, and never minding my own business." Someday that might be something to look back on and laugh about. Just not now.

"Yeah, there was a lot going on and Izzy wasn't sure who was tapping on her window at night, or who broke in...She went from frazzled and confused to having a very sudden sense of clarity. She never spelled out her thoughts to me, though. She just wanted our relationship to be more private. I didn't know how that would work, but I wasn't going to tell her no. I remember I kept asking her questions about what she was worried about or if she had an idea of who might have been trying to scare her, but I never got answers. I thought she'd tell me more in time, but we ran out of that.

"She was protective of those she loved, even Jessica," I say.

"I should have tried harder to find out more. I was just selfishly glad she believed that I had nothing to do with what was happening to her. In fact, I insisted she go to the police and report everything. I was scared something would happen to her."

I take a breath, wishing my heart would stop pounding so hard, listening to Griffin's thoughts mirror my own. "Yeah. I get it. Well, Izzy states clearly in the diary that Jessica broke into our house. Izzy had proof," I say. "She told my parents and me that she found a baseball in her room and some kids playing on the street must have hit it too hard and it broke through her window. It happens all the time. We had no reason to think she was making up a story. I know it's crazy, but I'm not ready to give up looking for her."

Mason's stare burns into the side of my face, but I won't stop looking for my sister until I have answers. Someone took her from me. He knows this. "You know, we should just bring the diary to the police?" Mason suggests.

"Mase...you know this case is cold. I'm not sure they'll reopen it for a diary that could have been tampered with by anyone especially seeing as it was in the attic of a house we were renting out for years," I tell them. "Look, my gut and heart tell me Jessica is responsible for what happened to Izzy. Taking her by storm might be the only way to find out if she's been hiding information about Izzy from us."

"How can we do that?" Griffin asks, swallowing hard after his question. "I live with her. She's my wife. I love her. We've been happy together. Her kids live with us." His hand wrenches around the back of his neck as his breaths grow quicker.

"I'm so sorry," Hannah says. "The last thing I would ever want to do is disrupt your life after what you've been through, along with the rest of us. But all I can wonder is why the two of you ended up together."

"She approached me at a school event. I had no clue who she was," Griffin says, his red hue becoming pale. "I asked her out later, and the rest fell into place."

"According to Izzy's diary, Jessica knew exactly who you were," I tell him. I won't be the one to tell him happiness can be the perfect disguise to dark buried truths. I'm sure he'll see for himself.

"Our marriage is based on a lie..." he says, his words hardly audible.

"I have an idea, okay? I just didn't want to act on it until we met."

"What—what idea?" he asks, his brows knitting together.

"I'm going write an email from Izzy's old AOL account, one Jessica will recognize. Depending on what Jessica truly knows about Izzy will be telling in the way she reacts to hearing from her all these years later. She spent years blaming you, Romeo, as she knew you. She tried to convince us that you had something to do with her going missing. We didn't tell you that because you were already hurting so much. Plus, everyone grieves differently, and Jessica needed someone to blame."

"I didn't go anywhere but home that night. The police questioned me like everyone else. I was cleared too," Griffin says.

"We know," I tell him.

"Jess must have checked out fine too, though," Griffin says. "Right?"

"She did, but things are different now that we have Izzy's words."

"So, you're going to email Jess, pretending to be Izzy?" he asks, confirming the plan.

"Yes, but that won't be enough to smoke out the truth from her. I need to take this a step farther."

"Hannah..." Mason says with warning.

"Trust me," I tell my husband.

"If 'Izzy' sends Jessica an email, confirming the story Jessica wanted everyone to believe about you being some crazy stalker... and tells her she's found out they're now married and living together, Jessica will be forced to question all of her past and current lies, knowing her ploy to blame you is no longer a secret. Because why would she marry the man who caused her friend to disappear and never mention Izzy's name to you?"

"But Jess didn't know who I was when we met—" Griffin says again. This is a lot to digest.

"Jessica knew who you were. We know that now," I remind him, placing my hand down on top of his.

"Right. Sorry," he says.

"Let's screw with Jessica until she starts to question everything that's happened in the past. She'll be left questioning if you know the truth about what happened to Izzy, which might force the truth out of her too. Do you think you can help with this part?"

"Help, as in, make the story about the psychotic stalker being me, seem true?"

"Yes," I confirm.

"I did study theater for a while in school. Plus, my rage and resentment for what she's done will spark my creativity too, I'm sure." He stares up toward the fluorescent lights, blinking slowly. "Jess is my wife." He makes his statement as if he still needs to believe this truth. "She must have always known who I am. How could I have been so blind?"

"Deranged people often know how to get away with way more than we can fathom. We don't want to drag our feet on this," I say, too nonchalantly as my mind goes wild with ideas for how I'll drive this nail into the coffin.

Griffin just said how much I look like Izzy, even after all this time. I can use that to my advantage. It won't be too hard with how small this town is. If Jessica did something to her, she might not be so calm when she spots the ghost of her best friend walking around.

"You know, I had thought Izzy's best friend was the one who stole my truck and ditched it down the road the night she disappeared...That would have been Jess," Griffin says, nervously tapping his fingers against his lips.

"Why did you think that?" Hannah asks, less sure all of a sudden.

"Well, when I went to sell the truck years later, I found this key chain that Izzy had given her 'best friend' for a birthday gift. I couldn't figure out how it ended up lodged in the fold of my driver's seat. I think I know now."

"Jessica is the one who stole your car and left it at the ledge of the cliff where Izzy was running. I sound so much more put together than I am but after more than twenty years of crying myself to bed many nights, I need to unravel this mystery for the sake of my parents and me—our sanity. We deserve that much.

I begin tapping out the email on my phone, the words shooting out like wildfire.

"Do you think she'd go to the police?" Griffin asks.

"I'm confident if Jessica is responsible for Izzy's disappearance, she wouldn't report any sort of email to the police. And regardless, you're still innocent. If anything, it'll eventually trace back to me and I'll tell them I was doing my own investigation since they stopped trying. I'm not worried."

"Don't send the email yet. I'm going to get my dad's IP address since he still lives in Spring Hill and he's friends with most of the police department. We can login into his network so she can't trace the email out of town. I can grab a burner phone or two if that helps," Mason says.

"Yes. It'll help." *Oh, the messages I can send that bitch...* "Can you write down her phone number and current email address for me, Griffin?"

"Sure...although, Jess still has her old email address forward emails to her current one. It would seem more legitimate if the email goes to her old AOL account since Izzy wouldn't know her current one." He seems hesitant or just thinking every possibility through. Or it could be fear of confirming this unfortunate truth. Something like this seems impossible to accept.

The energy from the plan rests over us like a heavy fog of grief. "Closure would be nice," I say. I don't know how hard it will be to get the answer we've been searching for all these years.

"Closure, yes. A divorce and a plan to get the hell away from her too," Griffin adds. "Her poor kids. God, they don't deserve this. Thankfully, they have their dad. I just—I can't believe this."

"We'll do whatever we can to help," I say, knowing I'll be doing much more than necessary. She won't get away with this and she'll pay. "We don't want you to end up missing too."

EPILOGUE

Hannah

The last message I received from Griffin was last night.

9:15PM

Griffin: *She's losing her mind. The police already left. That plan didn't work. But she's about to confess. She knows it's over.*

9:15PM

Me: *Be careful.*

9:15PM

Griffin: *I'm deleting these messages. Don't text back until I text you.*

There's no hope for a normal workday and I can't focus on creating a marketing plan for a new client. All I can do is stare out the window of my home office, wondering why Griffin never texted me again last night.

My phone rings. Mason's face shows up on my display and my stomach tweaks. I'm not sure if he would know something before me, but he doesn't usually call at this hour from work.

"Hi..."

"Are you okay?" he asks.

"Not really. I have a bad feeling."

"I figured. Well, Carol just called me from the school. Griffin didn't show up for work this morning. No one can reach him or his wife. He's never done something like this, so they sent someone over to his house to make sure he was okay."

Mason's dad and stepmom, Carol, are aware of what's been going on this last week. They let us use their house as a meeting spot for us and Griffin since their property is settled deep in the woods.

"Was he there? Is he okay?" I ask.

Mason releases a heavy breath. "His car was there, but Jess's wasn't. No one answered the door. But a window was boarded up. A wellness check was called into the police. They confirmed no one was home, and this was following a reported break-in last night."

"Griffin is the one who broke the window..." I say. "It was his plan."

"I know."

It was the only way to get the police at their house. He was supposed to turn her in when they were there. We don't know what came out of that, but it didn't seem to work.

"Do the police know anything more?" I ask.

"Not at this time."

"I think she did something to him," I tell Mason.

"We don't know that. We need to wait this out for more than a few hours." We both know a few more hours aren't going to matter right now.

"I can't just sit here. I dragged him back into this and God only knows what situation he's in now."

"Sweetie, you have to be patient. Please just take a breath."

"Okay," I say. "Tell me if you hear anything else. I love you."

"Love you too."

I open my laptop and connect to the IP address I've been using before logging into AOL.

I need to know...

I type up another email, my fingers pounding against the keys. Griffin said she was sure he was the one sending her emails from Izzy's account.

Mere minutes pass before a response pings in the inbox.

To: IzzyBee83isMe@aol.com

From: Jessica Peterson

Subject: Re: Re: Re: Re: Re: Re: Hey you...It's me...

I know you aren't Izzy. So who the hell is this?

Despite my fear for Griffin, I can't help but smirk.

Jess thought she could get away with murder.

Maybe two murders.

But she was wrong. And she's about to spend her life terrified of what will happen when the truth finally catches up with her. Because I will never let her rest.

There is nobody more dangerous than a little sister seeking vengeance for her big sister.

This is only the beginning.

A LETTER FROM SHARI

Dear reader,

I'm absolutely over the moon that you've chosen to read *My Husband's Past*. With all the books out there, I'm humbled and flattered to know you chose to spend your free time with one of my books.

Nothing makes me happier than being able to share a new book with readers, and if you would like to keep up to date with all my latest releases, just sign up at the following link. Your email address will never be shared, and you can unsubscribe at any time.

www.bookouture.com/shari-j-ryan

I loved every minute of crafting this story. Having the opportunity to write psychological thrillers is such a rewarding experience, developing unique colorful characters who bring twists and turns to each page.

I genuinely hope you enjoyed reading the novel, and if so, I would be grateful if you could write a review. Since the feedback from readers benefits me as a writer, I would love to know what you think, and it makes such a difference helping new readers to discover one of my books for the first time.

There's no greater pleasure than hearing from my readers—you can get in touch through my social media or my website.

Thank you for reading!

Shari

facebook.com/authorsharijryan
x.com/sharijryan
instagram.com/authorsharijryan

ACKNOWLEDGMENTS

Writing *My Husband's Past* has been a thrilling experience.

I'm so grateful for the opportunity to work with such an upstanding publisher, whose team and professionalism are unbeatable. As always, your kindness and commitment has been invaluable to me throughout the past few years of my publishing journey. Also, I would like to thank Lucy Frederick, my editor. Collaborating with you has taught me so much and given me so much inspiration. I'm very grateful to have the privilege to work with you on all the books we've put together so far.

Linda, your unwavering positivity and belief in me has brought me so much comfort and joy over the years. I cannot express enough how much I value our friendship.

Tracey, Gabby, Elaine, and Carla—my beloved Alpha-Readers, thank you for offering your time, support, and friendship when it comes to planning murderous plots.

My super supportive friends, Kelly, Susan, Erin, and Gosia who never give me the side-eye when it comes to sharing rogue book ideas, and also always cheering me on even when I may be annoyingly hard on myself. I don't know what I would do without you in my life.

To all the ARC readers, bloggers, influencers, and readers who are a part of this incredible community: thank you for your positive energy and influence.

Lori, the greatest little sister in the universe. Thank you for always being my #1 reader and my very best friend in the whole universe. Love you!

My family—Mom, Dad, Mark, and Ev, thanks for always believing in me and supporting my wild dreams. You all mean the world to me.

Bryce and Brayden—This is another book you can't read until you're at least thirty. You'll understand someday even if you think that day should be today. I love you with all my heart.

Josh, to have your support is everything to me, especially when the title makes the book sound like this story is about you. It's not. Again, just to make it very clear...This book is definitely NOT about you. You have never been killed off in any of my books, nor will you ever. I love you SO much!

PUBLISHING TEAM

Turning a manuscript into a book requires the efforts of many people. The publishing team at Bookouture would like to acknowledge everyone who contributed to this publication.

Audio
Alba Proko
Sinead O'Connor
Melissa Tran

Commercial
Lauren Morrissette
Hannah Richmond
Imogen Allport

Cover design
Emma Graves

Data and analysis
Mark Alder
Mohamed Bussuri

Editorial
Lucy Frederick
Melissa Tran

Copyeditor
Shirley Khan

Proofreader
Catherine Lenderi

Marketing
Alex Crow
Melanie Price
Occy Carr
Cíara Rosney
Martyna Młynarska

Operations and distribution
Marina Valles
Stephanie Straub

Production
Hannah Snetsinger
Mandy Kullar
Jen Shannon
Ria Clare

Publicity
Kim Nash
Noelle Holten
Jess Readett
Sarah Hardy

Rights and contracts
Peta Nightingale
Richard King
Saidah Graham

Made in the USA
Columbia, SC
25 October 2024